Travis

Travis loves you! Tracie x

By: Tracie Podger

Copyright

Travis

Copyright 2015 © Tracie Podger

All rights reserved.

ISBN-13: 978-1508744061

ISBN-10: 1508744068

About the Author

Tracie Podger currently lives in Kent, UK with her husband and a rather obnoxious cat called George. She's a Padi Scuba Diving Instructor with a passion for writing. Tracie has been fortunate to have dived some of the wonderful oceans of the world where she can indulge in another hobby, underwater photography. She likes getting up close and personal with sharks.

Tracie wishes to thank you for giving your time to read her books and hopes you enjoy them as much as she loves writing them. If you would like to know more, please feel free to contact her, she would love to hear from you.

Publicist, Paula Radell, can be contacted via email at Passionatepromos@gmail.com

Twitter: @Tracie Podger
Facebook: Tracie Podger, Author
www.TraciePodger.com

Available in ebook and paperback....
Fallen Angel, Part 1
Fallen Angel, Part 2
Evelyn - A novella to accompany the Fallen Angel Series
Robert - A prequel to Fallen Angel, Part 1
Fallen Angel, Part 3
Travis - to accompany the Fallen Angel Series

Coming soon....
Fallen Angel, Part 4
A Virtual Affair
The Passion Series

Acknowledgements

I could never have written the Fallen Angel series without the support of my family. My husband has been my rock, without him, I wouldn't be here.

My heartfelt thanks to the best readers, proofreaders and editors a girl could want, Janet Hughes, Paula Radell, Lucii Grubb, Karen Shenton and Alison Parkins - your input is invaluable.

Thank you to Margreet Asslebergs of Rebel Edit & Design for yet another wonderful cover.

A huge hug to the guys in Tracie's Fallen Angels, a fan page on Facebook - you cheer me up, encourage me and give me reason to keep writing.

And last but certainly not least, a big hug to my publicist and friend, Paula Radell. She is one of the kindest people I've come across on this journey called self publishing. Paula is responsible for getting my books out there and I am overwhelmed by her support and belief in The Fallen Angel Series.

Paula Radell - Passionate Promotions

As you read Travis you might notice a couple of familiar names. Karen Shenton and Alison Parkins not only beta read but star in the book - both ladies won the chance to be in Travis by being members of Tracie's Fallen Angels.

So how did this all start? It's been a long journey but my love of writing came about after I was encouraged to do so as part of my recovery from depression. I have always loved to read and lose myself in books, words soothe me.

One day, after a series of dreams, I sat with my laptop and the words flowed from my fingertips - pages and pages of them. I forgot my troubles and lost myself in the characters I have created. I hope you can too.

If you wish to keep up to date with information on this series and future releases - and have the chance to enter monthly competitions, feel free to sign up for my newsletter. You can find the details on my web site:

www.traciepadger.com

There is no friend as loyal as a book - Ernest Hemingway

Contents

Chapter One

As I cowered under the bedclothes my sister, Aileen, pulled me in close. She had tried to block out the screaming by covering my ears but I could hear the slap as a hand hit skin and the thud as a body fell to the floor. The cries from my mother echoed around the sparsely decorated apartment. My father's slurred voice boomed.

"Get up you useless bitch," I heard him shout.

Aileen sang to me in whispered tones, a song she had learnt years ago before the family ran away. I knew the song; she had taught me the words. It was a folk song sung around the fires back in Northern Ireland. A song she hoped would drown out the sound of my parents fighting.

****

I was the youngest of four, born in New York to a drunkard of a father and a weak, feeble mother. I think it was my mother that I hated the most. She would stand by and watch her husband beat us and then take a beating herself. Never once did she defend us, protect us from his fists, from the torrent of abuse we received on a daily basis. She ignored the looks from passers-by as we walked to school, with our bruised faces and tatty, torn clothes. She ignored the pleas from school to attend meetings and she lied to cover for him.

I didn't really know my family history other than my parents and siblings had fled Northern Ireland just before I was born. The family had been packed up in the night and sent away. In some of his drunken ramblings, my father would tell me that he had been in the Army. Not your regular Army - "One fighting for freedom," he would say. As he drank more he would get angry,

1

scream and curse. My mother would then usher us away from him to the one bedroom all the kids shared.

Home was a two bedroom apartment in a broken down block. Corridors that stank of piss were littered with discarded liquor bottles and needles. We would have to tread carefully to get to the main door and into fresh air. Neighbours screamed at each other day in and day out, and the kids ran wild.

The screaming from my mother stopped, the front door slammed and after a few minutes all we could hear was her gentle sobs. I crawled out from under the bedclothes and with Aileen we made our way to the kitchen. The place was a mess; the contents of cupboards and drawers were strewn across the room. What little food we had, had been spattered against the wall and the refrigerator door hung from one hinge. Its incessant buzzing echoed around the room.

I found my mom on her hands and knees trying to gather pots and pans, cutlery and plates. Blood dripped from a split lip and a cut on her cheek. I knelt beside her and placed my hand on her arm. I wanted her to look at me but, as usual, she pushed me away. In silence I helped clear the kitchen and threw out the broken chair. I left her leaning over the sink, holding a dirty washrag to her face.

Aileen was already outside sitting on the steps to the main door and puffing on a cigarette. I sat beside her and she placed her arm around my shoulders.

"Don't be worrying now, Travis, you hear me?" she softly said.

"Why does he do it?" I asked.

"Because he's fucking evil, that's why."

"Why does she put up with it then?"

I had so many questions floating around my ten-year-old brain, so much anger and resentment.

"She's scared of him, Trav. She won't ever leave, where would we go?"

We were stuck in a life of domestic abuse, living from one pay packet to the next, that's assuming dad worked that week of course. We scrimped, got by on charity and the kindness of an old woman living on the ground floor. Everyone called her 'Mad

Mary' but she was the only reason I had shoes on my feet. Someone told me that she'd once had a son. He had been killed in a gang fight, and she often gave me his clothes or his sneakers. Although nothing ever really fit me, I appreciated them. Some days she seemed madder than normal; her mutterings would grow louder as she walked the corridor or the sidewalk. But then there were times when she would let me in her apartment and we would just sit. She often read books to me - my reading wasn't great since I rarely made it to school. I liked to listen to her soft voice, it was calming - so very different to the shouts I was used to.

I left my sister and knocked on Mary's door. I heard the shuffling as she made her way to it, the pause as she looked through the spy hole and then the clunk of multiple bolts being released. She opened the door and let me in. No doubt she had heard my parents fighting; our apartment was directly above hers with paper-thin walls, she was probably expecting me.

"Come on in then, Travis, don't let the heat out," she grumbled. I closed the door and sat on the couch beside her.

"Bad one was it?" she questioned.

"Yeah, I fucking hate them both, Mary," I replied.

"Now, now, Travis. Enough of that language. How is your mother?"

"Bleeding as usual. Why doesn't she fight back? Why doesn't she leave?" I asked, tears were threatening to wash the grime from my cheeks.

"It's a difficult one that. Only she can answer it, dear."

She made her way to the kitchenette and poured a glass of lemonade for me.

"I remember when your parents arrived. It took your mother a long time to settle in, but she was kind to me when I lost my boy. She's a good woman, Travis, she's just having a hard time."

I couldn't believe what Mary said, that my mom was a good woman. Every day I would look at her and in my head scream the same thing over and over…"Fight back!" Yet she never did.

So what made me hate her? It wasn't that she stood by and let her husband beat her and her children. It was what she stood by

3

and let our older brother, Padriac, do to Aileen and me. That was what I could not forgive her for, not in a million years.

****

It had started the previous year, or maybe it was only then that I became aware of it. It had been one of those hot muggy summers. The streets of Hell's Kitchen shimmered as the heat bounced off the sidewalk. Steam rose from the ground when water hit the street as kids opened the hydrants to play and cool down in. Aileen, sixteen at the time, was playing with Carrig - my twelve year old brother - and me. We were darting in and out of the water as it sprayed from the hydrant, soaking our clothes and laughing.

Even at ten years old I knew my sister was the most beautiful of all the girls on our block. Her red hair flew around her face as she danced and skipped, holding our hands as we played. Her blue eyes would sparkle with laughter as she sang to us. She was the one responsible for feeding Carrig and me, for making sure we were up and dressed on the odd occasion we went to school. She was the one who cleaned and repaired the house after our dad trashed it. She was the mother we should have had.

Looking up the block I saw Padriac. Our older brother was nearing twenty and already an alcoholic. He was weaving his way along the sidewalk staggering from side to side, bouncing off the cars and singing at the top of his voice. As he got closer I saw his torn shirt and bloodied fists. He had obviously been in yet another fight. Sometimes he came home with a fist full of dollars from a fight in a back street. A group of men would form a circle and two of them would fight for money. He never gave any of that money to my mom but spent most of it in the bar on his way home.

I felt the tension from Aileen's hand, the hand that held mine. She quietened as she saw him and pulled Carrig and I closer to her. She started to cross the road but there wasn't enough time before Padriac closed in on us.

"What the fuck are you doing, showing your body off like that?" he shouted.

Aileen wore a white shirt and a long skirt. Like ours, her clothes were soaked through and the outline of her bra was visible.

"You're drunk, Padriac, go on home," she replied.

4

"You look like a whore. Trying to earn some money, are you?"

"Pad, we are playing, nothing more," she said.

"You should be out earning your keep."

"And who is going to look after these two, huh? It sure wouldn't be you."

He stepped closer to her, his face full of menace. I hated Padriac about as much as I hated my father. He was too quick to lash out with his fists for no reason, too quick to drag his younger brothers to the ground before laughing at our humiliation. He reached out to grab Aileen by the arm. Carrig stepped in front of her, his little hands trying to push Padriac away. I stood rock still, too scared to intervene. Padriac grabbed a handful of Aileen's beautiful hair, dragging her into the alley behind him. I watched as her hands covered his and her nails dug into his skin as she tried to work them loose. Carrig had started to cry.

"Pad, leave her alone, please," he said.

The other kids stopped their play and watched. Aileen was trying to fight him off but he was much too strong. He grabbed at her breast, laughing as he did.

"You want a man to touch you? Is that was this is about, huh?" he said.

"Take your filthy hands off me, Pad. I swear, I'll tell dad about this," she replied.

"Tell him what? You're standing on the street looking like a whore, he'd be pleased you've finally got a job."

A crowd had gathered; a man approached them and placed his hand on Padriac's shoulder, an attempt to pull him away. Padriac spun around with his fist raised, ready to strike whoever had interrupted him and the man backed off. Just the look on Padriac's face had most people watching, wary of intervening. However, it gave Aileen time to react. I watched her run down the alley, her hair flying out behind her and I smiled. She'd gotten away that time.

"What are you fucking grinning at?" he said to me.

"Nothing," I replied, turning away to head for home.

"Carrig, you better toughen up boy. Go and get Travis," he instructed.

I started to run. Padriac had decided that Carrig was going to be the next fighter in the family and for practice - or rather for his perverse fun - he encouraged Carrig to *practice* on me. The trouble was, Carrig was as scared of Padriac as I and if he didn't do as he was told he would be beaten instead. I remembered the last time.

Every time Carrig's fists rained down on me I could hear him whispering, "I'm sorry."

I never really fought back because if I got a punch in, Carrig would be punished for being careless, for letting his defence down. I would simply stand, defend myself as best I could, and wait for it to be over.

Carrig was as fast as me but somehow never caught up before I shouldered my way through the front door to the apartment block, taking the stairs two at a time. I stood outside the apartment door, my hands resting on my knees and I bent at the waist trying to catch my breath; or maybe I was just delaying having to go back inside. I had no desire to spend time in that apartment, watching my mother sit by the open window, smoking cigarette after cigarette and with a wistful, faraway look on her face. If she wasn't too lost in her thoughts she would notice me and smile, encourage me to sit with her but most of the time I would try to hide in the bedroom and do nothing to attract attention to myself.

I slowly opened the door. As I made my way to the bedroom, I could hear my dad snoring, no doubt passed out on the sofa after an afternoon in the local bar. Our room was small, barely big enough to contain what little furniture it did. There was one donated chest of drawers; we didn't have enough clothes to fill anything more, a double bed, a single pushed alongside it, and a mattress on the floor. The single bed was always left for Padriac; the rest of us just curled up wherever there was a space. Most nights that single bed was left empty, but none of us would take the gamble and sleep in it.

I crawled across the double bed, its tangle of blankets that were long overdue for a wash and curled up on our bed. I could hear the distant cries of a child, no doubt from the apartment above us and the thump of music from another. Somehow that mix of 'normal' sounds lulled me to sleep.

I was awakened by the crash of the front door being forced open. I heard my father shout, my mother cry out in surprise and the thud as someone hit the floor. I crept to the bedroom door, opening it slightly. Padriac was lying on the floor laughing. My mother bent to help him up and when he swung his fist, catching her lightly on the side of her head. As usual, she took it in her stride.

"Get the fuck up," my father growled, dragging him by his arm.

Padriac mumbled before he got to his feet, swaying and reaching out for the wall to steady himself. I noticed the stack of money in his shirt pocket; a few bills had fallen to the floor. I also noticed my mother look at them. She moved to Padriac's side to support him but as she did her foot swiped at the notes, quietly pushing them under a small table against the wall.

"Leave me alone, I'm not a fucking idiot. I can walk," Pad said, stumbling towards the bedroom door.

As the bedroom door was pushed open, I scuttled backwards.

"Look who we have here. Should have seen him earlier, dad, running away from a fight he was."

I backed into the corner as Padriac walked towards me. My father was standing at the door and I could see my mother behind him. I pleaded with my eyes for her to help me, but she cast hers down. I raised my clenched fists, using my arms to cover my head as the first blow connected with it. The force of the blow rocked me on my feet and tears sprang to my eyes. I would not let that bastard see me cry, so I swallowed hard, forcing the sob back down my throat. I tried to tune out the sound of my father's laugh as Padriac grabbed a fistful of my hair and dragged me towards the single bed. He threw me down, bouncing me against the hard mattress.

"Thinks he's a man now, dad. I see you, you little shit, playing with your cock."

I frowned, blinked a few times in surprise. I had no idea what he was talking about.

"Yeah, sees his sister and gets a hard-on each morning, he does."

"No I don't," I stammered.

"Oh, so maybe it's me then, is it? You're a fucking queer, are you?"

My dad was laughing so hard, but my mom stayed completely silent. I was terrified, I tried to use my feet to push myself up the bed and away from him. My heart had started to race. Padriac reached out, grabbed one of my ankles and pulled me towards him. As if in slow motion I watched his hand reach forward. He grabbed my crotch and squeezed, laughing until I cried out in pain.

"Yeah, it's me he fancies, dad. Fucking proof of it right here."

When Padriac was that drunk it was hard to understand him, his Irish accent was so strong. I kicked out my legs, catching the inside of his elbow and he let go. I rolled to the other side of the bed and tried to stand. It was hard with the pain but I sucked in deep breaths. Fun time over, my father turned to leave and pushed my mother to one side as he did. Padriac fell face first on the bed having finally passed out at last. Only then did I allow that tear to fall. I felt it roll down my cheek and I looked at mom. She never said a word. Her eyes were sad, I could see that, but she didn't speak. She didn't come forward and comfort me. That's when I started to hate her.

****

At every opportunity Padriac beat me, and worse, he seemed to think it amusing to grab my balls. At first I thought it was because he wanted to inflict pain but as time wore on, I saw a different look on his face and I felt sick to my stomach. I fought him every time, but I was no match for a drunken Padriac.

The summer wore on and the heat exhausted people, made them tired and angry. Most of the time we sat in a small park in the shade. Calling it a park was an exaggeration, it was really just a grassed area with a couple of benches in the middle of stifling apartment blocks. Even to call what we sat on 'grass' was wrong; it was more like scorched earth. Aileen took me there every day to get us out of the house, away from our parents and Padriac. Sometimes Carrig would join us, but most times not. He had started to idolise Padriac and wanted to join in the fighting. He loved to follow him to the bars and even at twelve years old he was starting to enjoy his first taste of beer. How he managed to get served was beyond me. No one seemed to care.

"How are you doing, Trav?" Aileen had been inspecting the latest round of bruises to my cheek.

"I hate them all, every one of them," I replied.

"I know you do. We need to get away, Trav. I need to get you away before..." She didn't finish her sentence.

"Before what?" I asked.

"Nothing, forget it," she replied, smiling as she brushed the hair from my eyes.

She winced as she stood and rubbed her lower back. I didn't need to ask why. Wincing and rubbing bruises was a normal occurrence for us. As we made our way home we walked past a couple of warehouses. One was being used to fix up cars and I noticed a guy stand and smile at Aileen. She smiled back before lowering her head to conceal the blush that had crept to her cheeks. Taking my hand, she rushed us on.

"Who was that?" I asked.

"Just a friend," she replied.

I hadn't known her to have any friends; she always seemed to be too busy looking after us. Judging by the way she blushed; even at my age I knew he was more than just a friend.

****

Thankfully the apartment was empty when we arrived home. We made our way to the living room and Aileen sighed as she sat on the worn floral sofa. Another item of furniture donated or found, I remember my dad and Padriac carrying it home one time.

"We had a nice house back in Belfast," she said, more to herself than me.

"Why did we end up here?" I asked.

"It's a long story, Travis, and not a nice one at that."

She patted the sofa beside her and I took a seat.

9

"Dad was a butcher, a *drunk* butcher but at least he had a job back then. Then he got into trouble and we had to run. Some men came in the middle of the night and we were all told to leave."

"What kind of trouble?"

"There was a war going on. Not a war with soldiers, not like the programmes you watch on the TV, a different kind of war. A war between people of different religions, of different nationalities," she said.

I wasn't entirely sure what she meant, she seemed lost in her memories as she told me the story.

"Friends fought just because one was Catholic and one wasn't. One of my best friends was killed. Some say dad helped a group of men, very bad men, kill some others. They called themselves the Shankill Butchers."

"Did he kill someone?" I asked, wide-eyed.

"I don't honestly know. Anyway, I shouldn't be telling you this. How about I make us something to eat?"

She left me sitting on the sofa while she rummaged through the kitchen cupboards, looking for anything she could use to feed us. She managed to put together a sandwich after scraping off the mould off the bread. We sat together in silence, the only sound being the grumbling of our stomachs telling us that half a sandwich apiece wasn't enough to satisfy our hunger.

"Aileen, did mom know what dad did? Is that why she's always sad?" I asked.

"She's always sad, Trav, because we had to leave our home and our family. You have aunts and uncles and cousins back home. Maybe she misses them too much. She doesn't have friends here. People don't want to get too close because of *him*."

Him, I assumed, was our father. Dad didn't like girls; I'd heard him say many times they were good for nothing, just 'breeding machines'. I didn't understand what that meant at the time. Aileen never called him dad, in fact she barely spoke to him and stayed out of his way as much as possible. He was always shouting at her to get a job, earn her keep but she was too afraid to leave me and Carrig unprotected. She had told me during one of our night-time chats that she would never leave us alone. She didn't spend all day with me, sometimes she snuck out on her own for a while. I had followed her one day and saw her meet the guy who fixed up the cars. They talked and laughed, and he held her hand. She looked happy, and I was excited for her. I hadn't seen her happy very often.

"Will you tell me a story?" I asked.

Aileen had the most wonderful imagination. She placed her arm around my shoulders and pulled me to her side. She told me of a place where the giant, Finn MacCool had lived, of a causeway across the channel with stones so he could cross and battle with a Scottish giant. She told me she would take me one day, we would leave New York, walk across that causeway and smell the grass that was so much greener than in America. While she was telling me the story I heard a small sob. Aileen and I looked towards the living room door. Our mom was standing there, her hand covering her mouth as tears rolled down her cheeks. I looked away, embarrassed. I had seen my mom cry many times but I couldn't find it in myself to hug her, but Aileen always did. She released me, wrapped her arms around her and I watched as mom sobbed into her shoulder.

"Let's run. Get back home," Aileen said.

"I can't," my mom replied.

"We can, there must be someone who will help us. What about your family?"

"He'll find us, Aileen. My family won't help, they begged me to leave him and I didn't. I made my bed and now I have to lie in it," she replied.

"What about us? Me and Travis don't deserve this," Aileen pleaded.

Mom shook her head. In frustration, Aileen pushed past her and left the apartment. Mom looked over at me and sighed. She gave me a small smile before making her way to the kitchenette to unload the groceries she had been carrying.

****

As summer moved into fall the temperature finally dropped. My dad and Padriac got more aggressive. I think, for my dad, the work on the construction sites started to dry up, or maybe his boss just got fed up with him not showing up to work most of the time. Padriac had no excuse. He just looked for any opportunity to torment me or encourage Carrig to beat me. Carrig stopped apologising a while ago, and now he seemed to enjoy it as much as Pad. It was then that I started to fight back. Before, when I thought Carrig would get a beating from Padriac if he didn't win, I let him. Not any more.

I was sitting on the stone steps at the front of the block just minding my own business. I was about to turn eleven and the only one excited about my birthday was Aileen. Every year she baked a cake for me. Where she got the ingredients from, I had no idea but she managed it. We would sit, just the two of us, make a wish, blow out the candle and eat until we felt sick.

I watched Padriac and Carrig walk down the street, laughing and shouting out nasty comments to people passing by. Over the past year Carrig had grown tall, not as tall as Pad, but at thirteen he was taller than most his age. I watched Padriac nudge him, motioning towards me and I knew what was coming. I stood and waited, I was going to fight back. Perhaps seeing my mom cry and hearing what she said had changed my mind. I didn't know, but I didn't want to be a coward anymore. I didn't want to be like her.

"There's the poof," Padriac said and Carrig laughed.

Calling me a poof was Padriac's favourite insult.

"I bet he likes to wear Aileen's clothes," Carrig chimed in.

"Or mum's lipstick," Pad added. "Fucking gay boy. I hate poofs."

"Maybe you want to stop grabbing my balls then, you're the fucking poof," I said, finding a little bravado inside.

Carrig smirked at me and I looked at his fists bunched by his sides. Padriac was laughing and it wasn't long before a group of people had gathered around us. Pad encouraged them to bet.

"$1 on the young 'un'," I heard an old man say.

"I'll gladly take that dollar, you won't see it again," Padriac replied.

I watched Carrig, the way he raised his fists to his face, and I copied him. He swung his arm; I ducked but felt it scrape across the top of my head. He was quick to follow up with another punch. That time I wasn't fast enough and he caught me on the side of my jaw. Tears threatened but I bit down hard on my lip; there was no way I was going to let them see me cry. I took a step closer instead. I was much smaller than Carrig so by getting close I limited his reach. I pulled my elbow back and punched this stomach as hard as I could. I heard the rush of air leave his mouth as he bent over slightly; I don't think he was expecting me to actually fight back. Padriac was shouting, people were laughing and I, finally, got mad.

I kicked, I punched, I even closed my eyes. I knew I was hitting something, I could feel the pain in my fists as they connected but I couldn't stop. I was lashing out at the years of abuse I had suffered from my brothers, my father and my mother. I swung my arms, I grabbed his hair and dragged him to the ground. I kicked and kicked and kicked some more. Then I heard a scream, I heard my name being called and felt arms wrap tightly around me. I stopped my assault and it was only then that I realised I was sobbing, my face was soaked with the tears I'd been holding back for so long.

"Travis, stop this now," I heard. Aileen held me tightly, my back to her chest.

"Fuck off, Aileen, I have money on this," Padriac said.

"Jesus, girl, leave them be. It'll toughen 'em up," the old man added.

"They're little boys, why do they need to toughen up?" she said.

I finally saw my brother, Carrig, curled in a ball on the dirty sidewalk. Blood dripped from his nose and his eyebrow. I looked at my own bloody fists in shock. I turned to Aileen, she must have seen the sadness in my eyes as she tried to comfort me. I heard the scraping as Carrig rose from the ground before I felt another punch to the back of my head.

"Enough, both of you," Aileen shouted.

"Fuck you," Carrig shouted at her.

"You get away from him now, Carrig, or I swear, I'll slap you myself," she replied. The comment caused a ripple of laughter from the onlookers.

With one arm she tried to shield me, pushing me behind her, and with the other she stopped Carrig from coming at me again. I didn't care that he was humiliated, I didn't care that Pad would be angry with him, I didn't care at all - about any of them. I was glad that I had finally beaten him, and I hoped they would leave me alone at last.

I was wrong. From that day on they targeted me. Carrig wanted revenge and we fought regularly. Sometimes he won and I was the curled mess on the sidewalk, bruised and bloodied, and sometimes I beat him. When I won I was forced to run and hide, as my reward for winning was Padriac coming after me. Aileen did her best to keep me away from them, but it was often at her own expense. Padriac and Carrig had no problem with punching me and they did the same to her.

Late one night I was sat on the mattress on the floor when a bruised Carrig came into the bedroom. He didn't speak; just lay on the double bed. It was unusual for him to spend time in the same room as me even.

"Why do you do it?" I quietly asked.

"Do what?"

"Anything Pad tells you. Why do you do it?" I said. I saw him shrug his shoulders.

"You know why. I see what he does to you and he ain't doing that to me. I do what he says and he leaves me alone. You should try it."

I thought I heard his voice catch at the end of his sentence.

"You could help me." I hated that I sounded weak and in need of him.

"Soon as I can I'm out of here, you should do the same. I promise you this, one day him and dad will be found dead in a ditch," he whispered.

In the dim light of the evening I saw him turn on his side, conversation over.

****

It was after one fight that my future was decided once and for all. Aileen and I were in the bathroom; she was wiping the blood from my face and holding tissue to my nose to stop the bleeding when a very drunk Padriac crashed through the door. She used her body to block his path. My mother was screaming at him to stop, which surprised me; she had never intervened before. Padriac grabbed Aileen by the hair and dragged her towards him. At first I thought it was so he could get to me and I cowered against the bathroom sink. Instead, he reached around Aileen with one hand and grabbed her by the throat, crushing her against him.

She fought, I watched as she dug her nails into his hand and elbowed him in the stomach to no effect. My mom pulled on his arm, trying to drag him away, but he swiped it back knocking her to the floor. I was shaking, terrified. Just the look on Padriac's face was enough to tell me he had totally lost it. As he squeezed her throat and her breathing became ragged, he ran his hand up her thigh and dragged her skirt to her waist.

I came around from the shock that had me frozen to the spot. Frantic, I pushed past and ran into the kitchen, stepping over my mom as she continued to lay on the floor. I was frantic; I could hear Aileen gasping for breath. I picked up a kitchen knife. My heart was hammering in my chest as I ran back determined to save her, even if it meant he'd kill me instead.

I didn't think as I stabbed the knife as deeply as I could in Padriac's arm, dragging it down his bicep. He howled as he let go of Aileen and spun around to face me.

"What the fuck? You fucking stabbed me," he said in surprise.

There was a moment of silence, Padriac held his hand over the wound on his arm, the blood seeped through his fingers and ran down his arm dripping onto the tiled floor. My mom was now backed against the wall, hugging herself, sobbing and mumbling. My gaze shot between her and Padriac as I took in the murderous look in his face. I watched my sister slump forwards, her hands resting on the sink as she tried to catch her breath. Then I heard someone speak.

"Run, baby, run," my mother said quietly.

The fact that mom spoke shocked us all, and it gave me time to do what she said. I dropped the knife to the floor, spun on my heels and ran. I was out and down the stairs before I heard the front door to the apartment smash against the wall. As I

15

approached the block door, Mary opened hers. Placing a finger to her lips, she beckoned me and closed her door quietly behind us. It was then that reality hit. A sob escaped; I had been trying so hard not to cry. My heart was still hammering in my chest and it hurt, everything began to hurt. I slid down the hall wall cradling my knees to my chest and gave in to it. Mary knelt in front of me; she placed her arms around my shoulders and held me. She let me cry myself out.

I don't know how long we sat, but Mary had trouble getting back up. When she finally managed to stand she took my hand and led me to the kitchenette. I sat at her table in silence as she busied herself making dinner. We could hear crashing and banging from above, and I prayed Aileen was all right. Mary put a plate in front of me, some kind of meat stew and I ate it all, I was starving. I hadn't spoken about what had happened and Mary let me be. She gave me some bread to wipe the juices from the plate and poured me a glass of milk. It was when I raised my hand to wipe my mouth that I focused on the bloodstains and broken skin and the tears came again.

"Hush now, Travis, it will be okay, I promise," she whispered, holding my hands in hers.

"No, it won't, Mary. Mom told me to run. Run to where?" I asked.

"You stay here tonight, let me talk to your mother in the morning."

"He's gonna kill me, I know it."

"What happened? Do you want to tell me?"

"He, Padriac, makes me fight with Carrig, he likes it. If I win, he beats me because he wants Carrig to win," I was trying to talk between sobs, the words were probably incoherent.

"Is that what happened today?" she asked, looking at my fists.

"Yes, I won and he came after me. Aileen tried to help and he strangled her. I was scared but for once mom tried to help and he knocked her down. I ran to the kitchen, there was a knife and..." I struggled to finish the sentence.

"What did you do, Travis?" Mary asked and a look of concern crossed her face.

"I stabbed him... in the arm, and he's real pissed now. What am I going to do?"

"Oh, Travis, you poor thing. I'll talk to your mom in the morning, okay?"

I nodded and wiped the tears from my face with the sleeve of my jumper. Mary rose from her chair and held out her hand to me; she led me to the bathroom and started to fill the bath. Placing a clean towel on the toilet seat she left me alone. I stripped off my dirty clothes and climbed in.

As I lay down I held my breath and let myself sink under the water. I kept my eyes open. I could hear my heartbeat and it was soothing, it was peaceful being submerged in the warm water. A thought flashed through my mind. *I could open my mouth, let in the water and it would all be finished. There would be no more fighting, no more tears and no more pain.*

At that moment dying was a better option than living.

When I could hold my breath no longer, when my heart hammered in my chest to the point it hurt, I sat up, gasping for air. Once my heart rate returned to normal I found some soap and washed my face, my hair and watched the water turn grey. I couldn't remember the last time I'd had a proper bath. As I climbed out, I grabbed the threadbare towel and wrapped myself up in it. It was scratchy against my skin but for the first time in a while I felt clean. I looked at my clothes on the floor, it was the first time I really noticed how grubby, how tatty they were. My jeans had holes in the knees and a broken zip, my jumper was torn at the shoulder and one sneaker was missing a lace. I couldn't put them back on, but I didn't want to walk around in just a towel. The noise of the water running away must have alerted Mary that I was done. I heard a knock on the door, it opened slightly and she handed over a T-shirt and shorts.

"Put these on for now," Mary said.

They were too big, but at least I had something clean to wear. Leaving the towel on the floor with my clothes, I made my way back to the living room. Mary was sitting on her sofa with the TV on and the sound muted. As I sat beside her I took a good look around the room. As many times as I had been in that room before, I had never *really* looked. The shelf above the little electric fire was full of photos, some in frames and some just propped against the wall. All were of a boy.

"Is that your son?" I asked.

She didn't answer immediately. "Yes, that's Glen. You look like him."

He was blond and in every photo he was smiling. He looked happy, not at all like someone who would have been in a gang. There were lots of gangs where we lived, most of the guys had tattoos and never smiled.

"I thought he was in a gang," I said, curiosity getting the better of me.

She laughed a little. "God, no. He was too sweet. He got caught up in a fight. He tried to help someone who was being robbed, so I was told. They stabbed him and left him on the sidewalk like he was nothing."

Her posture had changed, she sat upright and a flash of anger crossed her face.

"No one got caught of course. The police were never that interested. He was fifteen when he died, just a child. You don't expect your children to die before you, Travis."

I wasn't sure what to say so said nothing at all. After a while, she turned to me and smiled.

"Do you want to see his room?" she asked.

I nodded and followed her. Her apartment had the same layout as ours with two bedrooms, a bathroom, a living room and kitchenette. They were just big enough for two. Glen's room looked like it hadn't been touched since he died. The bed was made and the room was still full of his things. Books lined a shelf, there was homework on a desk and posters of football teams on the walls. It was clean and tidy, the total opposite to the bedroom I shared just one floor above.

"Why don't you climb in bed now? It's getting late," Mary said as she pulled back the bed covers.

She switched on a little bedside lamp as I climbed under the blankets.

"Aileen is going to be worried about me," I said.

"Do you want me to go upstairs and see if I can find her?" she asked. I nodded.

She left the room, leaving the bedroom door ajar. I heard the front door open and close. Mary had been to our apartment a couple of times, mainly to check on my mom but I worried about her. She was kind to me but everyone else thought she was mad and I wasn't sure what mom or Padriac would say to her. I sat in the semi darkness and waited. It wasn't long before I heard the front door open and the sound of footsteps making their way to the bedroom. Aileen came through the door first. I closed my eyes when I saw her, when I saw the bruises on her neck. Without speaking she sat on the bed and pulled me into her arms.

I felt her tears against my cheek and I looked over to Mary. She was standing in the doorway.

"I'm sure we could all do with something hot to drink," she said as she left the room.

"Travis, I am so sorry, are you okay?" Aileen asked, pulling away to look at me. Her voice was hoarse, strained.

I nodded, not wanting to speak for fear of breaking down again.

"I need to get you away, just for a while. Dan is heading to Washington, to DC tomorrow and he's going to take you with him. It's the only thing I can think of, Travis."

"Who's Dan?" I asked.

"A friend, a boyfriend. The guy you saw me with at the auto shop."

"Why can't you come too?"

"The police are coming and I need to speak with them. I need to tell them everything that happened. This has to stop, Travis. Pad is at the hospital and they called the police."

"Where am I going to live?"

"You'll stay with Dan. I will come and find you, I promise."

"Does mom know?" I asked.

"Yes, but not where you're going. I can't trust her not to tell."

I didn't want to go to our place, and I didn't want to leave Aileen either. I'd never been further than a few blocks from the apartment and I was scared. Mary came into the room with a tray.

19

She handed a cup of coffee to Aileen and a mug of hot chocolate to me. We sat and sipped our drinks in silence for a while.

"Aileen, Travis can stay here until this all blows over," Mary said.

Aileen shook her head. "Padriac will find him, he needs to get away."

"You can't leave him with a stranger, it isn't right."

"What choice do I have? If he stays here, Pad will hurt him. I trust Dan and it won't be for long. I'll get to DC as soon as I can," Aileen said.

Mary started to open cupboard doors, made a pile of clothes on the foot of the bed and found a backpack to carry them in. The last thing she pulled from the cupboard was a brown worn leather jacket. She held it to her face as if inhaling its scent before placing it on the top of the bag.

"Keep him safe, Glen," she whispered.

Before Aileen or I could respond we heard the block door open. Heavy footsteps made their way past Mary's door and up the stairs. We could hear crashing and banging, cursing and shouting. Padriac and my dad had returned home. Aileen climbed on the bed with me and lay down.

"Let's get some sleep for now, we need to leave real early," she said.

It seemed like I had been asleep for five minutes when I felt myself shaken awake. It was still dark outside; only the glow of the street lights illuminated the room.

"Time to go," Aileen said.

"What, now?" I asked.

"Yes, now. They'll come looking for you here and we don't want Mary caught up in that, do we?"

I climbed from the bed and reached for some jeans, socks and a jumper. I took them to the bathroom to change and find my sneakers. Dressed and with the leather jacket over my arm, I stood in the hallway. Mary, dressed in a robe and with her hair in curlers, checked her spy hole and unlocked the door. As I turned to leave, she pulled me into a hug.

"Take this, Travis. It's all I have right now, but you take it," she said as she stuffed some notes in the jacket pocket.

"When I'm older, I'll come back and visit," I said.

She nodded, wiped a tear from her eye and ushered us from the apartment. Although morning, it was still dark and chilly outside as we made our way to the warehouse to meet Dan. A light shone through a grimy window, the only indication someone was waiting for us. Aileen opened a small door and we walked in. Someone walked towards us with a smile on his face. He could only have been a couple of years older than Aileen and I assumed he was Dan. He looked different out of his overalls, with a clean face and hands.

"So this is Travis, huh?" he said, smiling at me.

"Hi," I replied shyly.

"Are you still sure about this?" he asked Aileen.

"It's the only thing I can think of right now. I'll follow as soon as I can, maybe a couple of days, no more," she replied.

"Okay, you've got the address, right?"

Aileen nodded and I turned my back when they embraced, when he kissed her. Dan picked up the backpack and placed it on the back seat of the car. Aileen wrapped her arms around me and whispered that she would see me in a few days, a week at most. Her voice caught as she sobbed before finally letting me go. Dan opened the door to the warehouse and with one last hug, I climbed in the front seat and we drove off.

"It's a long journey, Trav. You might want to get some sleep," Dan said as he lit a cigarette.

I gave him a small smile and nodded. I wasn't tired though, I was scared. I didn't want to leave but I didn't want to stay either. I spent a long time just looking out the window until finally nodding off.

****

Dan woke me with a gentle shake to my arm. It was daylight and we'd stopped at a roadside diner. Trucks were lined up and through the steamed up windows I could see the diner was busy.

"Need a pit stop, Trav," Dan said.

"Okay, I need a piss too," I replied.

With a chuckle, Dan stubbed out his cigarette and we climbed out. I stretched, my back and neck were sore from sleeping in the car, on top of the beating I had taken the previous day. A cold wind blew as we crossed the parking lot and I was thankful when we entered the diner. I made my way straight to the toilets while Dan took a seat in a booth by the window. I joined him as a waitress poured him a coffee and handed over two menus. It was the kind of place you'd see on the TV, with red leather booths, a counter where most of the truckers sat, and music playing in the background. Beyond the counter was the kitchen, where a couple of guys were cooking up breakfast orders. The smell of bacon wafted over and my mouth began to water.

"What do you want to eat?" Dan asked.

"I don't know. I've never been to a place like this," I replied.

"Want me to order for you?" he said.

I nodded and placed the menu back on the table.

"Where are we going to stay?" I asked.

"My dad has a place, my brother and some of his friends live there for the moment. We'll crash there until Aileen arrives then decide after that."

Did he intend for us all to live together? I wasn't sure how that would work. Aileen was only seventeen, and he was probably no more than nineteen himself. In one way I wished I was still at home, or at least at Mary's. But then my mom had told me to run, she must have believed something bad was going to happen to me if I'd stayed. She was probably right.

The waitress returned, Dan ordered eggs and bacon, waffles and more coffee for him, juice for me.

"You really have been through it, haven't you?" he said once the waitress had left.

I shrugged my shoulders; I wasn't sure what to say or how much he knew.

"Aileen told me what happened. Shame you didn't stick that fucker in the heart, you would have done the world a favour there."

"He's a bastard, I hate him and my dad, and Carrig and..." I left the sentence unfinished.

The waitress arrived with our order and we ate in silence. Every now and again Dan would smile at me; he seemed like a good guy and I almost started to feel safe. Breakfast over; he reached inside his wallet for some money. I fished around in the jacket pocket and pulled out some bills.

"Put that away, Trav. I promised your sister I would look after you and I will," he said.

We headed out to the car. Dan lit a cigarette on the way and we carried on with our journey with the windows down and the radio blaring out rock songs.

****

It didn't take long to find ourselves stuck in commute traffic on the streets of DC. Dan was trying to read the directions from a scrap of paper and keep his eye on the car in front at the same time. Eventually, he turned into a small street and slowed the car, looking for a house number.

"Shit," he said as we pulled alongside a building desperately in need of some repair.

There was a car in the front yard minus wheels and the grass was so overgrown it came up to its doors. A broken gate hung from one hinge.

"My dad's gonna freak when he sees this," he said as he turned off the car.

"Where is your dad?" I asked.

"Lives in Cali with wife number four, I think. Last time I was here and that was many years ago, this was a decent looking house."

We got out of the car and made our way to the front door. Dan moved a plant pot and found a key, not something you'd see in Hell's Kitchen. He opened the door and it was the smell that hit me first, a pungent sweet smell combined with stale sweat. The house was dark, all the drapes were closed and it looked like there had been a party. Beer bottles littered the floor. I followed Dan through the house to a living room. He flicked a light switch and the only sound was the groans of people either lying on the couch or the floor.

"What the fuck..." I heard.

A guy roused from the couch, red-eyed and dressed in crumpled clothes. He rubbed his eyes with dirty hands.

"Dan, bro, what time did you get in?" he asked.

"Just now and look at the state of this place. You better get your fucking ass in gear, Jake, and clean this up," Dan replied.

Dan walked around the room kicking the legs of the still sleeping occupants. Some groaned and eventually woke, others stayed still. Jake finally noticed me standing behind Dan.

"Who's this?" he asked.

"Girlfriend's brother, he's staying with me for a while. Now get these fucking people out of the house, Jake. Oh, Travis, this is my brother, Jake."

Jake smiled. "Welcome to the madhouse, Travis," he said.

Dan started to clear up the mess and I helped, collected empty bottles and emptied endless ashtrays into garbage bags. Jake went to make coffee and Dan and I continued to clean the place up. I might have lived in a run-down apartment block but at least my mom had kept it clean, this place was filth on top of grime.

Four garbage bags later, we could see the floor. Jake handed me a cup of coffee, something I had never drunk before, I sat on the edge of the sofa trying to keep out of the way. Someone lit what I thought was a cigarette; it had that same pungent odour I'd smelt when we first walked in the door. They handed it around, taking a puff or two before someone offered it to me.

"Stop fucking about, he's a kid," Dan said, taking it for himself.

I watched Dan suck in deeply, relax back and let the smoke swirl from his mouth. I guessed they were smoking dope, I'd seen some guys on street corners doing it back home. The smell made me feel sick and lightheaded so I made my way to the kitchen, pouring the coffee down the sink as I passed. I opened the back door and sat in the yard. I didn't want to be there, I wanted to be with Aileen and I wished I could have spoken to her. There was no telephone in the apartment and I had no idea how she would find me. I wanted to cry, I wanted to go home.

I don't know how long I sat there, but at some point during the day Dan appeared with a pizza. He sat with me and we shared it.

"The guys have gone now, I'm sorry you saw all that. Jake's a bit of a party animal and those guys are just fucking leeches," he said.

I nodded; I really didn't know what to say. I didn't know Dan and I had no choice but to trust him. I only hoped Aileen would show soon.

Chapter Two

It was two days later that everything changed. I decided to investigate the area, and pulling on the leather jacket, I went out for a walk. I must have been gone a good couple of hours and as I returned I saw a line of police cars out front. Cops were walking Dan and Jake from the house with their hands cuffed behind their backs. Dan caught sight of me, shook his head and his eyes darted up the street as if to warn me away. I crossed the road and kept walking until I came to a parked car. Ducking behind it, I watched. I had no idea what was going on but I knew not to go near the house. If the police caught me they would make me go back to New York, or worse, maybe they were after *me*. Maybe they wanted to arrest me for what I did to Padriac.

I tried to slow my breathing; my heart was racing. I watched as Dan and Jake were placed in cars and driven away. A cop stayed at the house, I saw him through the window walking around the living room. I stayed where I was until it grew dark. Only then did the police leave, but not before a maintenance man arrived to replaced the lock on the door. When it seemed all clear I walked over to the house. I felt under the plant pot for the spare key, but it didn't open the new lock so made my way around the back; that door was locked as well. I sat in one of the broken chairs and waited, wondering if Dan would return.

It started to rain, just a light drizzle but enough to chill me. I needed to find shelter and wondered how easily I could break the window. There was a small one above the kitchen sink, so I searched for something to smash it with. I took off my jacket and wrapped it around a piece of rock I had found hoping that it would deaden the noise. It took a few attempts but eventually the window shattered. I made a hole big enough to fit through and using the chair, I climbed inside.

The house was dark but I was too scared to turn on any lights and give myself away. The living room had been ransacked, the cupboards and drawers emptied. The police were obviously looking for something, and whether they found it I had no idea. My stomach was grumbling, I hadn't eaten that day. I found an old packet of cereal and settled on the sofa to eat out of the box. At some point I must have dozed off.

I woke up to a noise outside, talking and arguing. I crept to the window, making sure to stay out of sight. A man stood on the doorstep with a cop; I didn't recognise either of them. The cop handed over a key and before the man was able to open the door, I ran to the kitchen. As the front door opened, I fled into the yard, climbed over the low fence and ran alongside the houses until I was back out on the street. I kept my head down and walked away. I heard a shout, and since I wasn't sure if it was directed at me or not, I didn't turn around to look, I just ran. I kept running until I found myself under a bridge alongside the river where I leant against the wall trying to catch my breath. I was lost, I hadn't walked that far before and had no idea where I was.

I knew I couldn't just stand there all night so once I'd recovered I made my way out. The bridge crossed the river and connected to a major road. As I walked I tried to pick out landmarks, anything that would help me figure out where I was. I couldn't even ask for directions back to the house, I didn't know the street name. I just kept walking. I was so tired and hungry; I hadn't eaten properly for two days. Eventually I found myself in an alley, where I saw a group of kids, maybe older than me by a few years. I was wary as I approached. They were huddled together sharing food from a bag. They stopped the eating and watched as I walked towards them.

"What the fuck do you want?" one asked.

He had a grubby face, matted hair and scowled at me with half-closed eyes. A cigarette hung from his lips and the smoke swirled around his face.

"Nothing, just somewhere to sleep," I said.

"Go home then," he replied.

"I can't, it's too far."

"How far is too far."

"New York too far," I replied.

"Fuck, man, you came from New York to this shit-hole. When?" another kid said. He looked fairly friendly, well, he smiled when he spoke.

"A few days ago. I was staying with my sister's friend but he got hauled away by the cops yesterday," I said.

"Man, that's tough. You can sleep over there," he said, pointing to a doorstep beside a dumpster.

"He can fuck off," the one with matted hair mumbled.

I made my way over and sat down. I hugged my knees to my chest for warmth and rested my head on my arms. For a while they ignored me, I listened to their chat and kept myself quiet.

"You hungry?" I heard.

I looked up, one of the boys, the friendly one, was staring at me so I nodded. He started to walk over with a bread roll in his hand.

"We haven't got enough food as it is," I heard.

"Give it a rest, Slider, he's a newbie, we've all been there."

"I'm Tom and over there is Pete and Slider. Don't ask me why he calls himself Slider but you'd do well to stay out of his way." Tom lowered his voice a little.

"He's been on the streets a long time and mean as fuck," he added.

He handed me the bread roll. "Thanks, I'm Travis," I said as I stuffed it as fast as I could in my mouth. I was afraid it would be taken away.

Slider was the one with the matted hair and complaining about sharing the food. He was a big kid, bigger than me anyway, and wore an old army coat, dirty jeans and heavy boots. Pete didn't look up; he didn't acknowledge me at all. From the look of his fairly clean clothes, I'd guessed he hadn't been on the streets that long.

"What's his story?" I asked, indicating with my head towards Pete.

"Don't know really. He's in foster care but keeps running away. But you don't ask, okay. No one talks, it's just the way it is."

Tom joined his friends and ignored me for the rest of the night. As the evening wore on, the guys settled down. Slider had a blanket that he wrapped around himself, the others just settled near a door. I closed my eyes against the tears that threatened to fall. I didn't want to appear weak, to show fear, but inside I was terrified. I had no idea what I was going to do. All I could hope was that Dan would come and find me. At some point during the night I must have dozed off but was woken a short time later by shouting. I opened my eyes to see two men wrestling with Pete, Tom was trying to fight them off and Slider was running away.

"Fuck off, you fucking pervert," Pete shouted as he fought one of the men.

"Knife him," Tom said.

I saw a flash of metal as Pete lunged. The man backed off pretty quick. I was sat in the shadow of a dumpster and out of sight. My whole body shook at the sight of Tom and Pete fighting with two grown men and I covered my mouth so as not to let out a sob and be heard. I watched as Tom got a decent punch in which knocked one of them to the ground. The other ran, leaving his friend to pick himself up from the dirty floor and limp after him.

"Who were those men?" I asked, finally climbing out of my hiding space.

"They'll snatch you. Don't ever talk to them or take anything they offer you, you understand?" Pete replied aggressively.

He was pacing, pumped I guessed. I watched as he replaced the small knife he had wielded back in his jacket pocket. I nodded.

"They offer you food, it's drugged. You don't want to know what happens after," Tom added.

Fuck, I thought. It didn't take a brain surgeon to know what he meant and I felt sick at the thought. I closed my eyes and pleaded in my mind for my sister to find me. I don't think I got any real sleep that night.

So I learnt that no one told their stories. I had no idea how those guys came to be where they were, and no one asked me mine. It was just something not spoken about. Because I didn't *know* them, I felt very lonely. I had no choice but to stick to being the outsider where they were concerned. I knew I wouldn't survive on my own, not for a while. If those two men had come for me I couldn't have fought them off, I needed to stick with Slider, Tom and Pete whether they wanted me to or not.

****

The following morning we walked the streets; people avoided us and some were outright hostile. Eventually we found ourselves outside a small store.

"If you want to run with us, it's time to pay your way," Slider said, having arrived back at the alley that morning. "Go in there, grab as much food as you can then find us in the alley, just around the block."

I nodded and watched as they sauntered off. I'd never stolen anything in my life and I wasn't about to start. I entered the store and grabbed a basket, filled it with food then took it to the counter. I also asked for a packet of cigarettes. I pulled the money from my pocket and paid for it. The guys would never know and hopefully they would let me stay with them for a little longer. I made my way to the alley and handed over the bag I was carrying.

"What the fuck?" Tom said. "How did you get this lot? Slider, he has cigs as well."

"I found the bag by the door and the smokes were on the counter. It was easy, I just filled the bag as I went around then ran," I replied hoping they would believe me.

Slider looked at me through his usual half closed eyes. I guessed he was suspicious but he had cigarettes, he didn't care. We sat in the alley and ate. The problem was the guys then thought I was a master shoplifter and they wanted me to go again later that day.

The money ran out by day three.

The first time I really had to steal I was convinced the storekeeper could hear my heart pounding as I made my way round the aisles. I had the plastic bag in my hand and gently unfolded it, filling it with bread rolls and some salami before I heard a shout. I ran for the door. I was much quicker than the storekeeper and was out the door long before he had got around his counter.

Before I reached the alley I stopped to catch my breath and wiped my face. I didn't want the guys to see the tears that had started to fall. I didn't want to have to shoplift, I didn't want to have my heart racing in fear of being caught and more importantly, I didn't want to get picked up by the cops. I knew I'd be sent home and straight into the wrath of Padriac. A feeling of despair washed over me.

"Nearly got caught on that one," I said once I had found the guys. I planted a fake smile on my face.

****

As I walked the streets during the day I constantly looked around, searching for Dan. I was still convinced he would come and find me. One day I spotted a woman, just ahead of me with red hair hanging loosely down her back. My heart raced as I called out and started to run towards her. When I was close enough I reached out to grasp her arm. She spun around glaring at me.

"I'm sorry, I thought you were my sister," I said looking into the angry face of a stranger.

That was probably one of the worst days I'd had. The realisation that no one was looking for me hit at last. I wandered off and found myself in a park with a monument at one end. I slid down a tree and for the last time I cried.

I decided to stop looking for Dan or Aileen. I thought of the times I would catch sight of someone who resembled one of them, it would bring me to a halt and I held my breath, daring to hope to see a familiar face. I would stare for as long as they were in sight but deep down I knew it wouldn't be them and my heart would break a little more.

Dan, my sister, my family, they had all abandoned me, they had all forgotten about me and I felt very alone. I watched people, couples holding hands, families playing together and the pain I felt inside intensified. I was on my own and I had to make the best of it. I didn't leave the park, opting to lie on a bench once the night fell. It was a mistake. At night the drunks came and I guessed the bench belonged to one when he grabbed hold of my jacket and dragged me off. I landed in a heap on the ground. He was rambling, something about the war.

"Fuck off," he growled.

"I'm sorry," I said as I scrambled to my feet. I headed for a small wooded area, slid down a tree and waited for the morning.

The days had melded into each other, I lost track of what day of the week it even was. I only knew it was the weekend because the streets were less busy with suited people scurrying to and from work. The weekends were the hardest because that's when I would see families, moms and sons walking and laughing, brothers and sisters playing and that loneliness would hit me like a punch to the gut.

I noticed a couple of boys, slightly younger than me I guessed. They were playing ball, tossing it to each other. I watched them for a while, smiling at their laughter as they had fun. I was itching to join in, to do something normal like playing catch. One threw it too far and it landed at my feet, I was still sitting with my back to the tree that had been home for the past two nights. I picked the ball up, stood and walked towards them. They smiled at me and I smiled back.

"You wanna play?" one said. I nodded my head.

"Throw the ball," the other called out, jogging backwards and raising his arm, ready to catch the ball in his mitt.

It was nice to hear someone talk to me. That was until their dad appeared. He snatched the ball from me and without a word, grabbed the two boys by the hand. One child looked over his shoulder as he was hauled away and he gave me a small smile. Despite my promise never to cry again, I couldn't stop the tear that rolled down one cheek. I angrily wiped it away. I had no idea what I looked like, what condition my hair was in or how dirty my face was - there were no mirrors on the street. Those boys hadn't been bothered by how I looked; they had just wanted to play with me.

"Fuck you," I screamed to their retreating backs. "Fuck you all."

That day I hardened my heart. I would survive. I would shoplift and fucking enjoy it. I would wipe my family from my mind and fucking enjoy it. I would fight if I had to and fucking enjoy it. No one would ever see my heartache again.

That one simple act of dragging those children away from me, and I was no more than a child myself, confirmed one thing - no one was going to help me.

I had no choice but to toughen up and help myself.

Chapter Three

It was two days later that I caught up with the guys. They didn't welcome me as such just the nod of a head as I settled down on the cold, damp floor to sleep. My clothes reeked, my sneakers had holes that let in the rain, and my stomach constantly grumbled. I needed to get streetwise and quickly if I was to survive.

"I'm going for food," I said, causing Slider to raise his eyebrows. I was normally told to, I'd never volunteered before.

I had decided to walk a few blocks away for the food run. It was getting difficult to hit the local stores, I had become too well known. A light rain was falling and I pulled the leather jacket around me as tight as I could to keep dry. Although it was early evening the store I had chosen was still open. I followed an elderly lady in, the door chime alerting the storekeeper of her entry. I kept close behind her, using her as a shield from prying eyes. That time I picked up smaller items, loading my pockets and the inside of my jacket. I zipped it up to keep the food from falling out. I kept away from the counter as much as possible and when the keeper was distracted with the elderly lady I made for the door. When I was back on the street, I unfolded the carried bag I had kept in my pocket and filled it with the food.

It was time to replace my sneakers, the sole of one was hanging off and it made running hard. A cheap shoe shop that had racks just outside the door was easy pickings. I snatched a pair as I walked past, making sure they were left and right feet. They were two different sizes but it didn't matter, they were clean and they would keep my feet dry.

I started to make my way back and decided to take a shortcut alongside the river. It was not a route I liked to take at night normally, being alone at that time of the day was not always a good thing. It was safer to be in a crowd even if that crowd included Slider.

I hadn't noticed two guys following me until their footsteps echoed as I made my way under the bridge. Stupidly I turned to look, I should have just run.

"What you got there?" I heard.

"Nothing," I replied.

"Don't look like nothing to me," he said.

They were bigger than me, older for sure. One reached forwards to grab the bag I was holding and I gripped the handle as tight as I could. It was usual to fight to keep hold of food on the streets and I was prepared to fight. Whether I would win or not was another matter, there were two of them. Before it got out of hand and I took a beating the two guys stopped wrestling for the bag and looked over my shoulder.

"Fuck off friend, if you know what's good for you," one said.

"I'm not your friend. Now leave him alone," I heard, a deep voice came from behind.

I turned. Walking towards us was a man, or so I thought. My heart started to race, I was just about to drop the bag and run when he stepped closer and into the weak glow the one lamp provided. He wasn't a man but he was fucking big. By big I meant muscular, like he worked out. But that wasn't what had made the guys back off. There was something about him, something I couldn't put my finger on at first. It radiated from his body and it was scary. His face was totally emotionless and his eyes dead. It was his eyes that sent a shiver up my spine. He had black eyes, or they looked black from where I was stood.

The two guys turned and ran, I didn't blame them. I was about to do the same when his face changed, softened slightly.

"Thanks," I said and he gave me a small smile.

He turned and walked away; I watched as he slid back down the wall and sat. He looked just like I imagined I had when I'd first arrived in DC, lost. I felt compelled to walk after him, as if I was drawn to him in a strange way. I swallowed my fear and approached, sliding down the wall beside him. He didn't look up, didn't acknowledge I was there, he just stared straight ahead.

"I'm Travis," I said. He nodded.

"Are you hungry? I have some food," I asked.

Finally he looked at me and nodded again. I rummaged in the bag, pulling out a couple of bread rolls and handed him one. We ate in silence for a while.

"What are you doing here?" I asked. It took him a moment to answer.

"Same as you, I guess," he replied.

"You can't stay here tonight, the cops will show anytime. This is the place the drunks come and they get moved on. Half the time the cops end up fishing them out of the river, they get so drunk they fall in," I said.

I don't know what it was about him, he didn't look vulnerable, he looked like he could defend himself but I offered to take him back with me, it was safer in a gang. I stood and waited for him. He towered over me but when I looked closer it was hard to determine his age. Fuck knows what he had been doing to get so big. He didn't speak much and everything about him screamed of someone so much older. Then it dawned on me; there was something dangerous about him. I was confused because although I was wary of him, I wasn't afraid.

"What's this city?" he asked as we walked.

I stopped and looked at him, slightly surprised by the question.

"Are you kidding me?" I asked.

"Do I look like I'm kidding you?" he replied.

No, he didn't. His face was devoid of any emotion as he stared at me. I wondered where he was from as his accent wasn't entirely American. Even the tone of his voice made him sound much older.

"Welcome to the home of the President of the United States of America, Washington, DC," I said. "You have a strange accent, where are you from?" I added.

"I came from England four years ago, lived in Pittsburgh until this morning. What about you?"

"My mom and dad came from Northern Ireland but I was born here... well, in New York," I replied.

It felt good to have a conversation with someone, someone who appeared to be interested in me. It was a nice change from being ignored by the other guys. Eventually we arrived back at the alley. Slider and Tom were already there, the usual cigarette hanging from Slider's mouth.

"What did you get?" Slider asked.

I handed over the bag and while they delved in, my new friend and I took a seat on a stone step. I caught Tom glancing over on more than one occasion, probably wondering who the newcomer was. We didn't generally have people join us because of Slider's reputation.

"What's with your friend?" Slider asked.

"He's cool, leave him alone," I replied.

Slider obviously wanted to assert his authority. He sauntered over.

"Why are you staring at me?" he said as he kicked the newcomer's foot.

Big mistake. When my new friend stood, he towered over Slider and had that cold, hard look on his face.

"If I want to look at you, I will," he said.

Slider visibly shrank away. I don't think it was what was said that scared Slider; it was more the presence this guy seemed to have.

"Wow, man, that's cool. You scared him off and he's a real fucker," I said with a grin.

As he sat back down and closed his eyes, he spoke.

"I'm Robert," was all he said.

****

For some reason being around Robert made me feel better about my situation. There was something about him that I understood, yet I didn't know his story and I had only just met him. The following morning we took off on our own. We were both hungry and I took a chance on asking a donut vendor if we could have anything he intended to throw away. To my surprise, he handed us one each. Of course I couldn't leave it at that and maybe I was showing off a bit, but I stole a bag and we ran. I guessed I wanted to show Robert that I was a seasoned street kid, someone he could hang around with. I wanted to hang around with him; in one way he made me feel safer than Slider and Tom. I had always been an outsider where they were concerned and I thought maybe they just tolerated me.

"So this is Washington, DC," Robert said as we wandered the streets.

"Let me show you the White House," I replied.

It was obvious he didn't like authority when he spat on the lawn, he seemed like a very angry person. As we walked the streets, we talked.

"It's not so bad here, once you know where you can and can't go," I offered.

"Can't be any worse than where I came from," Robert replied.

He didn't offer any more information and I wondered what his story was. I decided to tell him mine. I changed it a little bit, I told him I had persuaded Dan to bring me to DC instead of the truth. I wasn't sure at first why I told him that. I guessed if I had said my big sister needed to get me away he might ask why and I wasn't ready for that conversation.

"My parents died when I was six, so I came here to live with an aunt. She thought she could beat the devil out of me and one day I'd had enough. I burnt down her house and here I am," he said.

I nodded. I wondered what had happened to the aunt, but I wouldn't ask. It sounded like he'd had a tough life too. I guessed that was why we bonded so quickly, we both understood what it was like to have a less than perfect childhood.

"So what do we do for food?" he asked as we passed a grocery store.

"Steal it, beg sometimes, not that it always works for me," I said with a chuckle.

"How many times have you hit these stores?"

"Too many, they can see me coming from a mile off now."

"And probably smell you too," he replied, teasing.

"Well, since you mention it, I guess I could do with a bath. Can't remember the last time I had one."

He laughed, I laughed, and it felt good to finally find something funny about our situation. At that moment, I knew we would be great friends. Something clicked with me, some understanding. Even at my age I knew that our survival and future were linked.

"Let me try to acquire us some lunch," he said.

"Acquire? How old are you?" I asked.

"Eleven going on twenty," he replied.

I was a little shocked; I hadn't imagined him to be the same age as me. He certainly spoke and looked like someone much older.

I watched him walk as casually as you liked into the store, pick up a basket and head off down the aisles. A few minutes later he walked straight out of the door, basket and all. No one challenged him; I doubt anyone would. We must have looked like an odd couple walking down the busy street, with Robert carrying a basket over his arm. We certainly received some odd stares, but nobody messed with us. Finding a park, we sat and ate.

"What the fuck is this?" I said, holding up an apple.

"Healthy food, Trav. It's bad enough that we look like tramps, we don't have to eat like them too."

We sat in silence for a while eating what was probably the best meal I'd had in ages. I chuckled as I bit into the apple. He wrapped up what we didn't finish and put the leftovers in our pockets.

"Get some candy next time," I said.

With raised eyebrows and a shake of his head he made to stand.

"Never eaten the stuff," he replied.

"You've never eaten candy?"

"Nope, never drank soda either."

"Fuck me. What did you live in, a monastery?"

I regretted the words as they left my mouth. A flash of pain crossed his face. Maybe he had. If his aunt tried to beat the devil out of him, maybe he had lived in some religious community... but to never have eaten candy? Boy, he had missed out. If I did the next dinner run, I vowed to get him some candy.

"We need clean clothes," he announced. We had stopped beside a hardware shop, a general store that sold everything.

"Here's what we're going to do. I'll go in and talk about splitters. I want you to sneak in behind me, go down the aisles and find T-shirts the same colour as you've got on, minus the dirt, of course. Put them on over the top. Remember to get me one much larger than yours. Grab some pants and stuff them around your waist, do up your jacket and head out," Robert said.

"Splitters?"

"Yeah, log splitters. Machines that split logs."

"Well, aren't you just a bag of knowledge," I replied.

"No, just someone who had to cut the fucking things every day of my life. You ready?"

We smiled at each other. I could hear the chatter going on at the counter and did as Robert said. I thought my T-shirt was originally white but probably looked quite grey at that point. I picked out some brown ones, they were close enough. Hiding behind a shelf, I removed my jacket, put on a small one and then a larger one over the top. I grabbed two pairs of jeans, having no idea what size to get, and hid them under my jacket. While the storekeeper was busy looking at brochures with Robert, I walked out the door.

It shouldn't have been that easy, really. I'd never been able to just walk in and out without someone noticing, but it worked. A few minutes later Robert left the store, the brochures under his arm.

"Next stop, swimming baths," he said.

"I can't swim," I replied.

"And you don't need to, although I'd rather you didn't drown under the shower. I'll show you how to hold your breath."

I followed Mr. Sarcastic to the corner of the block; there was an information stand with leaflets for tourists about the city. He scanned them until he found one with a map. I hoped he didn't give it to me; reading wasn't something I was great at back then. I mean, I could read, but some of the longer words confused me.

He marched off and I followed. We stood outside a building for a few minutes; he was watching the entrance, waiting for our moment. When a large group of men entered, we followed behind. While they queued at reception waiting to pay, we kept walking. Following the signs we found ourselves in a changing room full of lockers.

Having never changed out of my clothes in public, I was a little hesitant. I watched Robert pull his T-shirt over his head. My eyes widened when I saw the marks on his back, but I made no comment. He had slash marks all over his skin, some not completely healed. He turned to face me as he pulled off his pants.

"Fucking hell, Rob, for eleven you're big," I said. He stared at me, eyebrows raised.

"I mean your muscles, your shoulders."

"Trav?"

"Yeah?"

"Get in the shower and use the soap," he said as he walked past and into a cubicle.

Looking around to make sure no one was watching I stripped, wincing as my T-shirt passed my nose and I caught a whiff of it. Using the dispenser, I lathered my hands and washed, amazed at the colour of the water running away. I hadn't realised I was that dirty. I started to whistle to myself.

"Trav? Keep your mouth closed and breathe through your nose, that way you won't drown," I heard, followed by a chuckle.

"Yeah, yeah."

When the water ran clean I switched it off. Still dripping, I made my way to the bench Robert was sitting on. He had his T-shirt draped over his thighs, and I did the same.

"So how did you get big muscles?" I asked, genuinely interested.

"My aunt had me cut logs every day. I guess I got fit."

"I wonder if we could open those lockers," I said as I looked around.

"Trav, in the corner of the room, see? There's a camera. We won't get out this door before getting caught."

"So someone is watching us right now? Perverts," I said with a laugh. Although the laugh was partially forced as an old memory flashed through my mind.

"I don't suppose someone is looking at us," he said shaking his head. "Get dressed, let's get out of here."

We dressed in the new clothes, nothing fitted of course but we made do. I had to roll the legs on my jeans up a little, and although Robert's fitted him in length, they were too big around the waist. He tutted as he walked and they snaked around his hips.

"I'll sort out the clothes next time," he said.

I was amazed at the difference clean hair and clothes made. As we walked people would smile, and some even spoke to us. Before then, people moved out of my way, tutted and cursed if I blocked their path.

"Trouble is, we can't beg now, not looking like this. No one would believe we were homeless," I said.

"We're not begging, Trav. We get by any way we can - but we never beg."

The one thing I had learnt about Robert in the short time I had known him was that he needed respect. He needed for people not to look down on him, like he was nothing, like he was the dirt on their shoes. I didn't really understand why that was so important. I didn't care what people thought of me, but he did. He still had that scary look thing going on. If someone was rude to him he would stop in the street and just look back at them, sending them scuttling on with their heads bent low. I understood how those people felt. When I studied him and he thought I wasn't looking, I would see this hard, cold look on his face. And I swear, sometimes his eyes got darker. I was half tempted to cross myself, not really knowing what that meant.

"How did you get black eyes?" I asked him one day.

He sighed. "The same way you got your blue ones."

I looked at him, waiting for an explanation. "I was born with them, Trav," he said.

"They are weird though."

"Yeah, well, thanks for that."

We had been on one of our usual walks. Robert insisted on walking every day, discovering the city and planning, so he'd said. He was yet to tell me what he was planning, but I followed along. We stopped outside a church and Robert bent to tie his shoelace. A couple of priests made their way out the door and one stopped in front of me. He smiled, until Robert looked up and slowly stood. I saw the priest take a step back, his face blanched. Nothing had been said. I wondered what had made the priest turn and walk quickly in the opposite direction. I mean, Robert looked scary sometimes, but I was surprised by the priest's reaction. I just didn't see Robert the same way others did at the time.

We decided to visit a local store; we were hungry, and as we looked clean enough, we thought we might try something new. Robert had found a piece of paper on the sidewalk; he held it in his hand as if it were a shopping list. I held the basket. He checked the piece of paper before reaching for items from the shelf. We were half way around our shopping trip when he stopped. He looked at me and gave a slight sideways nod of his head. I stood still and looked back at him. He did it again. I shrugged my shoulders and frowned. He sighed; he always sighed when I didn't get want he wanted. On the third time, he nodded and shifted his eyes to the left. He stood and continued to look at me.

"What?" I said, getting fed up with the head nodding and the eye shifting.

"There is a security guard just behind you, following us. I was trying to subtly alert you. I guess you don't do subtle, do you?" he replied.

It was a comical moment. We both stood until I dropped the basket and we ran for the door. We crashed through, pushing past mothers with strollers, and we laughed as we ran up the street. Ducking down an alley, I placed my hands on my knees and doubled over, trying to catch my breath.

"Why didn't you just fucking say?" I said between wheezes.

"I was trying not to draw any more attention to us than necessary," he replied.

"Well, it didn't fucking work, did it?"

"Obviously not. Now, watch and learn," he said.

Okay, so now I got it. A slight nod to the left meant someone was behind. I had to clarify if that was behind on *my* left or *his* left. It was *his* left. If he straightened his hand it meant to stop, if he curled his fist, it meant turn around, and so on. We developed our own code so we didn't need to speak, and as time went on, our signals got more and more subtle. I imagine that if someone was watching us, all they saw were two boys looking at each other, when in fact we were having a conversation.

Chapter Four

It was a hot day; I was tired from all our walking and sure that we had covered the city multiple times. I still didn't know what our plan for the future was. I would ask and Robert would say that he'd tell me once he was sure. But I was more than tired; I was beginning to feel unwell. I had developed a cough and kept breaking out in a sweat. I needed to sit down and stop all the traipsing around.

We had long since moved away from Slider and Tom. We would see them occasionally, but Robert had found a fairly decent alley for us to sleep in. And by sleep, I meant to close our eyes and rest. We never slept. One too many times we had been disturbed by cops or men looking to pick up young boys. I had watched wide-eyed as Robert punched one who came too close. He'd lashed out without a second thought.

I settled down on the step and although it was a warm afternoon and despite the beads of sweat on my brow, I couldn't stop shivering. Robert sat close by, he never left my side. As the night drew in I began to feel worse. I couldn't stop the coughing and my sides and chest hurt from it.

"This is because you eat shit, Trav. You don't eat healthily," Robert had said. I flipped him the finger.

I knew Robert worried about me, I could tell from his face. He would stare at me and flinch every time I coughed and winced with the pain, but he wasn't good at showing it. I was wrapped in a blanket he had stolen some time ago. When we went on our daily jaunt we would stash what little belongings we had behind a burnt out car, the only thing sharing the alleyway with us. We could only hope that our worldly goods would still be there when we returned.

"I need to get you some water," Robert said.

Robert stood, and with one last look at me he headed off. I was completely alone for the first time in months. We hadn't left each other's side - other than to rob a shop - since we'd met. I don't know how long he was gone, and I think I might have even dozed off before I heard him again. I felt a hand on my forehead, but my eyelids were too heavy to open.

The next thing I heard was a woman's voice saying, "He's so hot, he must have a fever."

My eyes would only open half way, my vision was blurred, but I could make out Robert and a woman... a young, A brown-haired young woman was kneeling in front of me. She smiled as she smoothed the hair from my forehead.

"You're right, he needs medicine to reduce the fever and make him more comfortable. Just around the block is a pharmacy. Ask them for Tylenol, and get a bottle of water too," she said.

I heard the sound of running feet moving away but her hand stayed on my forehead, soothing me. I could hear her whispering but not really make out what she was saying. I caught just the odd words, "Poor boy."

Robert returned a short time later, I could sense it. I also felt my head being lifted and a bottle placed against my lips. Cold water ran down my chin before I was able to sip from it.

"You need to take these," I heard the woman say.

I managed to open my eyes a little more and saw her. She had kind brown eyes and she was smiling at me. In her open hand she held two small white tablets. I looked over at Robert, unsure at first. He nodded to me. She placed the pills in my mouth because my arms were too weak to raise them from under the blanket; I took another sip of the water and the pills she offered.

"When did the two of you eat last?" she asked Robert.

"Yesterday. I'll get us something later, I didn't want to leave him," he replied.

"Okay. Let me see what I can find," she said.

I watched as she walked away, her hands clutching the bag she was holding under her arm.

"Who was that?" I asked, my voice hoarse.

"I didn't get her name, maybe she'll come back, maybe not," Robert said.

"She wasn't just walking this way, was she?"

"No, I brought her. I tried to steal her purse and she cried, so I gave it back."

Robert sounded upset, and I knew it was a big thing for him to have done that. We had no problem with stealing food from a store; somehow that didn't feel personal but neither of us had ever stolen from a person walking past before. I was surprised he had even considered it.

"What happened when you gave it back?" I asked, as I rested my head back down and closed my eyes again.

"I told her I needed money for a sick friend. I wanted to get medicine and she asked if she could help."

"You did that for me?"

"You're the only sick friend I have right now."

"Wow, thanks. That's real good of you."

"Yeah, well, I won't do it again."

Robert couldn't take a compliment; it was already perfectly clear that he wanted to help me but was uncomfortable being thanked for it. I had thanked him in the past for being my friend and he'd brushed it off. We sat in silence for a while until we both heard footsteps echoing down the alley. I tried to raise my head to look, to see if I needed to get up and run, not that I thought I would get very far. It was the woman. In her hands she carried a paper bag and two takeout containers.

"You need to eat something, and drink this, it will warm you up," she said as she got close.

I could smell the hot food and my tummy grumbled in appreciation. Robert stood and made way for her to crouch down next to me. With her help, I shuffled up the step and into a half sitting position. She handed me a pie and a coffee. It was probably one of the best meals we had eaten in a long time. I couldn't remember the last time I had hot food or drank coffee. In fact, that might have been the very first cup of coffee I ever drank.

"Will you be here tomorrow?" she asked Robert.

"Yeah, unless the cops come of course, then we will have to move."

Until I was well enough to run, we were hoping we would be left alone. There was no way I could outrun anybody. She smiled as she stood and smoothed down her skirt.

"What's your name, lady?" Robert asked her.

"Evelyn, but you can call me Ev if you like," she replied.

Robert introduced himself, told her my name, and with one last smile she turned and walked away.

"What a nice lady," I said.

"Maybe. Maybe she'll be back with the cops before we know it."

The difference between me and Robert was that he trusted no one, but I trusted and believed everyone. That's one reason we needed each other, I think. We settled down for the night. Robert woke me periodically to take more tablets and water, as instructed by Evelyn. I would rather have gotten a good night's sleep. The following morning we both looked like shit and Robert was grumpy as hell.

Our morning was brightened by the sight of Evelyn walking towards us; even Robert gave her a broad smile. She had cartons of milk and salted beef bagels for us. She pulled a bar of chocolate from her bag, and snapping it in half, she handed over one part to me and one to Robert - who shook his head.

"You don't want some chocolate?" she said.

"No, never eaten it before."

"You've never had chocolate?" she replied, surprised.

He just shrugged his shoulders while I reached out for his half. There was no point in letting it go to waste. I tried to eat it slowly, to make it last, but I had a sweet tooth and candy wasn't something I got very often. I savoured every mouthful.

"How are you feeling, Travis?" she asked.

"Better, don't know what was in those tablets but they're working."

"I think you should still rest for today and I'll pop along later and see how you are doing, okay?"

"Why are you doing this?" Robert asked.

She took a moment to answer. "You look like you need me and right now, Robert, it's nice to be needed."

With that, she rose and went about her day. It was late afternoon that I felt well enough to actually get up off the step and was dying for a piss. Robert had rules, we were not allowed to piss near where we slept, so I walked a way down the alley and ducked behind a garbage bin, which served as our makeshift toilet. It wasn't the most pleasant of places, but we made do - it was all we had.

As the days wore on I got better. Evelyn came and checked on us frequently and she always brought food. Sometimes it was just a sandwich, sometimes it was pasta, still hot and served in little plastic containers that she would take away when we were finished. She stayed with us for a half hour or so and chatted. We made her laugh; she was beautiful when she laughed, and she reminded me of Aileen. When she threw her head back, her eyes would shine.

We also started to walk with her to work. She worked in an office, importing stuff from Italy. It was clear she was Italian, with olive skin, dark hair and dark eyes, and it was only when she stood next to Robert that I wondered where he had really come from. He had the same colouring. He'd told me he came from England, but never spoke about his parents; I often wondered if they were Italian too.

****

We had been together on the streets for nearly a year when Robert announced that he thought it was his birthday. We had picked up a discarded newspaper, initially to keep behind the garbage bin for toilet use, but he had seen the date. July 28 was printed across the top left-hand corner.

"What do you mean, you think it's your birthday?" I asked.

"I think my birthday is July 28th," he said, with that sarcastic tone to his voice.

"You either know or you don't."

"I seem to remember, back in Pittsburgh I found out my birthday when I was ten. I'm sure it's July 28th."

"You never had a birthday cake or presents?"

"No. No one ever remembered my birthday."

I thought back to the days when Aileen would bake me a cake, and it saddened me that Robert had never experienced that. Having that cake and sharing it with Aileen was always the best day of that year for me. No matter what came before or after I always knew there would be one day a year where I would be happy. I didn't want Robert to feel sad that he wasn't sure - or that he had never had cake - so I lied to him for the second time.

"I don't remember when my birthday is either, but I know my sister used to bake me a cake every year," I said.

We fell silent for a while. A sadness descended on the two of us. I don't know what saddened him, but I thought about how terrible it must be not to not know your own birthday.

"What happened to your sister?" Robert asked.

"She left me here. She said she would come and find me and she didn't bother. Fuck her, fuck my whole family, I hope they have all died a terrible death."

"Don't say that, Trav. You don't know why she didn't come. She might have tried, you never know."

"Dan said he would come and find me, but he never did. No one wants us, Rob, and I don't care anymore. I would spit on them if they found me now."

I saw a flash of sadness cross his face. He had no family at all. He'd told me a long time ago that he found it hard that I hated mine with every part of my body. I meant what I'd said - I would spit in her face if she ever found me now. She didn't care, she lied to me. She probably had no intention of coming to DC, and why would she? She had a house, albeit a violent one, but she had a roof over her head and food in her stomach every day. Why would you leave that?

"So pick a date," Robert said.

I looked at him, not understanding. "Pick a date and that's your birthday. Today is mine, whether it's real or not," he said.

"I don't want to. I don't want to celebrate another birthday. I know how old I am if you know how old you are. We're the same age, I think."

"Okay, we're both twelve."

We did a high five, smiled and went for one of our usual walks around the city. We loved to walk through Columbia Heights. Its mix of old and new, and its Italian and Spanish quarters were fun places to be both during the day and at night. It was also where Evelyn worked. Sometimes we would meet her and walk her home. We never got to her house before she ushered us off. We never questioned why, either. I guess we knew. She wanted to help us; she was kind and she fed us, but having two homeless kids in your house was a whole different ball game. Maybe she didn't trust us fully then - after all, Robert had tried to steal her purse. Perhaps she thought we would steal from her if we got too close.

It was also on our twelfth birthday that our lives changed again.

****

It was a hot day and we were both thirsty. We had tried to keep the bottle that Evelyn had brought to refill it whenever we could, but we'd left it behind. Robert did his nod of the head thing as he ducked into a store, one we had hit before. Just after he entered I watched a huge black car pull up next to the sidewalk. A man, flanked by what could only be described as his goons, entered the store. There was nothing I could do to warn Robert other than watch as they collided in the doorway. The man grabbed Robert by the scruff of his neck and hauled him in with him.

I hopped from foot to foot, eager to know what was happening. I tried to get as close as I could without being seen. The goons were blocking the window, but I could just about see Robert. He straightened his T-shirt and held out his hand. I watched the man shake it; he seemed familiar, but I couldn't place him. I stepped back as he turned and opened the door, holding it for Robert to exit before him. I saw the slight nod of his head and his open palm, and waited until they stopped at a door between two takeout stores. I held back as instructed. I trusted Robert and his decisions, he would make sure it was safe before including me. It seemed that he knew who this guy was, and I wracked my brain to remember where I had seen him before.

Just before they made their way through the door, Robert looked over to me; the man followed his gaze and beckoned me to join them. We climbed a flight of stairs to some sort of office. It was a mess, the place stank and people lazed around. And then I remembered. *Fuck*, we were sitting in an office chatting and laughing with the local gangland boss. The guy who seemed so familiar was someone I had seen around the neighbourhood; I'd seen the goons acting as his security, and I'd heard the gossip about him.

"Nice place you've got here," Robert said. I was kind of hoping Mr. Sarcastic wouldn't surface, especially not while we were socialising with the Mafia.

"Say's he whose office is a doorstep in an alley," came the reply. I wondered how he knew that.

"At least I keep it clean and I know where everything is," Robert replied with a smirk.

"If you pay us, me and my friend will clean this place up," he added. I looked sharply at him in surprise.

I'd never cleaned anything in my life. Well, other than the step and the surrounding sidewalk that Robert insisted we clean that one time. And here he was offering us up for $5. It was genius.

Robert's offer was accepted, and as Guiseppi Morietti and some of his henchmen left, - leaving one behind to watch us - we started the big clean.

"You think you might have got us a different job, you know, maybe as a getaway driver or look-out or something?" I grumbled.

I held a bucket and mop, unsure of where the tap was, while Robert lugged out broken furniture and moved what was left to one side. After his usual sigh, he grabbed the bucket from me and headed for the small kitchen. He came back with it full of warm water and I started to mop the floor. He signed some more when the floor started to resemble the swimming pool we had been using for our showers.

"Watch," he said as he took the mop from me.

On top of the bucket was a grid thing, he squashed the mop on it to release some of the water and showed me how to mop the floor before handing it back to me.

"Show me that again?" I said. His stare told me I hadn't fooled him, so I took the mop and carried on.

It took most of the day to clean the floor, the furniture and the grimy cracked window, but the difference when we had finished was unbelievable. The room was bright and airy; the stench of stale cigarettes had started to be replaced by the fresh air wafting in through the open window. My clothes were soaked, my hands and face were filthy, but we had done a great job. When Guiseppi arrived back he seemed impressed as he handed over $5 each. I quickly scrunched the bill up and placed it in my pocket.

"Well, well, you did good kids," Guiseppi said.

"Of course we did. Now, do you have any other jobs we can do?" Robert replied.

I watched Guiseppi run his hand over his chin, thinking before he answered. He told us to return the following morning, and with huge grins we turned to leave the office. We were pulled up short by the sight of Evelyn in the doorway.

"Papa, I see you've met Robert and Travis," she said.

Fuck, she was his daughter. I was so glad Robert had given back her purse. No matter how big Rob was, those goons, as I called them, were much bigger. She gave us a wink as we left the office. No wonder Guiseppi knew we lived on the streets.

It felt great to walk down the street with money in my pocket. We stopped outside a candy store. Bearing in mind Robert didn't eat candy, I wondered why - but I wasn't going to question it. I headed straight for the counter, collecting as much candy as I could while he made his way to the stationary rack. I bought candy; he bought a pad and pen.

And so started our careers with Giuseppi Morietti - or Joe, as we called him.

****

The following morning we were there bright and early and sitting on the doorstep to Joe's office. We watched as his car arrived and he climbed out. This time we received a smile from one of the goons, a scowl from the other. Before we entered the now clean office, Joe pulled a wad of bills from his pocket. I don't think I had ever seen so much money in my life. He peeled off $50 and handed it to Robert.

"If you're going to work for me, you need clean clothes. Go and get some then get straight back here," Joe said.

We turned and walked down the block.

"Oh man, look at all that money," I said, wanting to hold the $50 bill.

Of course Robert kept hold of it. "We could live off that for a month," I added.

He told me off and he was right. We did what Joe asked and headed into a surplus store. We bought new T-shirts, jeans and sneakers, some new underwear, and with the clothes in a bag, the change and Joe's receipt, we made our way back.

Joe seemed surprised to see us; perhaps he had thought we might take his money and run. I guess if it had been up to me, I would have, but Robert had a plan; a plan I was still waiting to hear about. Joe gave us our first job - he wanted his dry cleaning collected and brought back to the office. Without comment, we headed off.

"We've got to pick up his dry cleaning?" I said as we left.

"Yep, and anything else he wants us to do. Think of the bigger picture, Trav. We start at the bottom and work our way up."

"We are twelve, not twenty. How many trips to the dry cleaners do you think it will take before we hit the big time?" I replied.

"I don't care, and neither should you. If takes a thousand trips, that's what we will do."

I had no problem working for money, but I wasn't about to be anyone's slave. However, Robert had decided that was what we were going to do, and that was the end of it. I didn't mind really; my life had improved and he made sure I was included in everything he did. I knew I should be more thankful. After all, if it hadn't had been for Robert I doubted I would still be around.

The one time I thought I had the upper hand where knowledge was concerned was when we were asked to deliver a small package. Robert held it in his fingers, rolling it around, looking at it with a furrowed brow. I knew instantly what it was and began to realise Robert had, in fact, led quite a sheltered life. We were delivering drugs. Drugs were always packaged that way; I had seen Slider open the same style packages. We were to deliver those little packages and sometimes collect money, sometimes not. There were times when the packages were larger and these would often be taken to huge mansion type houses. The ones I hated were the small packages that had to be delivered to the run-down apartment blocks, because those reminded me of home.

At the end of the first week, Robert had $30 and I had nothing. He spent some of his money but saved most of it. He only ever spent on essentials and he wrote down everything he earned in that little notebook. Early the following week he announced he was going to keep my money and give me an allowance. I wasn't bothered by that, I trusted him. I instinctively knew he would do right by me.

****

One day, Jonathan, Joe's right-hand man, asked us "Where do you sleep?" We liked Jonathan, he always took the time to talk to us. He wasn't a goon.

"Depends. Usually an alley not far from here," I replied.

He looked at Joe, concern etched on his face.

"How did you end up on the streets?" he asked.

Before I could answer Robert cut in. "That's a long story, we'll tell you one day, won't we, Trav?"

I wasn't entirely sure why we couldn't say but just nodded. Robert always had his reasons and he would share them with me when we were alone.

"I don't want you on the street at night. You stay here, okay?" Joe said.

He made a call. A little later Evelyn arrived, followed by Paul, a guy both Robert and I were unsure of. Paul was carrying two pull-out beds and Evelyn had linen and pillows. The beds were new and wrapped in cellophane. As Robert and Evelyn unpacked them she handed me a piece of paper.

"Trav, read out those instructions will you?" she asked.

There was a moment of silence as I looked at Robert. "Give it to me," he said.

The comment hadn't gone unnoticed but nothing was said. Robert read how to assemble the beds and soon enough they were up in the corner of the office. I watched as Evelyn went to speak, but Joe shook his head before she could.

Later that night with the lights off and just a streetlight illuminating the room, I asked Robert why he didn't want Jonathan to know how we ended up homeless.

"I don't want people to know what I did, Trav, not yet. If Joe knows what I did he might not want us around and right now we need this."

In the dark I nodded, I understood. Robert had burnt down his aunt's house, that wasn't just having a falling out and running away. I often wondered why he burnt down the house, what made him angry enough to do that. I mean, Robert was someone who didn't actually show any emotion. I'd seen him hit a man and the expression on his face hadn't changed. I fell asleep content, with a belly full of the food Evelyn brought us earlier that evening. It was the first time I had slept soundly in a year. I was woken by Robert shaking my arm.

"Trav, time to get up," he said.

I groaned and rolled to my side. He whipped the bed covers off exposing my half-naked body to the cold room.

"What time is it?" I asked.

"How the fuck do I know, but its light outside, time to get up," he replied.

"Can you even tell the time?" I asked.

"Of course I can tell the time, dumbass, but I don't have a watch."

"We need a watch, it might be too early."

"We'll buy a watch, now get your lazy ass up."

I groaned and grumbled as I sat up on the side of the bed and rubbed the sleep from my eyes. Robert was already busy making his bed, tidying away his small pile of clothes and opening the window to let yet more cold air into the room.

"Shut the fucking window, at least," I said.

"Fresh air, Trav. We need fresh air, it stinks in here. And you need a wash."

He was like my bloody mother. No, he was nothing like my mother, he cared for me. I grabbed my clothes from the screwed up pile on the floor and made my way to the small bathroom. By the time I had splashed some water over my face and dressed, he had folded all my clothes and placed them on his bed, leaving mine still unmade. Apparently he didn't like the mess; he looked at me and then the messy bed until I got the hint and made it.

It wasn't long after that Evelyn and Joe arrived. We dived into the breakfast she brought then waited for instructions on the jobs we were assigned that day. It was the usual, deliver a package and collect the money. Robert and I headed off. We held our breaths as we climbed the stairs in a dank and dark hallway, the block looked like it was about to fall down. When we came to the apartment we were looking for, there was no need to knock, the door was hanging off its hinges. It was pure filth. The apartment block I had lived in, in New York, would have been called a palace compared to where we found ourselves.

A guy was slouched on a sofa and it was obvious he was a druggie. He had that same look Slider had towards the end, his eyes and nose were red and watery, and he had that faraway look, just staring into space. He didn't even care that we had just walked in, not that he had anything worth stealing anyway. I noticed Robert look around in disgust. It wasn't that he was a snob but he did have a thing for cleanliness and order.

I stood and watched as he asked for payment and chuckled when the druggie refused.

"Fuck off," he told us.

"I want the money, and you know I can't go back to Guiseppi without your payment," Robert replied.

What I liked the most about Robert was that he never raised his voice, he didn't shout, in fact, his voice got lower the angrier he was. It was quite chilling if you wasn't used to it.

"Beat it, kid," the man said with a laugh.

I watched as Robert pulled back his fist and quick as a flash, punched the guy square in the face. Blood squirted from his nose and he slid off the sofa. Robert nodded to me and signalled with his eyes to a small table. I spotted the money and decided to take an extra $10. Why not? I handed the money to Robert, minus the $10 dollars at first. Robert just looked at me with his hand outstretched until I handed it over.

"Why can't we keep it?" I asked as we made our way back to the office.

"Wait and see," he replied.

I had learnt over the past year what he meant when he said 'wait and see'. I knew whatever he had planned, Robert would cut me in; we shared everything. As we walked back to the office I noticed people stare at Robert, their attention drawn by the fresh blood splattered on his shirt and his fists.

Paul was sitting in his usual chair just inside Joe's office door with a cigarette hanging from his lips. He nodded as we walked in. Jonathan sat opposite Joe and the two goons, whose names I never knew, we sat down in the corner. Robert held out his bloodied hand with the bills, I watched Joe look at his hand and then back up at his face.

I smiled as Robert recounted the tale of how we had gotten the money and then as he asked for the $10 back as a bonus because we had done an extra job. If he hadn't have hit the guy, Joe wouldn't have been paid. Joe was laughing so hard he had to wipe a tear from his eye. He gladly offered the $10 back. Paul was then sent to remind the guy that he always had to pay; it didn't take a genius to know what that meant.

"Kids, tomorrow I want you to meet someone," Joe said.

Later that evening Evelyn arrived with dinner. She served from plastic containers and sat with us at her father's desk as we ate.

"Travis, I want to ask you something and I don't want you to be embarrassed," Evelyn said.

I looked from her to Robert. "Can you read?" she asked.

I didn't answer at first, I was embarrassed. Robert knew, but to confess to Evelyn was not something I was comfortable with. I used the excuse of having a mouth full of food to delay my answer.

"Yes, a bit," I replied.

"Would you let me help you learn?" she said.

I looked at Robert who nodded very slightly to me. I knew that if we were to succeed in whatever plan Robert had up his sleeve I ought to be able to read properly.

"I'm not going to school," I said.

"I'm not suggesting you go to school, although it's a shame you don't. There is a great one locally you both could attend."

"No school," Robert said firmly.

"Okay, no school. But I can teach you. One night a week maybe, we'll have dinner and learn, no one will know, just us," she said with a smile.

I was hesitant but after a while nodded.

****

The following morning we waited for Joe as usual.

"I wonder who we're going to meet?" I asked.

"Don't know, sounds interesting though," Robert replied.

We heard the car pull up outside, its throaty exhaust making it easy to recognise, and we made our way down the stairs. The car was huge and as I slid across the leather seats I nodded in appreciation. I vowed that I was going to own a car as big as this one someday. Joe was sitting in the back with us, puffing on his cigar. Robert was trying to cough discreetly and cover his face. Up front was the driver and one of Joe's goons. I would have to find out his name, not that he ever spoke to us.

We pulled up outside a run-down warehouse. That wasn't surprising, every building in the neighbourhood was run down. Goon got out first and opened the door for us. I liked that and smiled up at him, but as usual he ignored me. We entered through a small metal door and found ourselves in a cavernous space filled with boxing equipment. There was a ring, punch bags hanging from the ceilings, mats and weight equipment. There were also quite a few very large guys working out.

Joe signalled to an older man, who made his way over. He had a broken nose, short grey hair and a cigarette in his mouth. With one eye half shut against the smoke swirling around his face, he smiled at us.

"Kids, this is Ted. Ted, these are the kids I told you about," Joe said.

Ted reached out and shook our hands. He had huge hands with gnarled fingers. Joe told us that he had been one of his best fighters and that he was going to teach us to box. I had seen Rocky; I knew what to do and was very excited by the prospect. Robert stood and looked around before nodding. We were shown to a changing room and handed some shorts and a vest to wear.

"What do you think of this?" I asked Robert.

"Looks cool. I'm looking forward to it."

"Bet I can beat you," I said.

He just looked at me with that expressionless look he always had and did his signature sigh before turning around and leaving the changing room.

"I can, you know. You've never seen Rocky have you?" I called after him. Fighting was something I knew a lot about.

We stood on the mats and I warmed up well, to be honest I threw some punches in the air and danced around a bit. Robert looked at me with raised eyebrows; I figured he was impressed with my skills already. I tried not to puff and pant too much but could already feel the sweat beading on my forehead.

"Now boys, I'm gonna teach you to dance," Ted said as he called over one of the largest guys I had ever seen. He made Goon look like a child.

"Fuck off mate, we don't dance," I replied. Dancing was for girls, I wanted to box.

Ted introduced us to Mack, who I guessed to be in his twenties, and I couldn't help but stare at his muscles. He had to be a heavyweight for sure. Mack took us off to a corner away from everyone and taught us how to stand, where to hold our hands, how to defend and how to throw a punch. I knew all this, or I thought that I did. Mack had Robert and I square up against each other; we were not allowed to hit but only throw soft punches so the other could learn to deflect it. I went first. As I threw my fist forward Robert moved, so my arm swung through thin air. I tried again. Rob didn't need to block my punches, I wasn't getting anywhere near him. He was fast and before I knew it, it was his turn. I hadn't had a chance to blink before one of his 'soft' punches caught me on the side of the head.

Mack had to repeat that we were not allowed to put force behind the punch and when Robert told him he hadn't, I took a sharp breath in; that had stung a little. If that was a soft punch I would need to tighten my game before we really sparred. It seemed that we had only been there five minutes before Mack looked over at the door. Joe had arrived back and was calling us over.

"How long have we been here?" I asked.

"Couple of hours, I think," Robert replied.

"Shit. Do you think Joe will let us come back?"

"I hope so, that was about the most fun I've ever had," he replied.

"You can come back tomorrow after you've run some errands for me," Joe said as we caught up with him, he'd obviously heard our exchange.

Both Robert and I had huge grins on our faces as we made our way to the changing rooms.

"Thought you said you could beat me," Robert said as we pulled on our clothes.

"I bet I can. I was just testing you out there. You know, make you sway about a bit."

"Really?"

I chuckled. "One day, bro, one day."

He stilled and looked at me, I wasn't sure why. He had a strange look on his face.

"What?" I said.

"What did you call me?"

"Bro, why?"

He smiled, not one that reached his eyes, more a sad smile at first.

"Yeah, brothers in all but blood. That's what we are," he said before heading out.

At first I didn't understand the significance of what either he or I had said. But then, watching him walk away it dawned on me. We were brothers, street brothers, we were the only family we each had.

****

The following days were pretty much the same. Deliver a package, return with the money, then hit the gym. We trained every day and I soon realised I knew nothing about boxing. I never had the same level of aggression Robert displayed. Sometimes just the look on his face when he hit the punch bag sent a shiver up my spine. He seemed to enjoy every punch he delivered in a way I couldn't begin to understand.

In one way, we got the most exercise being the delivery boys. We walked for miles each day. Joe would often offer us a car and someone to drive but Robert preferred to walk. On occasion, we would visit Evelyn in her office. We would collect items from her and take them to restaurants or houses. Most days it was a joy to see her, but not always. She could be pushy, especially with me.

"Good morning boys, how are you both today?" she said as we entered her office.

"Great. It's a lovely morning, Ev, you should get out and about," I replied.

She peered at me. "Come here, Travis."

I stepped forward and before I knew it she had one of my ears in her hand.

"When was the last time you washed your ears?" she asked.

"I don't know, two years ago?" I joked.

Using my ear as a handle, she pulled me behind her. Robert was chuckling at my discomfort. We made our way into the ladies restroom thankful she was the only lady so we wouldn't bump into another. Wetting some tissue she shoved it into my ear. I twisted and turned trying to get out of her hold. She was like a dog with a bone, she just wouldn't let go. Robert was openly laughing until she glared at him. He promptly cleaned his own ears.

"Show me your teeth, did you clean your teeth?" she asked. I clamped my mouth shut.

"Travis, do you remember how sick you got? Please don't make me come to that office every day to check that you have washed and cleaned your teeth, okay? If you don't look after yourselves you will get sick."

I nodded. Who cleaned their teeth every day anyway? But if it meant avoiding having my ears torn off, having her hands trying to pry open my jaw, I would make sure I cleaned my teeth and washed my ears. When she was satisfied I was clean, she let me go. I grumbled as I followed her back to her desk.

We were to collect some boxes from Evelyn's office and deliver them to a restaurant nearby. They weren't particularly heavy boxes, and Paul would meet us there to collect whatever payment was required. The restaurant was empty; it was too early in the day for diners. Hearing voices, we made our way to the kitchen. Paul was talking to the person I assumed was the owner.

"I've got to take a piss, let Paul know we are here," Robert said.

He left me to push through the kitchen door. Before I could make myself known I watched as Paul took a stack of bills from the guy. He counted out some, separated them off and placed the two stacks in two different pockets. At first it didn't bother me. I didn't really understand what I was seeing. On hearing the door open fully, both turned to look at me.

"Trav, put those boxes just down there, and where's Rob?" Paul asked.

"Taking a piss, anything else you need?"

"No, I'll walk back with you."

We caught up with Robert as he exited the toilets and made our way back to the office. Paul was quiet on the journey but I did catch him looking at me a few times, and so did Robert. As we fell very slightly behind Paul, Robert looked over to me, his brow furrowed in question and I shrugged my shoulders. Paul was never the most talkative, but he was looking at me as if he wanted to say something, yet he never did.

We climbed the stairs to Joe's office and found him sitting behind his desk, with Jonathan seated to the side. I watched as Paul removed the larger stack of money from his pocket and hand it over to Jonathan. As he turned to leave, Paul glanced at me. I held his gaze but kept my mouth shut. He hadn't handed over all the money he had received.

I was unsure whether to say anything, or even if it was my business to speak up. Perhaps that was normal; maybe that was Paul's cut and Joe was aware of it. I could be a snitch and tell, and if I fucked up I'd be on the wrong side of Paul. And if the guys thought I would run to Joe every time I saw something I didn't understand, would they shun us? I decided to think on it some more.

Evelyn arrived later that day with a meal for us, not just a meal but some comics as well. We ate as Robert and I flicked through the comics. He wasn't really interested in them but as Evelyn sat beside me we read aloud. The comics were old and had belonged to her brother, Joey. Although I found the stories dumb, they were a fun way to learn to read. If I stumbled over a word, Evelyn corrected me. Robert would lie on his bed and leave us to it. It was nice to have her teach me and I appreciated the effort she took. It reminded me of days with my sister and I enjoyed the time we spent together, just the two of us.

Chapter Five

Robert and I were walking through Columbia Heights; we had a small package to deliver. From the corner of my eye I noticed Robert half turn his head, as if to look over his shoulder before he turned to me. He nodded his head slightly to the left, indicating that someone was behind us. We continued at the pace we had already set until we saw an alley just to our left.

"Down there," Robert said quietly. "Trav, keep walking, I think the cops are on to us."

"How do you know?" I said, turning to look behind.

Robert grabbed my arm and told me not to look.

"You sure it's the cops? Wouldn't they have picked us up by now?" I said.

As we rounded the corner we ran. A couple of blocks away we found a pizza place and pushed through the door. Its glass windows were steamed up from the cooking and we took a seat in the far corner but with a view of the door.

"What do you think they wanted?" I asked, craning my neck to see if I could see anyone outside.

"I don't know but I can't get picked up by the cops, Trav, not ever."

"Why?"

"I just can't. I'll tell you but not here. Let's eat and then get to the gym."

We shared a pizza, ignoring the stares of the other diners. We must have looked odd sitting there with one pizza and one bottle of soda between us. The one pizza and soda was Robert's idea, because we were still saving as much of our earnings as possible. I was yet to find out what we were saving for, but it was nice to know I had a stack of money sitting in the safe at the office.

When we thought we had been there long enough, we paid the bill and made our way out. Checking to make sure the coast was clear, we headed for the gym. By then we knew our way around most of DC like the back of our hands, and it didn't take long to get to where we were going. The usual guys were there and Mack looked like he had already done ten rounds with someone. Robert asked Ted to call Joe and explain why we didn't make the drop. He knew what we were delivering by then and I also knew he wasn't at all pleased about it. I didn't have any feelings one way or another, as long as we didn't end up in a jail cell; I could still remember the stories Slider told us about that.

Ted taped up our hands and we left to change while he made his call to Joe. Robert had decided to take a run on one of the treadmills and I worked with Mack on the heavy bag. I was getting faster and bolder with my moves and enjoyed working out with him. He would swing the bag towards me, making me duck and swerve out of its way while following up with a couple of punches.

I took a breather and watched as Robert made his way to the bag. Something was bugging him, that much was obvious. Maybe it was the cop thing, but he hit that bag over and over with such force Mack had to hold on tightly. To be honest, I was in awe watching him, totally speechless until I saw the look on his face. He wasn't in the gym, he wasn't punching a red leather heavy bag hanging on a chain from the ceiling, he was someplace else. He was *fighting back*.

"Whoa kid, steady up," I heard, and noticed that Ted had silently made his way to Robert.

Robert didn't stop immediately but by the look on his face I knew he had heard. He slowed his pace until he came to a stop. He was covered in sweat, even his hair was stuck to his face. Ted grabbed hold of his wrists and it was only then that I noticed the blood. The white tape was stained red across his knuckles.

I wanted to talk to him, I wanted us to be alone. I knew he wouldn't speak in front of Mack or Ted, but then I spotted Joe entering the gym. He strode over to us and taking Robert's fists from Ted, he inspected them himself.

"What happened today?" he asked.

Robert told him of the cop, or the person he thought was a cop. He was able to detail exactly what the guy was wearing and where and how many times he had seen him throughout the morning. I hadn't noticed the guy at all. I would have to be more observant in the future. It was strange because if you watched Robert it would never have been obvious that he was scanning, looking around. Yet he knew everything that seemed to go on around him.

****

The next days, weeks and months followed the same pattern. One or two evenings a week I learnt to read; during the day, we ran our errands then hit the gym. Every day we worked out, competing on the treadmill to see who could run the fastest, the longest, who could lift the heaviest weights and skip the most. Not that I would ever tell him, but Robert was far fitter and more muscular that I was. And as each week wore on, he got bigger. I think we were evenly matched on speed but he was stronger, his punch harder.

It wasn't long after that we were allowed to get into the ring and spar, first with each other and then with some of the other guys that trained. Most would mock us and no matter how hard I tried not to, I always bit. Robert was as cool, or perhaps as cold, as always. I think he took boxing a lot more seriously than I did. He meant every punch, he wanted to hurt his opponent and it wasn't long before I noticed wariness from the other guys when they climbed into the ring with him. I sensed he was unpredictable; you were never quite sure what you were going to get with Robert.

Our birthday kind of crept up on us; well, I say ours, but if it was July 28th, it was technically Robert's. Regardless, we always *celebrated* together. We hadn't told anyone it was our birthday, and Evelyn was distressed when she found out a day after. We had decided that we would treat ourselves to some new clothes and needed some of our savings from the safe.

"Jon, can you get some of our money out for us?" Robert asked him.

"Sure, Rob, how much do you want?"

"$50 dollars each should do it."

"What are we celebrating then?" Jonathan said. It was an unusually large amount of money for us.

"We need new clothes, some boxing boots and stuff," Robert replied.

"And it's our birthday so we're treating ourselves," I added.

"You're kidding me? It's your birthday, on the same day?" Jonathan said.

"Well, sort of. It's Rob's birthday anyway," I said.

Unbeknown to us Jonathan told Joe, who then told Evelyn. She came into the office the following morning with a cake. Before we were allowed a slice she told us off for not letting her know.

"We don't really bother with it," I said.

"Why ever not?" she asked.

"No one ever celebrated my birthday," Robert said quietly.

It was not often that he spoke about his life, and most unusual that he had done so in front of an office full of people. I was quick to divert attention. It was clear Joe had heard and he was looking at Robert, apparently waiting to see if he would explain.

"My sister used to make me a cake every year but I bet yours is much better, Ev," I said.

Robert just sat on his own with his cake and picked at it, not having a sweet tooth. I devoured mine then finished off his and an extra slice. Even Goon gave us a smile on that day. When the office emptied, the doors were locked and Robert and I settled down for the night, I asked him if he was okay.

"Sure, why wouldn't I be?" he replied, somewhat aggressively.

We were lying in the dark but the blinds stayed firmly open on the two windows in the room. I never questioned it, Robert just wouldn't have them pulled and his bed was the one next to the window. I would catch him just looking out, up to the sky for hours sometimes.

"You don't seem very happy, that's all," I said.

"I'm fine."

"You're fine like, when a girl say's 'I'm fine' or like, you really are fine?"

"Trav, what the fuck are you talking about?"

"Oh, I know the difference. My sister used to say she was fine when I knew she wasn't. It means you don't want to talk about it. Or you're fine as in really okay."

I was a bit of an authority on women, far more knowledgeable than Robert on the subject of the female species even at our age. I smiled at the thought. It was good to have something I was better at than him.

"You talk shit, you know that don't you?" he replied.

"So, are you fine or fine?"

"Go to sleep, Trav."

We fell silent for a while. Just as my eyelids were about to drop I heard him very quietly speak.

"I'm fine like your sister says, Trav."

"Okay, but if you ever want to tell me, I'll listen. We're brothers, Rob, we don't have to have secrets."

He never answered, but in the dim light I could see him nod his head before he turned on his side. I lay awake for ages after, worrying. I knew he'd had a bad life but there was a lot more about Robert that I didn't know, and it saddened me that he hadn't shared. I wasn't sad that he wouldn't tell me, there were things I had never spoken about; it saddened me that he might feel he *couldn't*.

I think that was one of the things that bonded us - we knew without the need for words. He knew I wasn't just beaten by my dad and my brothers, and I knew he wasn't just beaten by his aunt and burnt her house down. There was more to both of us and we accepted that in each other. One day we would open up completely, I was sure of that, but only when we had dealt with the demons inside ourselves.

****

Time seemed to fly by and as it did we got closer and closer to Joe; he became a father figure as such. Many a time he had invited us to his house; he wanted us to live with him, but for some reason Robert always declined. Although we stayed the odd night, he was comfortable at the office despite the fact that we had really outgrown it.

"Why don't you want to live at Joe's?" I had asked him one day.

"I don't ever want to be reliant on someone. You can, I won't mind, but this way I can walk away anytime without feeling like I'm trapped."

"Would you ever consider walking away?"

"No, what we have is good but if I get comfortable in his house and he finds out about me, he might throw me out - and then what?" Robert said.

Whatever was in Robert's past was worrying him enough that he would never get close to anyone. He always held a little of himself back. But then I did the same. Trusting people was harder for Robert than for me. There was also Joey; he was Joe's son and not someone Robert or I had taken to. There was just something about him we didn't like. Maybe it was the permanent sneer or the fact he was so fucking lazy that bugged us. He would slouch around the office and even though he was just a little older than us, he smoked his cigarettes and tried to be one of the gang. It was clear some of the guys tolerated him, not many liked him. But he was Joe's son, so we formed an uneasy and somewhat distant friendship with him.

Evelyn still fussed over us every day and I wondered if Joey resented that. She brought us meals, clothes, and presents, and spent time chatting with us. Over the time we had known her, she had become very important to us. I had stopped thinking of my family, of the disappointment and hurt I felt with my sister, and Evelyn seemed to take her place. She became the one who had found me, Robert became the brother who actually liked me, and in my mind I started to erase all my life prior to the age of eleven.

****

Robert and I were sitting on the grass in a small park area surrounded by apartment blocks, blocks that Joe owned. It was a bright spring morning and we were waiting for Richard. He collected the rents for Joe, and like Jonathan, was someone we got along with, I noticed Robert watching a family, a mom and dad, a son, all playing ball.

"What was your mom like?" I asked.

"I don't really remember her. I know she had blonde hair, but I can't picture her face anymore," he replied.

"Does that bother you?"

"No. She was a drunk, I think."

"How did she die?"

"They told me it as a car crash that killed her and my dad. I don't know any other details, I never even went to their funeral."

"Does that bother you?" I said.

He looked at me. "You say 'does that bother you' a lot, don't you?"

He had a half smile on his face.

"I'm just asking if things bother *you*, I know they would if it was me."

"So what bothers you then?" he asked.

"That I hate my family. Is that wrong?"

"Hate is a waste of energy, bro. Do what I do, block them out."

"What happens if they turn up one day?" I said.

"We'll deal with it. You won't have to face them alone, I'll be with you," Robert replied.

"I don't ever want them to know where I am, in case they come for me. I stabbed my brother, Rob," I said.

He looked at me for a long time without answering.

"Did you kill him?" he asked.

"No, he was hurting my sister so I stabbed him in the arm with a kitchen knife."

"Should have killed the fucker," he replied.

"I don't know if I could ever kill anyone," I said, lying back down on the grass and letting the sun warm my face.

"You'd be surprised what you can do," he said quietly.

I didn't answer, I wasn't sure what to say, but by the way he had spoken, *I knew*. I knew then that he had killed someone. We sat in silence for a while, and I thought hard about what he had said. It didn't make me feel any different towards him but, fuck, he had actually *killed* someone. It had to be his aunt; maybe he killed her then burnt down the house to cover his tracks. My mind started to race, so much so that I didn't realise he was looking at me.

"Come on, time to get back," he said. Richard was walking towards us.

I should have said something but I didn't, and I worried that he might clam up again. That might have been the one chance we had to open up but the moment had passed.

"You all right?" Richard asked.

"Sure," I replied.

Joe wanted us to head over to a warehouse, there was a truck being unloaded of kitchen appliances and a few extra bodies were needed to stack the boxes. We had done this once before, and I often wondered if the drivers of the trucks were aware we were relieving them of their cargo. They never seemed to be around.

Robert was quiet as we worked but I whistled away, anything to break the silence. Goon was at the warehouse, leaning against a metal pillar and puffing away on a cigarette. 'Directing operations,' I believed it was called. Every time I passed I gave him a big smile. His frown would grow deeper and deeper. It was like tormenting a dog on a chain, except he wasn't tied to that pillar and I should have remembered that.

"What the fuck do you keep grinning at?" he said on my tenth pass.

"Ah, he speaks," I replied.

"Of course I speak, now stop fucking smiling and get on with it."

"Yes, sir," I said, nodding my head.

"He'll smack you one someday," Robert said as he caught up with me.

I chuckled; antagonising Goon was a good way to pass the day. I doubted he would smack me; by the size of him he'd never be able to catch me. I imagined I would be able to walk faster than he could run. His pot belly hung over the top of his trousers and his shirt strained against his chest. Goon had no neck; it was as if his head just sat atop his shoulders, or perhaps he actually had one, but too many donuts had obscured it.

Once we had finished unloading the truck we started the journey to the gym. Robert was still in a bit of a funk and I tried to be happy, to cheer him up. By the time I had bid a good afternoon to the fifth woman that passed by Robert was about ready to explode. He sighed.

"You always sigh when you're miserable," I said.

"No I don't."

"Yes you do."

"I don't, Travis."

"You do, *Robert*."

"Trav, I'm not arguing with you," he said.

"You are," I replied.

"I am what?"

"Arguing with me, you always argue with me. You could just accept that I might be right sometimes," I told him.

We had stopped in the middle of the sidewalk facing each other. I was smiling, Robert wasn't.

"You know, if you smiled just a little every now and again you might not look so scary," I said.

"Do I scare you?" he asked in a surprised voice.

"Not me but you sure as hell ain't going to get a girlfriend anytime soon with that scowl."

I saw a twitch, just a small one at the side of his mouth.

"All those women we passed? They love me because I smile at them," I said.

The twitch had developed into a tight-lipped smirk type of smile.

"Go on, do it. Smile. The world is a better place when you smile," I said. I'm sure I'd heard someone say that once.

He huffed, shook his head but at least he smiled. Then he got me in a headlock and forced me along the sidewalk. We both laughed out loud and once he released me, we raced to the gym.

We had changed and were warming up, I was working out with the speedball and Robert was about to go in the ring with Mack. Joe had come to watch us train. He did that sometimes, he would take five minutes out of his day and stand beside Ted as he coached us. By that time we knew that Joe owned the gym, and all the guys would box for him at some point. There were times when one or two would come in for training, bruised and with half-shut eyes. Sometimes they were allowed to stay, and sometimes not. It seemed that Joe didn't take too kindly to those that lost.

I paused my training and watched Robert. The moment we had entered the gym his earlier, very brief spell of cheerfulness had vanished. Looking at him now, in the ring, it was difficult to imagine he had actually been smiling just an hour or so before. He wasn't concentrating when Mack threw a punch. What should have been easily deflected wasn't, and even I heard the crack of Robert's nose as it broke. I winced. Robert did the complete opposite to what was expected, he dropped his arms and stared hard at Mack. The look on his face was murderous. He threw just one punch, so quick Mack had no chance to defend himself and I watched, open-mouthed as he fell backwards onto his ass.

Ted jumped in the ring and surrounded Robert with his arms, the gym fell silent as everyone stopped and watched. For a moment Mack was motionless and I breathed a sigh of relief as he moved and propped himself up on his elbows. But it was Robert's face that had me walking towards him. For someone who normally showed no emotion, he was utterly devastated. I climbed up the side of the ring and leant over the ropes. He had blood dripping from his nose, over his lips and down his chin; it had splattered on his T-shirt. He looked at me, I returned the stare. We didn't always need to speak, don't ask me why, but somehow we communicated.

He pulled the string of the gloves loose with his teeth before placing them between his knees and pulling his hands free. He walked over to Mack who, thankfully, was being helped to his feet, still a little groggy. Mack smiled, gave him a soft swipe to the head and told him he had anger issues before chuckling and being helped to the changing room.

Robert sat on the floor of the ring and I climbed under the ropes to sit next to him, shoulder to shoulder. Nothing was said; just a very slight shoulder bump was enough to let him know I was with him, and not just physically. We sat in silence, heads bowed with only the sound of a drip every now and again as blood fell and hit the floor. Ted climbed under the ropes and knelt in front of Robert. He held a wad of cotton in his hand, which he then placed against Robert's nose to stem the bleeding.

"You okay, bro?" I finally asked. Robert nodded.

"Want to tell me what went on there?" Ted asked.

Robert finally looked up and shrugged his shoulders. "Guess I just kind of lost it for a bit," he said.

"That was one powerful punch," Ted said with a chuckle.

"I tasted the blood and I didn't see him, I saw..." Robert never finished his sentence.

"Who did you see, kid?" Ted gently prompted.

Robert shook his head; he wasn't going to say anymore.

"Okay, let's get you back to the office, someone needs to fix that nose. Gonna hurt like a bitch, I warn you," Ted said.

Goon was waiting outside with a car; I waited for him to open the door for us. He didn't, he just stood looking at me, or was it a scowl? I could never really tell with him, he had a face like a bulldog, but less friendly. I opened the door and Robert and I slid across the back seat. We were driven to the office and as we climbed the stairs Paul and his wife followed us in. Paul's wife, Rosa, was a petite Irish woman; she kept to herself and rarely came to the office. But she had been a nurse so we were told that she would fix Robert's nose. She had protested that he ought to go to the hospital for fixing but Robert refused. The hospital would want information - information we couldn't give, an address for starters. With shaking hands she stood in front of him, her fingers on either side of his nose. Then, with a twist of her hands, she straightened it. He never made a sound. My stomach turned at the noise and even Goon screwed up his face in disgust. Robert walked off to the bathroom to clean himself up.

"How the fuck did that not hurt him?" Joe said, shaking his head.

"He doesn't feel, Joe," I replied.

All heads turned my way. I shrugged my shoulders, there was no explanation needed. Robert didn't feel anything; he had no emotions, that much was obvious to me.

"Did you see that punch? Fuck, that kid can box," Joe said. The conversation then moved on to how Rob had put Mack on his ass.

Joey sat in his usual chair, his feet up on the corner of his father's desk, ignoring the conversation, sneering and puffing away on his cigarette. He smirked at me as he deliberately flicked the ash to the floor.

****

One night Robert said, "I've had enough of being an errand boy, I'm going to talk to Joe about letting us do more."

It had been obvious over the previous few weeks that he was getting bored just picking up laundry, running packages around and sitting about the office. To be honest, so was I. For the past few years we had been running around DC and it had gotten tedious.

"Like what?" I asked.

"What does Jonathan actually do? Or Richard, or Paul for that matter? I want to learn what they do, maybe move about a bit," he replied.

"Do you think Joe will let us?"

"Don't see why not. It's not like we don't know the kind of business he runs here, is it?"

"I guess not. Does that bother you?"

"No, I just want to earn enough money, Trav."

"Enough for what?"

"Enough to know I'll never be hungry or poor again."

"How will you know when enough is enough though?"

"I guess we never do, but this isn't what I planned for us."

"You gonna let me in on this grand plan?" I asked.

He chuckled. "One day."

"You don't actually have one do you?"

"Oh, I have a plan. I told you, we are never going to be hungry again. I want a place to live and I don't want to have to rely on someone the rest of my life for that."

So that was the grand plan. Seemed okay to me, not that we were going hungry anyway. Evelyn still brought us meals, although not every day. There were times we went out for a pizza or to a local restaurant where we had become regulars. The manager of that particular restaurant, one owned by Joe, always took pleasure in serving us. At fifteen years old we both looked older; we weren't just a couple of kids looking odd and awkward. Robert hated junk food, candy or soda but sometimes I would grab a burger while he ate the pasta Evelyn brought.

The following morning Robert announced to Joe that he wanted us to do more. There was no asking; Robert never asked for anything, he stated what he wanted. Of course, Joe said no at first. But we were relentless. Day after day Robert would badger the guys, asking them questions and trying to learn. We learned that Jonathan was Joe's right hand man; he managed all the money, and he advised Joe. Paul looked after any construction projects Joe had going on and Richard dealt with all the tenants. Goon was just a driver, we knew that, and then there was Mack. Mack boxed and when he wasn't boxing he accompanied Joe on his *business dealings*. It was obvious to us that he was Joe's personal security.

Eventually Joe gave in.

"Quit with the nagging will you? You sound like my daughter. Fine, you go with Richard and help with the rents," Joe said.

Robert gave me one of his 'I told you so' looks as we followed Richard from the office.

We accompanied Richard to the first block, probably the worst one that Joe owned. It was run down and not in the nicest part of DC. As we entered the front door Richard handed us a book and pen. We were to collect rent and write the apartment number down. Robert was to start on the bottom floor and I was sent to the top. Richard went to meet with the supervisor.

I made my way up the stairs, opting to avoid the elevator with its broken light and stench of piss. At first I was unsure of the reception I would receive. I was just fifteen years old; would the tenants take me seriously and pay up? However, after I knocked on the first door, I knew I had found my calling. Standing before me, dressed in a top that was way too low and a skirt way too short, was a goddess. Well, I say a goddess; she would have looked better had she not had a cigarette hanging from her blood-red lips and did something with the bleached blonde hair with black roots.

I didn't care though, she looked me up and down and smiled, obviously pleased with what she saw. I leant against the door frame making sure to flex my muscles.

"Hey, beautiful," I said.

She smiled some more.

"Hey yourself, handsome," she replied. "What can I do for you?"

"I'm here to collect the rent but how about I take your name first," I replied, trying to sound as sexy as I could.

She looked at me and licked her lips before replying. "My clients call me Mistress Spanx."

She took her time to spell out her name so I got it right.

"Well, Mrs. Spanx, we're updating our records and need a telephone number if you have one," I replied, chancing my arm.

"How about I give you a card?" She handed over her business card.

"Oh, you do massages," I said.

"It's one of the services I offer. Now, what do I call you?" she purred as she spoke.

"Travis, but my friends call me Trav."

"Well, Trav, how about you come back and visit me another time?"

"Sure, when were you thinking?" I asked, a grin spreading from ear to ear.

78

"In about three years, when you're a man," she said before closing her door.

I stood for a minute, wondering what I had done wrong. Fuck her; she didn't know what she was missing. I put a big cross beside her name and the words 'no rent' then moved on to the next apartment.

The next door I knocked on was opened by another goddess, although maybe not so forward as Mrs. Spanx. She was shorter than me, maybe just a little over five feet with short brown hair and big blue eyes. I watched as her eyes widened, a sure sign she liked what she saw, right? I consulted my notebook.

"Good morning, Mrs. err..." I said.

"Shenton, Karen Shenton," she replied.

"Oh, right. Well, good morning, Mrs. Shenton, and how are you today?"

"I'm very well, what can I help you with?"

"I'm here to collect the rent and to update our records," I replied.

"Oh, okay. Please, come in," she offered, appearing slightly surprised.

As she opened the door wide and stood to one side, I entered her apartment. It was tidy and comfortable. I stood in the middle of her living room while she fetched her purse. Counting out notes, she handed me that week's rent. There was an awkward moment of silence as I counted the bills, not that there was a need to.

"You said you needed to update your records?" she said.

"Ah yes, do you have a telephone number? You know, just in case of emergencies," I replied.

"Emergencies? Wouldn't the supervisor take care of notifying us?" she asked.

"He should, but he might *be* the emergency."

"Mmm, I see. Sorry, but I don't have a telephone."

I think she had caught on to my game, but the banter was fun and I liked her. She was pretty, petite and looked like she would fit nice and snug into my side. I felt a stirring in my pants and turned from her trying to subtly adjust myself.

"Is there anything else I can help you with?" she asked.

It was on the tip of my tongue to tell her what she could *help me with* but I refrained. I smiled at her, my killer smile, the one the ladies always respond to.

"I think that's about everything for the moment, Karen. Can I call you Karen?" I asked.

"I guess so, let me show you out," she replied.

She didn't ask my name, I assumed she was just overwhelmed by my personality. I made my way out of her apartment and paused before moving onto the next.

"So, I'll see you next week?" I said.

"I imagine so," she replied with a smile before closing the door.

Smiling, I nodded to myself and put a tick beside her name in the notebook. Yep, she fancied me for sure. I'd only got to my fourth flat before I heard Robert on the floor below me; his bored tone of voice was not going to help him make friends.

"You only did four apartments?" he said when he saw me smiling.

"I was building relationships," I said.

"You were chatting up the ladies, I heard you," he replied.

"Yes, same thing. You should try it. I bet I get laid before you."

"I don't care who gets laid first, but I've done three fucking floors here and you've done four apartments. Four," he said holding up four fingers as if I hadn't understood.

"But I got one phone number, look," I said waving the business card under his nose. He snatched it from me.

"Mistress Spanx, really?" he said as he handed it back.

"She told me to come back and visit with her," I replied, giving him a wink.

"You'll catch a fucking disease from that one," he said.

"You don't even know her, she seemed like a nice lady."

"I'm not sure *lady* is the right word, Trav. She's a hooker."

"You don't know that, it says here she does massages."

Robert looked at me, his eyebrows raised. "Mistress Spanx, Trav. What do you think she *really* does for a living?" He sighed and shook his head before turning away and walking back down the stairs.

I followed flipping the card over in my fingers. It was an unusual name to have, for sure. Robert was still chuckling to himself as we caught up with Richard and the supervisor. Richard was going through a list of repairs, or rather, how *not* to repair and keep the tenants happy at the same time.

"What's funny?" he asked Robert.

"Trav here thinks Mistress Spanx is a nice *lady* who does massages," Rob said.

I was a little annoyed to see both Richard and the Super doubled over in laughter. I huffed and made my way out of the building. All right, so she had blown me off, so to speak, but I wasn't giving up that easy. And so what if she was a hooker? Everyone had to earn a living, didn't they?

****

The next few weeks followed the same pattern. Robert got increasingly stressed as he covered most of the blocks we collected rent from.

"PR my friend, that's what I'm doing," I'd told him one day.

"You don't even know what the fuck PR stands for," he'd replied.

"Yes I do, Private Relationships, that's what I'm building here. You might want to try it."

I was determined to get laid first; I wanted something that I managed to do before Robert. He was faster than me in the gym, a better boxer, more educated - but he wasn't going to get laid anytime soon unless he changed his attitude. And the ladies didn't like him; he scared most people, even more so as he got older.

My PR'ing finally paid off. I knocked on Karen's door, ignoring Mistress Spanx, and planted a huge smile on my face. My smile slipped somewhat when she answered. It was clear she had been crying; her eyes were red-rimmed. She didn't greet me with the smile that she usually did, the smile that made her eyes sparkle and little dimples appear on her cheeks.

"Oh, Travis. Hold on, let me get my purse," she said, leaving me standing in the hallway.

When she returned I took the money and pocketed it.

"Are you okay?" I asked. I was genuinely concerned.

"Sure. Just a bad day, that's all."

"Want to talk about it? I'm a good listener," I said.

She chuckled. "You don't want to hear my problems."

"Sure I do. How about I make you a coffee and you can tell me what has those pretty eyes so sad," I had been waiting to use that line forever.

She opened the door and I followed her to the kitchen. The outdated kitchen had a cupboard door that needed fixing, and a tap that required a jiggle so the water would flow into the coffee machine. Karen sat on the sofa, and while we waited for the coffee to brew I sat beside her.

"So, what's up?" I asked.

"Life, Trav, that's what's up. I lost my job the other day; I don't know how long I can stay here before the money runs out."

"What about your husband, doesn't he work?"

She chuckled. "I'm not married."

"Oh, I thought... assumed you would be."

"I let people believe that, I don't know why," she replied, as she handed me a freshly brewed coffee.

"So what did you do, for a job?" I asked.

"It was nothing much, just cooked at the local diner. You know the one around the block, Hot Rods?"

I knew the one, Joe owned it. On the odd occasion I'd managed to persuade Robert to eat a burger, it's where we went, but I hadn't noticed Karen there before.

"I know it, I know the owner too. Want me to have a word? See if we can get your job back?" I asked.

"I don't know. The manager isn't very nice. He wanted to take me on a date and when I refused I lost my job."

"Wait here," I said.

I left the apartment and made my way down the stairs. Robert was talking to a cat, a cat being held by the one tenant I never wanted to call on, Mrs. Wrenn. He looked up as I approached.

"I need to do something," I said.

"Do what?" he asked.

"Beat the shit out of someone," I replied as I carried on walking.

"Sailor, tell Mrs Wrenn I'll be back in a minute. Trav, wait up," I heard him say.

"Sailor?" I asked as he caught up.

"It's the cat's name, don't ask. So who are we beating the shit out of and why?"

I told him about Karen losing her job and he shrugged his shoulders. "Seems a good enough reason, let's go."

It took less than a minute to walk the block to Hot Rods. It was lunchtime and the diner was full. As we entered I spotted the manager just behind the counter, he appeared to be leaning a little too close to a waitress. I could see the forced smile on her face as she turned her head slightly away from him, trying to angle her body so he wasn't pressed up against her tits. I strode over.

Reaching forwards I took the arm of the waitress and with a smile pulled her towards me and away from him. I then swung my fist back and punched him square in the face. He fell backwards, landing on his ass as blood squirted from his nose.

"My girlfriend, Karen Shenton, will be back at work tomorrow. Don't make me come back here again," I said.

I heard a chuckle from behind; it was audible because the whole diner had fallen silent as they watched me. Turning, I saw Robert. His arms were folded across his chest and he had a large grin on his face. As I walked back around the counter the waitress whispered, "Thank you."

The manager hadn't said a word. He rose, grabbed some napkins to hold to his face and shuffled off with his head bent low. Robert and I made our way out.

"Your girlfriend?" he asked.

"He doesn't have to know she isn't, does he?" I replied with a grin.

Back at the apartment, Robert continued talking to Sailor, who was still in Mrs. Wrenn's arms, and I made my way up to the top floor. I knocked on Karen's door and she opened it immediately. She had a phone to her ear and a smile on her face.

"Yes, he's back here now. I'll see you tomorrow, early shift," she said to her caller.

She reached out and held my hand; she pulled me into the apartment as she placed the phone on its cradle in the hallway.

"Thought you didn't have a phone," I said as she raised her arms and placed them around my neck.

"I didn't, but then I didn't have anyone to call until now."

I placed my arms around her waist and pulled her to me. She rose on tiptoes until her lips were millimetres from mine. I'd never kissed a girl properly before but instinctively parted my lips and followed her lead. Her tongue swept along my lower lip until finding mine, she tasted of the coffee we had drunk earlier. She pressed herself further into my body and I could feel my cock growing hard. I tried to pull my hips back, embarrassed, but she had me pinned to the wall. Her kiss was getting deeper and I heard a small moan from her. Fuck, this was serious. I pulled my head back slightly and smiled down at her.

"I need to get back to work," I said as one hand circled her lower back.

"You sure?" she asked.

I nodded. "How about I come visit later, when I'm done at the gym," I said.

"I'll look forward to that," she replied.

With a brief kiss and a wink, I left her apartment. As her door closed, leaving me in the hallway, I slumped against the wall and adjusted my cock which was now painfully straining against the zipper of my jeans. I couldn't stop the grin from spreading as I knocked on the next door and greeted the elderly, very grumpy owner of apartment number fifteen. As usual, Robert had completed most of the block before we met half way on the stairs.

"What are you grinning at?" he asked.

"I got a rather nice thank you from Karen," I replied.

"You got laid?"

"Not yet, later though."

"Does she know you're not quite sixteen years old and a virgin at that?" he said with a smirk on his face.

"Of course she doesn't, I'm not that fucking stupid," I replied.

"How old does she think you are?"

"Fuck knows. Who cares, I'm in there. Watch and learn, bro, watch and learn."

"Make sure you get protection," Robert said.

"For sure, heading to the drugstore right now. Reckon they do extra large?"

Shaking his head and laughing, we left the block. The drugstore did, indeed, stock extra large but I opted for large instead; I'd rather they be too tight than loose. I bought a pack of three, stuffed them in my back pocket, and we made our way back to Joe's. I whistled all the way, while Robert scowled.

"Jealousy is not a nice trait, Rob," I said. He rolled his eyes, did his sigh thing and we carried on in silence.

After depositing the rent with Jonathan and making sure our notebooks were up to date, we headed for the gym. I talked about Karen and THE KISS all the way although I spared Robert the raging hard-on details; he looked like he was getting a little pissed.

We warmed up with a run before making our way to the speed ball and finally the heavy bag. My mind wasn't totally on my boxing and when Mack swung the heavy bag at me it caught me in the balls, knocking me to my ass.

"Watch the merchandise, Mack, he's got a date later," Robert called out.

"You got a date?" Mack asked with a laugh.

"Yeah, nothing funny about that," I replied, indignant.

"She know how old you are?" he asked.

"No, she doesn't fucking know how old I am, okay? What's with the fucking age anyway? My cock works the same way yours does," I said.

Mack nearly spat his gum shield out he laughed so hard. "Trav, it isn't just about your cock my friend. Let me give you some advice, tell you what the chicks like."

He placed his arm around my shoulder and, with Robert, we sat on a bench lining the wall.

"First, they like the kissing. Especially their necks, they like that. You got to take it slow, have them begging for more," he said.

"They like the pussy eaten too," someone called out.

I looked up to see Lou, a huge black man with a scarred face, making obscene gestures with his tongue. It then occurred to me that most of the guys in the gym had heard our exchange and were listening in.

"Right, so kiss 'em slow, eat the pussy, what else?" I asked.

"Fuck her hard, Trav, so she can't walk after. The women, they love that," another called out gyrating his hips. In fact, he looked more like he was having a fit than simulating a fuck.

"Look, I'm fucking serious. She wants me, help me out here," I said.

Robert appeared to be crying until I looked closer. He was laughing so hard that tears leaked from his eyes. I stood.

"Fuck you lot, I'll work it out myself," I said, stomping to the changing room.

"Trav, come back, we're sorry," Lou called out with a laugh. I flipped him the finger over my shoulder.

I was muttering to myself and getting dressed when Robert walked into the changing room.

"I'm sorry, bro. Just take it slow, she'll show you what she wants," he said.

"How the fuck do you know?" I mumbled.

"I don't, but ignore those guys, they're just teasing."

"I'll see you back at the office, yeah?" I said as I patted the back pocket of my jeans to make sure I had the condoms.

"Sure," he replied. We headed to the gym door and went our separate ways.

The closer I got to the apartment block the more nervous I began to feel and my palms sweated slightly. My earlier bravado had run for the hills. I had a key to the main door and slowly took the stairs to the top floor. As I paused on the landing, the door to Mistress Spanx opened and I watched an old, flabby guy with red cheeks leave. Mistress Spanx gave me a wink before closing it. I stood outside Karen's, took a deep breath and knocked. She opened the door with a smile and stepping aside, she ushered me in.

"What can I get you to drink? A beer?" she asked.

I shook my head. "Just a coffee would be good," I replied. I hadn't drunk beer before.

While Karen bustled around the kitchen I sat on the sofa, not entirely sure what to do with myself. I took a good look around. She had a small TV in one corner sitting atop a chest of drawers. Around it were photos in frames of what looked like family. There was one with an older couple, a child in their arms. There were a few of Karen with a guy and I wondered who he was. One of the plain cream walls was full of paintings much too abstract for me to understand what they were meant to be, but they brought colour to the otherwise plain room. The leather sofa creaked as I shuffled around, its worn cushions cracked but comfortable. I sat back, crossing one foot over my knee and waited.

Karen returned with two coffees, sat beside me and smiled. For a moment there was an awkwardness between us; I wasn't sure what to say so sipped my coffee in silence.

"My manager rang earlier, to make sure I would be back at work," she said.

"That's good. I don't think you'll have any trouble there," I replied.

"Yeah, he said he hadn't realised I had a *boyfriend*."

"Err, yeah, sorry about that. Thought it might make him keep his hands to himself if he thought you did," I said.

She chuckled as she placed her cup on the floor beside her and shuffled closer to me.

"Thank you, whatever you said helped."

She shuffled closer still until she was snuggled into my side. As I imagined, she was a perfect fit. I placed my arm around her shoulders. She lifted her face and angled her body towards me until eventually she moved to straddle me. She placed her hands on either side of my head and kissed me. As my hands crept up her back my fingers caught hold of her T-shirt; we broke apart as I pulled it over her head. She had the most amazing tits spilling out over the top of her bra. I cupped each one, pushing them together, squeezing them. She reached around and unclipped the bra, sliding the straps from her shoulder and threw it to the floor. Her nipples were hard.

"Suck them," she whispered.

Fuck me, I thought I had died and gone to heaven. I greedily sucked a nipple into my mouth, still squeezing until I she yelped and pulled away. Karen grabbed the hem of my T-shirt and pulled it over my head. She pushed herself from my lap and stood before me, unzipping her skirt. It fell to the floor, leaving her standing in the skimpiest lace panties which she then peeled off. I fumbled with my jeans, rushing to remove them. I watched her eyes travel the length of my body, coming to rest on my impressive cock. Well, I thought it was impressive anyway.

As she took a step towards me, one hand wrapped around my cock, she gently squeezed and massaged. I couldn't stop the moan that started in the pit of my stomach and travelled the length of my body before escaping. With her other hand, Karen gently pushed me back on the sofa. She fell to her knees and I prayed to God that she was about to do what I thought she was. But as her tongue gently touched the tip I exploded.

"Fuck, fuck, fuck," I said.

"Wow, Travis, that was quick," she replied.

"It's been a while, give me a minute." I was frantically pumping away on my own cock to keep it hard.

She sat back on her heels, smirking.

"That wasn't your first time, was it?" she asked.

"Of course not," I replied breathlessly.

My efforts paid off; my wrist ached but my cock was rigid again in my then sticky hand. I reached out for her, subtly wiping my hand on her sofa. I grabbed her wrist and pulled her towards me; she straddled my lap and lowered herself, my cock just brushing against her entrance.

"Condoms, they're in my jeans," I said, trying to reach down without her falling off.

"It's okay, I'm on the pill," she said.

She lowered onto me and it was the most wonderful feeling. Her wet pussy tightened around my cock; it was hot and wet as she moved, slowly at first. I grabbed her face, pulling her towards me for a kiss - albeit a sloppy kiss that had her wipe her mouth with the back of her hand. As she rode me, I recited the alphabet in my head, forwards then backwards, anything to stave off the need to come. I felt a strange sensation in my stomach as she upped the pace, my balls tightened, then pulsed slightly before I shot my load into her. I moaned loudly into her mouth before she pulled her head away. She frowned at me, her frown deepening the wider I grinned.

"Baby, that was fucking awesome," I said.

"Erm, yes, for you I guess it was," she replied.

She climbed from my lap and my now flaccid cock fell to one side. I rested back, placed my hands behind my head and closed my eyes. Taking a deep breath, I let out a sigh. When I opened them, Karen was already dressing herself. She had her panties back on, was fastening her bra and then pulled her T-shirt over her head.

She cleared her throat before speaking. "Can I get you a drink or something?"

"Sure, I could do with something cold," I replied, still with that stupid grin on my face.

While she was back in the kitchen I pulled on my jeans and T-shirt, not bothering to clean myself up first. Karen came and sat on the sofa, this time at the other end, and handed me a glass of water. My throat was so dry I gulped it down.

"Trav, how old are you?" she asked. The question startled me somewhat.

"Nineteen," I lied.

"Oh, I, erm, I have to get ready for my shift," she said.

"I thought you said you were on tomorrow."

"Yeah, I was, but someone called in sick."

I took that as my cue to leave; perhaps she wanted some time to recover before work. I rose from the sofa and walked to where she sat. Leaning down, I kissed her on her lips. That time, though, she didn't open her mouth. I smiled as I made my way to the door.

"How about I call you tomorrow?" I said.

"Yeah, okay. I might be a bit busy the next few days. You know, catching up on work and all that. Need to pay the rent," she said with a chuckle.

She rose and followed me to the apartment door; before I left I stopped and turned towards her.

"Thank you for today, it was fun. Shall I take your number?" I said.

"Oh, okay."

She pulled a piece of paper from a pad beside her telephone and hastily scribbled down a number. Without looking, I folded it and placed it in my pocket.

"I'll call you tomorrow," I said as I left.

I raced down the stairs and with a bounce in my step, I made my way back to the office.

****

"Bro, you here?" I called out as I climbed the stairs.

"Yeah, good time?" I heard Robert say.

As I walked in I saw him lying on his bed, his hands behind his head.

"Fucking epic, man I was good," I replied.

"So you actually got laid then?"

"For sure, she rode me like a fucking cowgirl, couldn't get enough of me."

"Spare me the details. Are you seeing her again?" he asked.

"Maybe. You know me, bro, fuck 'em and leave 'em."

"Travis, this is the first girl you have ever fucked and I guarantee you will be on that phone tomorrow calling her. Go and shower, you stink like a fucking alley cat."

I chuckled as I made my way to the small bathroom. After much nagging from Evelyn, Joe had recently installed a shower for us, just a plastic cubicle with lukewarm water but it did the job. I stripped off and climbed under the dribble of water. I soaped my hands and washed my cock; it was a little sore but hardened as I recalled my time with Karen. While the water ran cold I stroked, giving myself a little relief.

Chapter Six

I'd slept like the dead and was only woken by the noise of Robert stomping about the office. I assumed it was time to get up. I stretched and grinned, still recalling the previous afternoon's activities. By the time I finally rolled out of bed, Robert was showered and dressed, having made his bed and tidied the space we called home.

I dressed, and as we waited for Joe to arrive I took the piece of paper from my jean pocket and sat on the edge of the desk, deciding what to do. I must have picked the phone up and replaced it three or four times.

"Make the fucking call," Robert said.

"I will. I just want to make her wait a little," I replied.

"Well, since it's just eight o'clock in the morning and you saw her only a few hours ago, you're not exactly making her wait long."

I picked up the phone again and dialled. A continuous tone informed me I had dialled the wrong number. I tried again.

"Something's wrong with this phone," I said as I replaced the handset.

"Or she didn't give you the correct number," Robert replied.

"Of course she did. I'll try again later."

I folded the piece of paper and returned it to my pocket. Rob and I sat and waited for Joe to arrive. We heard the car pull up outside, and footsteps as Joe and Goon made their way up the stairs to the office door.

"Good morning," I said, smiling at Goon. One day I was sure he would smile back.

"You want to head out with Richard again today?" Joe asked.

"Sure," Robert replied.

We made our way to the door where Richard was waiting.

"Oh, Trav, don't fuck the tenants," Joe said with a chuckle as we left.

"What can I say? She wanted me," I called over my shoulder.

We climbed into a car and drove off. Instead of collecting rents at apartment blocks, we made our way to a row of stores. We followed Richard from one to the other. Sometimes we were offered a coffee or, as was the case with the deli, something to eat. As we hadn't had breakfast we accepted all offers. Richard introduced us to every person we met and it was immediately obvious how uncomfortable people were around Robert.

****

It was a week later before I finally managed to catch up with Karen again. I had gone back to the apartment after it became apparent the phone number she had given me was wrong, but she was never in. However, it was rent day and as usual I climbed the stairs straight to the top floor while Robert started at the bottom. Richard no longer accompanied us, we knew what to do and Joe was happy for us to be left to it. I ignored Mistress Spanx, opting to start with Karen. I knocked on her door and waited with a smile on my face. However, that smile soon slipped when the door was opened by a guy. The same guy I had seen in the photographs with Karen.

"Is Karen in?" I asked.

"Who wants to know?" he replied.

"Tell her it's Travis."

He turned his head to shout over his shoulder. "Some kid called Travis is asking for you."

I glared at him. He was about the same height as me, a lot older with a pouch of a belly hanging over the top of his jeans. A cigarette hung from his mouth, and he had an attitude, one I didn't like. I stared at him, unsmiling. Karen came to the door; I noticed how she put her hand on his back as she stood beside him.

"Rent's due," I said.

"Oh, of course," she replied.

She was struggling to look me in the eye as she collected her purse from a table near the door.

"I think your phone's broken," I said to her.

"Nothing wrong with the phone, buddy," the guy said.

"Not your buddy, buddy," I replied.

Karen looked uncomfortable, obviously feeling the tension radiating from us. She fumbled around in her purse before handing over a stack of bills. I took my time writing her receipt, liking how uncomfortable she began to look. She kept her eyes cast down and shuffled from foot to foot. After the guy had taken the receipt and had started to close the door, I caught her eye. She mouthed the word, "Sorry," before the door was finally shut.

"Fucking bitch," I mumbled to myself before moving on to the next apartment.

I brooded the whole day. Robert had asked three or four times what was wrong with me, why I was so quiet but I just shrugged it off. The more I thought about it the angrier I got. We had finished our last rent collection for that day and started to walk back to the office, passing the apartment block on the way. I paused as we got close.

"You want to go and see her?" Robert asked.

"No, I think she lives with a guy, although he looked old enough to be her dad," I said.

"How do you know?"

I told him what had happened that morning. He offered to go around and investigate, but he had been in a strange mood all day and there was no telling what his version of investigation was. We returned to the office, leaving the rent and our notebooks, before heading to the gym. As we walked I tore up the paper with the phone number on it and deposited it in a trash can.

I encountered Karen again the following week. I knocked on her door expecting the guy to answer; she opened it instead.

"Hi, Travis. Rent day again? Seems to come around so fast," she said with a chuckle.

"Sure is," I replied, opening my notepad ready to record her payment.

"Do you want to come in? Have a coffee with me?"

"Sure your dad won't mind?" I asked, the sarcasm dripped off every word.

She sighed. "I'm sorry about that, I should have been honest. Come in, let me explain."

I followed her to the kitchen and leant against a counter top while she made coffee.

"So, who is he?" I asked.

She paused, not looking at me. "He's my boyfriend. Correct that, my ex-boyfriend, should he ever get his ass in gear and move out."

She finished making the coffee and we sat in the living room, sipping our drink in silence for a few moments.

"Why won't he move out?" I asked.

"He says he can't find anywhere to live. He doesn't work; he drinks too much and likes to be waited on."

Karen placed her coffee on the floor and slid closer to me, she rested her hand on my thigh, letting her fingers trail over my jeans. I could feel my cock stiffen as her hand wandered farther up. She took my coffee cup and placed it next to hers before she stood and held out a hand to me. I took it and she led me to her bedroom.

It was a small room, with a double bed under the one window and a wooden closet against the opposite wall. Beside the bed was a nightstand with yet another picture of the happy couple. If he was her ex, why all the photographs? I stopped caring the moment she gripped the edges of my T-shirt and pulled it over my head. Her nails scraped down my chest, leaving small scratch marks in their wake. She unbuttoned my jeans, and falling to her knees, dragged them to my ankles. I didn't wear shorts normally and when my cock sprang free, she wrapped one hand around it. I started my silent alphabet recital.

Her lips closed around my cock as her hand cupped my balls. I gripped her hair as her mouth sucked and her teeth scraped gently against me. I drew in a deep breath. By the time I had made it through three sets of the alphabet, forwards and backwards, I was struggling to hold back. I pulled her head from my cock. As she rose she dragged her T-shirt over her head, undid her jeans and let them fall to the floor. She unhooked her bra, sliding it off her shoulders, and then slid down her panties. Just the sight of her stripping in front of me had my heart racing.

She lay on the bed and beckoned for me. As I lay beside her she took my hand and placed it between her thighs. Her fingers guided mine, showing me what she wanted. She was so wet, her clitoris swollen and hot. I pushed my finger inside her as I leant over her body and kissed her. I tried to take my time, I listened to her breathing and when she moaned I smiled. I was obviously doing something right. Karen pulled my hand away and as I covered her with my body she guided my cock inside her. I leant up on my elbows as I fucked her. I tried to keep it slow, calm, but when she wrapped her legs around my waist, forcing me deeper, I lost it. I pumped faster and harder into her as her moans grew louder. When she cried out my name I came. Sweat ran down from my brow and I collapsed on top of her. She wrapped her arms around me and chuckled.

"Better than your first time, huh?" she said.

"How did you guess?" I asked.

"It was fairly obvious."

I rolled to one side and stretched, feeling a little drowsy, that was until there was a knock on the front door.

"Expecting anyone?" I asked.

"No." Karen climbed from the bed and pulled a robe around her.

While she went to the front door, I dressed.

"Can I help?" I heard her say.

"Is Travis here?" came the reply, and I knew instantly it was Robert.

I made my way to the door, still pulling my T-shirt over my head, with a huge grin on my face. Of course he did his sigh thing, with his eyebrows raised, unsmiling. I pecked Karen on the cheek and told her I would see her again before joining him.

"I've done the whole fucking block, Trav," he said.

"Sorry, got a little distracted," I replied.

"I gather that. We need to go, we have a driving lesson."

With that, we made our way back to the office. Joe had decided we needed to learn to drive and I was pleased about that. I'd had enough of walking and since we were carrying more money, it felt safer to have a car. It would have been great to have a driver but we weren't high enough in the pecking order for that.

****

I found learning to drive easy. We spent most of the time in a car lot at night, and I'm not sure learning to spin away from a standing start was part of the test, but we mastered it. Robert was an aggressive driver and I was nervous when it was his turn behind the wheel. For me, roaring around at night was fantastic; but it was the freedom that I loved the most. It didn't seem like we'd had too many lessons before we were taken for some photographs. It always amazed me the influence Joe had over people when I saw him hand over a stack of bills in return for our permits.

Our first car was an old Mercedes, a classic according to Goon, beat up and uncomfortable according to Robert and me. It was about a week later that the car ended up wrecked after we spun it in a lot and hit a brick wall. We were lucky not to be seriously hurt; we only received a few cuts from the flying glass as the side window shattered. As we walked back to the office late that night both of us were nervous about what Joe would say.

The following morning, Joe stomped, waved his hands around, cursed in Italian and then checked us over for cuts or bruises. Evelyn was frantically trying to keep up with the translation. He was annoyed about the car, naturally, but he was more concerned whether we had been hurt or not.

"You're not to have another car," Evelyn said, translating.

"Papa, they can't do that," she said in response to whatever it was Joe had said.

"He's upset because you could have been killed." She was looking between Joe and us.

"He's not happy is he?" I whispered to Robert. He raised his eyebrows at me and shrugged his shoulders.

Robert and I watched the exchange, Joe ranting in Italian and Evelyn in English.

Evelyn sighed. "You're to ride a motorbike from now on," she said. She shook her head at her father.

According to Joe riding a bike around DC would be enough to scare us into being more responsible drivers. Robert and I looked at each other with huge grins on our faces.

Later that day we were back in the car lot roaring around on two small motorbikes, trying to figure out how to change gear and racing each other from one end to the other. Goon shook his head, Evelyn pleaded with her father to change his mind and Robert and I had the most fun we'd had in ages. We loved the bikes, much to Joe's annoyance. If anything we were more reckless, weaving in and out of the traffic and racing each other through the streets at night. It took about a month for Joe to realise his mistake and we were given another car.

****

I saw Karen once a week; we never went out anywhere, just fucked on rent day. For me, it was the perfect relationship. Whether she knew or not, she wasn't the only woman I fucked. It all came to an abrupt halt one day though. I had Karen bent over the sofa; my hands held her hips as I fucked her hard. I was determined to make her come, to scream out my name. As I was about to pump my load into her I heard the sound of the door opening and then a voice.

"What the fuck...," he said.

Turning, I saw the not so ex-boyfriend and his face was blazing with anger. Karen had been a little economical with the truth when she'd told me he had just moved out.

"What the fuck are you doing?" he said, wheezing a little with the effort.

"Fucking, that what's what the fuck I'm doing," I replied as I pulled out of Karen.

She grabbed her T-shirt from the sofa and hastily pulled it over her head. For a couple of seconds there was a silence and then he came at me. Well, when I say came, he staggered towards me as quick as his pot belly and short legs would allow. I laughed and darted to the other end of the sofa, grabbing my clothes as I did.

"You fucking punk," he shouted.

I ran around the sofa laughing, then out the front door hopping on one leg to get into my jeans. I was half way down the stairs by the time I had gotten them on and passed Robert, who was standing just outside the apartment block.

"Trav?" he said, as I shot past and into the car.

I watched in the rearview mirror as I sped off. The boyfriend was doubled over trying to catch his breath; I flipped him the finger and laughed as I made my way to the gym.

****

Robert and I had started to visit the club, a place that Joe owned. Each Friday we would get dressed up and go to a place reserved for us at the bar. They would hand us a bottle of bear and we'd watch a group of girls trying not to show us how much they wanted our attention. Robert would nurse two, maybe three bottles of beer a night; he would never get drunk, whereas I would down them like water. After a couple of weeks of seeing the girls sway their asses to the music, toss their hair and try to subtly glance over at us to make sure we were watching, Robert made his move. I watched in amazement as he strode over, grabbed a brunette by the arm, and with no conversation, lead her to the toilets. Half hour later he was back, straightening his clothes, and she was excitedly telling her friends all about it. Robert would then ignore her for the rest of the night.

"Bro, you need to treat the ladies right," I said.

"Really? She just let me fuck her in a stinking toilet without even telling me her name," he replied.

"But if you want to fuck her again, you need to at least talk to her."

"Maybe I don't want to fuck her again," he said.

We weren't old enough to be in the club, let alone to drink alcohol, but since Joe owned the place and we had been in many times to collect the rent, we were welcome. A few of the locals knew us, some were tenants, some were just people who knew of Joe and therefore knew about us. Some would nod, offer a drink - which we always declined - and others would stay as far away as possible. The longer the evening wore on, the closer the girls got to us; especially the one Robert had fucked in the toilet. She didn't look too bad and I fancied my chances with her myself. However, there was a blonde who looked a little shy that caught my eye. I gathered her name was Carly, as I'd heard her being called. When I finally caught her eye I gave her the full killer smile and watched the blush creep up her neck and cover her cheeks.

"Carly, what can I get you to drink?" I asked. She looked a little shocked that I had addressed her by name.

"Oh, a beer would be good, thanks," she replied.

I noticed her friends nudge her towards me a little. I called the bartender over and ordered another beer. By the time I had turned back to her, the group of girls had moved closer. I watched Robert tense; he hated anyone encroaching on his space. The brunette he had fucked earlier was practically hanging off his arm. She whispered in his ear, he put his bottle down on the bar before leading her back to the toilets, giving me a wink as he passed. I wondered how he did it, he hadn't spoken a word to her and she was throwing herself at him.

"So, tell me about yourself?" I asked. I leant one arm on the bar giving her my full attention.

"Me and Christy, Christy is the one who has just gone off with your friend, share an apartment just around the block. We work together."

I liked the fact she had her own apartment. Although Robert had relented and we were spending more time staying with Joe, I couldn't exactly invite a girl back there. I think Evelyn would throw a fit. While she talked, she twisted a strand of hair around her fingers. She told me about her work - an office of some sort - and I began to tune out a little. I found it hard to keep my eyes fixed on her face. She had removed her jacket and probably didn't realise the top buttons on her blouse had popped loose. I could see the creamy white skin of her tits spilling over the top of a white lace bra.

Robert returned with the brunette following in his wake, struggling on high heels to keep up with him. She didn't look too pleased.

"Carly, we need to leave," she said, tugging her friend by the arm.

"See you another time," Carly said as she shrugged on her jacket.

I mentally said goodbye to the tits and turned towards Robert.

"What did you do? I was in there," I said.

"Fucked her."

"Can't have been good if she's rushed to leave," I said.

"Trav, she came, what more does she want?"

"You could have bought her a beer or something, even told her your name."

"She knows who I am, they all know who we are," he said.

"How?"

"Look around you, see how many people glance away, won't catch our eye. It's because we work for Joe."

I hadn't noticed it before, but Robert was right. As I stared at the first guy next to us he immediately dipped his head, and the longer I stared the more he shuffled further away. Rob was an imposing character; he was over six feet tall built like a brick shithouse, and I guess I wasn't that far behind. It was a far cry from the days when we were skinny kids on the street. Okay, Rob had *never* been a skinny kid but I'd spent many a night cowering, and seeing these older men intimidated by us gave me a sense of power, of importance. Damn, it felt good.

****

It was one lunchtime that I got the full story of what happened to Robert's aunt. Evelyn had come to the office with lunch. We headed off to a park and sat on the bench to eat.

"Rob, I've never asked, but how did you get to be here?" Evelyn asked.

He told us how he had burnt down the house, this we knew. Then he told us his aunt was still in the house when he'd done it, and he'd killed her. I guessed I should have been shocked, but deep down I already knew. However, it was the look on Evelyn's face that had me worried. Robert didn't do pity; he hated for anyone to feel sorry for him, and it was her look of sadness that had him standing, brushing the crumbs from his lap and insisting we make our way back.

"You didn't kill her; it was an accident, wasn't it? I doubt you could have done anything to save her, you were so young," she said.

"No, that's where you're wrong. I watched the fire for a while, watched it take hold of the basement. I had plenty of chances to do something about it but I didn't. I had plenty of time to get her out of the house, but I didn't. I stood at the edge of the woods and watched until there was nothing left of the house or of her," he replied.

I didn't know what to say, how to respond. I knew about his childhood, the beatings and the preaching he had endured, and whether it was right or wrong, I sympathised with him. Would I have done the same? I don't know. I often wondered if I'd stuck that knife in my brother's heart - if I had killed him - would I feel bad, and the honest answer would have been no. To grow up in a home full of conflict and anger, to suffer the beatings as we had, meant we became immune to pain, and immune to inflicting it. Like Robert, when we beat someone to get paid for the drugs we delivered, I felt no remorse. I felt nothing for the man lying at my feet, bleeding from the wounds I had inflicted on him. Robert was often troubled by his lack of empathy; I didn't care one way or another.

What came out of that conversation, though, was my understanding of Robert's desire never to get pulled over by the cops. I was the one to drive normally, and I assumed he had more reason than me to stay out of the cells. He had murdered someone, and I wasn't sure if he could still be charged with that.

He had no one. There was not one person left on earth that he was related to - that he knew of - no one that he could call family other than us. He would always be my brother. He would always be the brother or the son of Evelyn - however you wanted to look at it - and the more we stayed at the house, the more he became Joe's 'other' son.

At first I was envious of the relationship Robert was developing with Joe. They would converse in Italian - I wasn't educated enough to learn another language. They would spend time alone together, sitting in Joe's garden room and chatting, drinking coffee and planning. I wasn't sure what they were planning, but I knew it was our future, and I would be eternally grateful to Robert for taking me on that journey with him.

****

It was with a lot of reluctance that I started working with Jonathan. Accounts were not my thing; I would look at a list of numbers and it meant nothing to me. I understood basically what went on - the rents were reported much higher than they actually were so that the drug money we made could be filtered in and 'laundered'.

"Rob, what the fuck does this mean?" I asked.

We were sitting in the office with paperwork spread over the desk. I had no clue what most of it was, and watched as Robert scribbled constantly in a large accounting book.

"Look, this is the rent we've collected this week. If we leave it like that, Joe will pay tax. So we have to find receipts to make sure we lower the amount of tax he pays," he replied.

"Okay, so how do we do that?"

"Go find Paul, we need receipts for materials that could have been used for repairs. Don't come back with a receipt for a stack of bricks, though. I want invoices for taps, paint, door locks, that kind of thing."

I would then spend the day chasing after Paul for invoices, and Robert would sit in the office with Jonathan learning how to manipulate the books. It amazed me and Jonathan how *creative* he could be with the figures, even early on. His suggestions, the ones that were accepted, had started to move Joe's businesses towards a more legitimate state, while still making him the maximum amount of money. Paul was the one who seemed the most troubled by that. I sensed reluctance from Paul when he was questioned about what building materials had been paid for, and whether the missing stacks of bricks were found. It was clear to Robert and me that he was skimming off payments, and perhaps selling off materials then pocketing the money. We never mentioned it to Joe, but as Robert became more involved in the accounting, Paul was reined in.

Joey was still Joey - lazy, always keeping a small portion of the money he collected, and he spent most of his time sneering at us. Everyone felt his resentment. He looked down at us, something Robert hated; and the more he did, the more Joe conferred with Robert. Joe drew Robert closer and involved him more in the business while pushing his own son, his flesh and blood, to one side. Little were we to know the consequence of that choice.

Chapter Seven

Boxing was becoming important to Robert and I; it was the only legal outlet we had for the aggression we both seemed to harbour. It felt good to work out, to see my body change and bulk up. I loved when the guys at the gym challenged me and I held my own against them.

Robert was the first one to get a fight. We had known for some time the guys fought for Joe, making money for him if they won, standing the chance of being *dispatched* if they didn't. To Joe, the gym, the fighters, were all a business. I was excited for Robert, but underneath there was a small amount of anxiety. For Robert to unleash the aggression inside him, the aggression he kept contained, might be dangerous for him *and* for his opponent.

We arrived late one night at an abandoned warehouse similar to the ones we used when we unloaded the trucks. Robert, Ted and I went directly to the changing rooms. He was quiet, calmly taking in his surroundings.

"Are you sure about this?" I asked him. "Are you nervous?"

He looked at me and shook his head. "No," he said. However, I did notice his eyes darker than usual, a sure sign he was fired up.

In the first round, Robert wouldn't allow his opponent to get close. People were calling out his name, and Ted was getting agitated.

"Fuck, Rob, step it up a bit. People have come to see a fight," he called over the ropes.

I was positioned in the corner while Ted stood on the platform, leaning over the ropes and shouting instructions. Whether Robert heard him was another matter, because he certainly never acknowledged him. Watching Robert fight was like seeing an animal about to be unleashed from its cage. His anger had been pent up for so many years, and boxing gave him a way to release that. When he decided he'd had enough of his opponent he opened his cage and all hell broke loose. Something changed in him; a flash of recognition seemed to cross his face. The man in the ring wasn't the Robert I knew. He was relentless, his opponent half dead by the time Robert finally let him fall the floor, ending the match.

Although Robert and I sparred together, he had always said we would never fight for real, and looking at that man being dragged to his corner, dazed, beaten, bruised and bloodied, I was glad.

In the car on the way home Robert was quiet, but I was buzzing. That had been the best thing I'd ever seen. Joe and I relived the fight second by second and when we pulled up at the house, I placed my arm around a worried Evelyn and told her all about it. She had been pacing the drive waiting for us to return.

"Man, that was amazing," I said as Robert and I settled down in the twin bedroom at Joe's.

"It was okay, I guess," he replied.

"You fucked him up big time. His corner team were in a total panic at one point, did you see?" I asked.

"I didn't see anything and I didn't hear anything. All that went through my mind were memories."

"Memories?" I asked.

"Yeah, memories. Go to sleep, Trav. I'm fucking exhausted."

I knew he hadn't fallen asleep, and we lay in the dark in silence. I thought on what he'd said. He was fighting back, I believed, the way he should have all those years ago. Perhaps that was what he meant. It was the memories of his aunt and the beatings he endured that he was fighting against in that ring; the man in front of him was just a punch bag.

****

The following day Joe had a job for us. There was no resting for Robert, it was straight back to work. A store owner had failed to clear the loan Joe had given him, and time had run out. Robert and I were to collect his last payment; in fact, we were told not to leave the store without it.

It was a rundown store, and on entering I turned sign over to indicate the store had closed. Behind the counter sat a fat, dirty, greasy-haired guy in a stained white vest. Robert was always the one who asked for the payment, and when the guy spat at his feet I knew we were in for some fun.

A second guy appeared from behind a door. With a quick glance at me and a subtle movement of his hand, Robert told me what to do. As quickly as I could, I crossed the room and with my fist already pulled back, I punched him in the face; he fell like the proverbial sack of spuds and was knocked out cold.

By the time I had looked around, Robert had the storekeeper over the counter and the money the guy owed in his hand. We left the store, climbed into the car and sped back to the office laughing. Joey was sitting in his father's chair with his feet up on the desk when we arrived.

"Is Joe around?" Robert asked.

With a sneer and a cigarette hanging from his lip, Joey replied. "No. What can I do for you Rob?"

Robert was very particular about who called him Rob; only the people closest to him could call him that. To everyone else, and especially Joey, he was Robert. He took the nickname as an insult. I leant against the desk, interested in how this exchange would develop.

"I have some money for him, that's all. I'll catch up with him later," Robert said.

"Give it to me," Joey demanded.

"It's cool, I'll give it to him in the morning," Robert replied.

Joey slid his feet to the floor and stood. He was about a foot shorter than Robert and I chuckled as I watched him square his shoulders to butch himself up a little.

"I said, give it to me," he said.

The amusement on Robert's face was evident; the twitch of his lips gave him away. That smile faded the moment Joey grabbed

Robert's arm. I pushed myself from the desk, sensing what was would happen should the tension between them escalate.

"Joey, do yourself a favour, take your fucking hand off me," Robert said, his voice so low it was almost a growl.

"You need to watch yourself," Joey replied as aggressively as he could, although I noticed his hand shake.

Robert spun to face him, leaning close. "From who, Joey? You?"

With a laugh, Robert and I left the office.

"Who the fuck does that prick think he is?" Robert said.

"He thinks he's the boss in the absence of the boss," I said, chuckling.

****

I was preparing for my first fight, the same night as Robert's second one. We had been at the gym every day, sparring, training and getting fitter than we had ever been. I was looking forward to it, to winning and having that stack of bills in my pocket. Robert was fighting an unknown, I was up against a seasoned pro but I had no worries about it. I could hold my own.

We arrived at the warehouse, driving past the row of cars waiting to drop off or park, and made our way to the changing room. We changed and warmed up. Joe was met by a tall, obviously Italian man. Their conversation possibly involved Robert and me, as they would look over at us occasionally. Robert took no notice, but I was intrigued. I couldn't understand what was being said, but at the end of their conversation, they smiled and shook hands. Ted was doing his motivational speech - the usual 'go out and fucking kill 'em' talk. Robert had shut himself off and I found myself a little nervous. The level of noise filtering through the changing room walls suggested the place was packed. The smell of cigar smoke wafted through the door and every now and again some bimbo dressed like a hooker arrived to collect the next fighter.

When it was my turn, Robert walked with me to the ring. Joe had taken his seat ringside and Ted climbed up to hold the ropes open for me. My opponent was bouncing around on his toes, throwing punches in the air. He smirked at me. I could hear Ted call me back to my corner just a few seconds before the ref was to call us together.

"Watch those gloves, kid. They've roughed 'em up," he said.

I nodded and made my way to the centre of the ring. Staring at the smirking jerk in front of me was making my blood boil. I caught a quick glance of his gloves and noticed the shine missing. I was about to find out what he had done to them. The bell rang and I took a slight step back. We danced around for a moment, just sizing each other up, until I thought I saw an opening. I steamed in, throwing punches and making a big mistake. I let my guard down, and as I did, his fist connected with my jaw, putting me on my ass. It hadn't hurt but I was fucking livid. I could feel blood seeping from the graze the gloves had made. I lost focus and got careless. I could hear Ted and Robert shouting instructions from the corner, but all I thought about was how that prick in front of me had cheated. I then understood what 'roughed the gloves up' meant. It felt like sandpaper had been rubbed over my jaw.

The bell sounded for the end of round one and Ted cleaned up my face. I was pumped, so pumped I didn't hear a word he was saying. I pushed him to one side, eager to start round two. I managed to get some decent punches in and I watched as my opponent stumbled backwards a little after a good uppercut from me. However, for the second time I let him get to me. I lowered my hands too much and found myself sitting on my ass again. I was embarrassed. I knew I wasn't fighting as well as I could, I knew I was letting his goading get to me. It was Robert that pulled me out of my funk as I returned to my corner at the end of round two.

"What the fuck are you doing, Trav?" he said as he leant over the ropes. "Back off bro, watch what he's doing and wait for your moment."

I nodded as Ted pasted Vaseline over my face and the grazes I had already sustained. The rest of the fight went to plan and I fought well. I'd taken Robert's advice, backing off, watching - and when I could, landing some great punches. It wasn't enough, though. At the end of the fight, the ref raised my opponent's arm high in the air - I had lost.

Robert walked me back to the changing room. I was deflated. I knew I could have done better, I knew I could have won that fight, and I was pissed. I pulled off the gloves and angrily threw them to the floor. I paced the room, growling at anyone who came close, feeling sorry for myself. When the bimbo came to call for Robert, I followed him. He had stood by the ring to watch me and I wanted to do the same.

Robert was chillingly quiet, his face totally devoid of any emotion. He climbed under the ropes, ignoring Ted, and made his way to the centre. He stood with his arms at his side as the ref spoke. Not once did his eyes leave his opponent's.

"Ted, this doesn't look good," I said.

"I know. I've never seen him this quiet before," Ted replied.

"He's really pissed, big time pissed. Something bad is going to happen here."

The bell sounded and my premonition was right. Within a minute Robert had his opponent backed onto the ropes and he was relentless. The room had quietened; people were unsure what they were watching. Was this a boxing match or a slaughter? It was so quiet that when Robert threw an uppercut and caught his opponent under the chin, I heard the crack of his neck as it broke. I saw his eyes roll back in his head. He was dead before he hit the floor. Ted and I stood in silence, in shock.

"Get him out of there," I heard from behind.

Joe had risen from his seat to join us.

"Get my boy out of there," he said again.

Ted climbed under the ropes as Robert screamed at his opponents corner. Ignoring Ted, he made his way across the ring, climbed under the ropes and pushed his way past people to the changing room. His opponent was left lying in the centre of the ring with his corner team too stunned to move. Ted and I ran after Robert. We caught up with him in the changing room but felt it best to leave him be. We stepped aside, I changed and the three of us left for the car. We drove back to Joe's in silence.

Sitting at the kitchen table, Evelyn fixed up my face. Robert asked Joe if he knew about the gloves, if he was aware they had been roughed up. Of course Joe hadn't known, and although Robert's tone of voice was accusing, I believed him. Joe wouldn't do that to us; he wanted us to win, he earned money if we did. As Robert rose to head upstairs, to the room we were to stay in that night, he turned to Joe.

"Set him up another fight, soon as," he said, nodding his head towards me.

****

Things took a dramatic turn in our relationship that year. Joe wanted us to pay off a truck driver and supervise the unloading of his cargo. Crates of liquor were to be stacked in a warehouse. The driver was paid well to ensure he had no idea how he had lost his cargo when reporting the *crime* to the cops.

After a morning in the gym we returned to the office to collect the payment. Joe was out of town and Joey sat in his place with his feet on the desk, flicking cigarette ash everywhere. With an uncharacteristic smile, he pushed a small parcel wrapped in brown paper towards us. As we drove to the meet, Robert told me to pull into a parking lot. He took out a small knife and pierced a hole in the package. As he withdrew the knife we both saw white powder on the end. It wasn't exactly a surprise that the package contained cocaine; money wasn't wrapped that way and assumed Robert just wanted confirmation Hiding the package, we continued on to the warehouse.

"Something's wrong," I said as we pulled up outside.

"No shit. The absence of the truck gives that away," Robert replied.

"What do you want to do?" I asked.

"Go take a look. Someone's set us up, and I think I know who. You up for it, bro?"

"For sure."

We made our way as quietly as possible through the door and into the darkened room. The only light came from the moon shining through the window, bathing the centre of the warehouse in a subtle glow. We made our one and only mistake that day - we separated.

Robert took one side of the warehouse and I took the other, making my way around the room to the stack of crates piled at the back. I heard the shuffle of feet, the clank of metal and before my brain could register it something wrapped around my legs and I fell to the floor. I was dragged backwards. As I tried to sit, to reach the chain that was digging into my ankles, a man, one I recognised, emerged from the shadows and punched me squarely in the face. I smiled back at him and spat the blood from my split lip onto the floor at his feet.

He leant down close. "Where's Robert?" he whispered.

I shrugged my shoulders, I wouldn't answer him. I couldn't answer him once a boot connected with my stomach and the air was forced from my lungs. The kick had me lying on my back, and hands roughly grabbed my shoulders, turning me over. My arms were pulled behind me and tied together. The sound, that click of plastic as it passed through a hook, and the bite into my skin made me believe they used cable ties.

"Call for your friend," he said.

"Go fuck yourself, you fat prick," I replied as I tried to catch my breath.

The guy holding the chain was the same guy I had beaten when we had been sent to collect a payment from the storekeeper. The storekeeper, Sam - or Fat Sam as I liked to call him - was kneeling at my head. He had a handful of my hair in his fist, raising my face and smashing it down on the concrete floor. All the time I smiled up at him. He'd need to do worse than that to provoke the reaction he wanted from me.

Fat Sam leant so close I could smell the stench of him and my stomached turned, revolted by the stale sweat and his bad breath. He had a knife that he placed to my throat.

"Where is it?" he said.

"Where the fuck is what?" I replied.

"My coke, you prick. What do you think you should have brought here?"

I laughed, I knew this wasn't just about a kilo of coke — Joey had set us up.

"Where's your boyfriend?" the guy holding the chain called out.

I knew Robert wouldn't reply, he would silently be making his way around the warehouse. It was then that I saw two others. They had been standing in the shadows out of sight until they moved, each taking one side of the warehouse. It was only then that I realised that we were in some serious shit.

The knife pierced my throat, not enough to hurt, just enough for me to be able to feel a small trickle of warm blood, enough to make my heart start to race . I could no longer see the two men that had gone after Robert, although I could hear them; their footsteps echoed in the abandoned building. They didn't know enough to be stealthy, all they were doing was giving themselves away. Altogether, things weren't going the way Fat Sam had planned. He wanted Robert. Perhaps he had been paid that kilo of coke to deal with him, but all he had was me trussed up on the floor.

"Call for your fucking mate," he said again.

I shook my head and took another punch to the face. My teeth rattled, I spat more blood and saliva at his feet, which pissed him off. Fat Sam took his knife and drew it slowly down my stomach, cutting through my shirt. At first I felt no pain, just a searing heat following the path of the knife. But as the wound opened and the blood started to flow it hit me. I clamped my teeth together and sucked in a deep breath. I felt beads of sweat form on my brow, even though the warehouse was cold.

A second slash came shortly after, and I couldn't stop my scream. It was an angry scream, not one of pain, despite the burning sensation. Slash after slash came, all over my stomach and shoulders. I no longer felt the burn or the pain; it all seemed to merge. I writhed on the floor, my body in agony as spasms of pain washed over me. Even the noise that left my lips seemed to come from someplace else, or perhaps it was the echo in the empty space. As my screams bounced around the room, all I hoped was that they covered any noise Robert made. I needed him.

For the first time in years I was scared. Fat Sam and his pricks, despite not having a brain cell between them, meant us harm, serious harm.

A thought flashed through my mind - *today is the day I'm going to die.*

"You better fucking kill me. You let me live and you're fucking dead," I shouted.

"You fat prick," I screamed through gritted teeth as the knife drew slowly across my chest, the deepest cut yet.

I bucked my body from the floor, which was a mistake as all it did was drive the knife deeper into me. Vomit filled my mouth as I heard the scrape of metal against bone. I swallowed it down, the burn of acid causing my throat to constrict, and I screwed my eyes tightly shut.

A strange sensation flowed over me, a kind of numbness I'd never experienced before. I could no longer feel the burning pain across my body, but a coldness instead. Blood ran down my sides and my skin prickled in its wake. Individual sounds merged into one noise in my head. Screaming resonated through my mind and evoked memories. Memories of my mother crying out for help and being ignored. Memories of myself as a child and the inner voice that screamed constantly in frustration at the violence I witnessed and could do nothing about.

However, one sound broke through all the screaming. It took a moment to understand what it was, and it was the smell that made me recognise it. It was a gun shot. That one sound stilled the noise in my head. All was quiet for a while as everyone looked towards the corner of the room. Who had been shot?

"Lou, where are you?" Fat Sam called out. There was no reply.

I watched as Robert walked towards me. As he crossed the circle of light the moon had created he held the gun steady in his hand. I don't think I had ever been so pleased to see him.

"Rob, these pricks here want to have a friendly chat with you," I said.

As I spoke, the effort caused the wounds to bleed more and the pain to take my breath away.

Robert stared at me but I noticed something, a very subtle sharp intake of breath. I knew then that I was in a badly hurt. I looked down at my chest; the shirt I had worn was no longer white. It was shredded and red, completely soaked. He very gently nodded. The coldness in his face had Fat Sam moving slightly away and behind me, closer to his mate. For a moment Robert stood still and quiet with his eyes fixed on the guy holding me captive. I could feel the slight tremor vibrate down the chain as his hands started to shake.

"Tsk, tsk. You have both made a big mistake today," he said.

"Lou," Fat Sam shouted, panic laced his voice.

"Lou isn't coming. Neither is the other one. If I let you live, you will find one dead over there, and one dead on that side," Robert indicated with his head the location.

"Now, you," he said, pointed the gun at the guy holding the chain. "You are going to help my friend up, you've already ruined his shirt."

I chuckled, although that turned into a wince as I stood. My hands were cut free and despite the pain I felt, I spun around and snatched the knife from the hand of the guy behind me. I plunged it into his throat.

Blood spurted, splashing onto my face, and his hands clasped around his neck, frantically trying to stem the blood as it pumped through his fingers. I watched in fascination as he gurgled, bubbles of bloody saliva foaming from his mouth as he fell to his knees and then flat on his face. He bled out in front of us. A river of blood, bright red in colour against the grey concrete floor, slowly ran to where Fat Sam was kneeling.

Fat Sam tried to scramble backwards, his tears mingling with snot. He held his hands up in surrender - I'm sure he didn't expect the evening to turn out as it had.

"I know who sent you, but I want to hear it from your fucking mouth," Robert said, as he crouched before Sam.

Fat Sam shook his head.

"Right now who are you more afraid of? Because it should be me," he growled.

Looking at Robert right then was like looking at an animal, something deranged, something unnatural. His eyes were black and his features hard. Even I succumbed to a shiver up my spine; fuck knows what was going through Fat Sam's mind.

We got the confirmation we needed; we learnt that we were to die that night. Robert stood, and with his foot he kicked the guy who was lying face down on the floor onto his back. He pulled the knife from his throat. As he walked back to Fat Sam he gave him a very frightening smile. I watched, my hands holding my stomach to stem the blood, as Robert grabbed Fat Sam's hair, holding his head still as he drew the knife across his eyebrow.

"Every time you look in the mirror you'll see that scar and you'll remember this night, you'll remember me. I will watch you for the rest of your life and one day, when you least expect it, when you think I have forgotten you, I will be back."

The sound of bones breaking echoed around the room as Robert stomped as hard as he could on one of Fat Sam's ankles, he did the same to the other. The high pitched screams hurt my ears as I ground my boot onto his hand, first one then the other, twisting my foot to grind them into the floor, crushing as many bones as I could.

I kicked over and over into his ribs, any part of his body I could, and when I was done a wave of nausea and lightheadedness washed over me. We left Fat Sam sitting in his own and his friend's blood.

It was only as we left the warehouse and into the cold air of the night that I collapsed. For most of the evening I had been running on adrenalin. I felt Robert's arm around my waist as he practically carried me to the car and placed me in the passenger seat. I begged him not to smack my car before I passed out.

The next few hours were a blur. I knew we had arrived at Ted's and he was forcing whiskey down my throat like it was going out of style. I hated whiskey but it worked. I heard Joe speak, and Paul instructing his wife, Rosa, to help me. I felt nothing as she went to work, stitching my wounds.

I looked at Robert as Rosa wove the needle that closed the slashes, all the time grumbling that we should be in the hospital. As she finished I managed to say the words that had been swirling around in my mind.

"You saved my life, bro." Then I passed out.

****

I woke the following day, bandaged and aching from sleeping on a sofa. Robert was asleep on a chair; I could see a line of stitches running down his side. I hadn't even noticed he'd been hurt. I tried to move, wincing as I did. I needed a piss, I needed a drink.

116

My mouth was dry and my head thumped. Robert woke, disturbed by my rustling.

"Hey, you okay?" he asked.

"Sure, you?"

He shrugged his shoulders before a smile slowly crept on his face and he shook his head and chuckled.

"What's so funny?" I asked.

"You. All you were fucking concerned about was your car. *Don't smack my car,*" he mimicked my accent.

I tried to laugh but it hurt too much. Instead, I managed to swing my legs off the sofa so I was at least in a sitting position.

"Fuck off, and did you smack my car?" I asked.

"Yes, totalled it. Coffee?"

"Of course I want coffee," I replied.

Our conversation brought Ted into the room, holding two steaming coffee mugs and a packet of Advil.

"How you boys doing?" he asked.

"I'm okay, he's just worried about his car," Robert answered.

"The car's totalled and Mack's going to organise a clean up," Ted said. I hoped to hell he was teasing. Robert nodded.

Someone would have to go and remove the bodies, and Fat Sam, assuming he was still there. In the meantime Robert and I needed somewhere to stay. We couldn't go back to Joe's; we didn't want to alert Joey that his *hit* had failed. Robert told me that he'd spoken to Joe and had a set of keys for an apartment in Columbia Heights; we would stay there until we healed completely. It went without saying that Joey would be shown the error of his ways, and he would pay for what he'd done.

****

While we were recovering I got to know more about what brought Robert to DC.

"Trav, there's something I need to do and I don't want to involve you in this," Robert said.

117

We had been sitting in the living room after a gentle session at the gym, just exercising.

"Bro, everything you do involves me," I replied, looking at him.

He sat forward on the sofa, his elbows resting on his knees, with his chin in his hands. The look on his face was one of sadness, something I hadn't seen that often in Robert. Looking back over the past couple of days, it was clear something had been on his mind. Quietly at first, he told me of his life in Sterling, the abuse from his aunt, the priest at his school, and how he had lost his best friend, Cara. She had been killed by her father after spending years being abused by him. He also told me that he had confided in Joe because he wanted advice. He wanted to know if he could be charged with his aunt's murder.

At first, knowing that Joe knew Robert's story and I didn't stung a little. But then I had to remember that I'd never confided in him, either. It seemed strange that we were brothers, we were closer than family, and yet we both had a dark past we couldn't speak about until then. It could have been my opportunity to tell him about Padriac, but I didn't and I never really knew why. I felt something in my gut, though, a surge of anger that not only had this happened to him, but memories of *my* childhood and the abuse I'd suffered came flooding back.

I stood, picked up my coat and the car keys, and smiled. I was up for revenge. I was up for a little payback and I would take great pleasure in dishing out that punishment. Robert looked at me; a slow smile crept across his face as he stood up beside me. Silently we made our way to the car and headed to the freeway. The journey to Sterling took a little under three hours.

"Tell me about Cara," I said.

"We were kids but she was my only friend. The only person who spoke to me, well, I say the only one. Some of the other kids would try and taunt me but they backed off pretty quick," he replied.

"It's your fucking devil eyes that probably scared the shit out of them," I said with a chuckle.

He laughed. "My aunt would beat me, trying to drive out the devil as she said, and the more she beat me, the more I smiled back her. It drove her fucking nuts. You know, after a while it just didn't hurt anymore. I felt nothing, not one blow from her fucking belt. She would preach to me from her Bible and I'd see her mouth moving, but I couldn't tell you what she said, I heard nothing."

"How do you want to play this?" I asked.

"Head for the house, or what's left of it, first. I had a camp in the woods, it's where I used to hide out. If Cara could get away from home she'd meet me there. I'd like to see if it's still there."

"You must own the land then?" I said.

"Probably, and if there is a building still there, I'll have it razed to the fucking ground."

We continued our journey in silence. I saw an involuntary shiver run over Robert as we passed a wooden sign announcing we had arrived in the wonderful town of Sterling. It should have been called Hicksville. Having come from New York, this town was totally backward to me; it was like something from a TV show. One road led through the town and there were wooden houses on either side. Most had either burnt-out cars or trucks without wheels in the dusty front yards. Dogs roamed free as did the kids. It looked as though they didn't get visitors too often in Sterling; the kids stopped their play and watched as we drove slowly past.

We arrived at a patch of ground that contained what was obviously the remains of a house. Over the years the burnt wood that lay there had been covered with weeds and ivy, the ground bare of grass. We climbed out of the car and walked past the ruins, skirting around towards the woods behind. Robert knew exactly where he was going and it wasn't long before we came to a small clearing. There was a wooden frame nailed to two trees, and a tattered piece or tarpaulin strung across the top. He walked straight to one of the trees, and I watched silently as he ran his fingers across a carving. There were two initials carved into the bark, and although now green with moss, I could still clearly see the R + C.

"I used to beg her to run away with me," Robert said quietly.

"Maybe she was just too scared," I replied, thinking back to my own childhood and knowing how many times I had wanted to do that but didn't.

"Yeah, and I guess we wouldn't have gotten very far, not then."

I heard Robert take a deep breath; he held it for a while before releasing it and turning towards me.

"Let's go visit Father Peters," he said.

We walked back to the car and drove off. Parking outside the church, I could see the school attached. As we climbed out and walked towards the doors, the sound of children singing could be heard. The church doors were open and we walked the aisle to the front pew. Robert paused looking at the hard cold bench. I guessed he had spent many an hour sitting there. It was clear the church was empty so we made our way back out in the daylight, the brightness momentarily blinding us. Attached to one side of the church was a small cottage, and walking alongside it, we saw a man. He was hunched over, wearing a black cassock. He had his back to us and was using a cane to walk. He paused, sensing someone behind him, and used his shaking hand to hold on to a bench to steady himself. Very slowly, Father Peters turned around.

"I've been expecting you, Robert," Father Peters whispered. "For years, I've been expecting you."

The priest looking back at us had obviously already paid a price. One eye was blue, blinded by whatever object had hit him over the head; a scar ran across his brow and down his cheek. His hands were gnarled with obviously broken and badly repaired fingers. Robert and I stood in silence, watching him shuffle towards us. Before he got too close, Robert turned his back and started to walk down the garden path. I watched the Father reach out as if to touch Robert.

"I'm sorry. God, forgive me, I'm sorry," he said.

Robert stopped and half turned, looking back over his shoulder. "You carry on asking, Father, He isn't listening. He never did to those that needed Him and He sure as fuck isn't going to listen to you now."

We left and walked back to the car. As we passed the small school, children were leaving the building. There was none of the laughter and running or playing that I had experienced on the odd occasion I'd been at school. Just sad faced kids making their way from one hell to another. I shivered; the place gave me the creeps. There was something sinister, and for only the second time in my life I had an urge to cross myself. How the fuck Robert grew up in a place like that was beyond me, and it certainly answered any questions I had as to why he was the way he was. Just the couple of hours I'd experienced in Sterling had me fucking depressed.

We made our way out of town, driving slowly so Robert could remember the route. He pointed to a rundown shack of a building. It resembled a house only in as much as there was a front door and a couple of windows. Take those away and it could have been something seen in a third world country. Corrugated tin lined the roof along with tarpaulin and rope presumably to cover the holes in it. A mesh screen door hung off its brackets and as we came to a halt, a woman appeared with a child.

Both were grubby, and as we walked towards her a flash of recognition crossed her face. She pulled the child close, holding his head against her stomach. She nodded, just once, before pointing to a shed.

Quietly entering the shed, Robert and I watched a man, crouched down doing something to the still-spinning rotor blades of his tractor. He stilled, having either heard or sensed us. Slowly he stood and turned. Before he had a chance, Robert punched him back down to the ground.

"What the…," was all he managed to say before he recognised Robert and his eyes widened in fear.

I stood and watched as Robert crouched down beside him. He grabbed a handful of hair, raising the man's face to look directly at him.

"Payback for Cara. Remember her? The daughter you abused, the daughter you killed," he snarled.

Robert pushed the man away from him, he stood and paced, running his hand through his hair. His eyes were black when he looked over to me and the hatred on his face for the man at his feet even sent a shiver through me. Fuck knows what that guy was thinking.

"You see, there isn't a day that goes by where I don't see her face, where I don't hear her cries. Do you? Does she haunt you like she does me? Do you close your eyes at night and see her face, the split lip, the bruises? Do you see the blood running down her thighs? I do, and I never forgot."

Until that point I had been standing slightly away from Robert. I could hear the anger in his voice and I could see it flowing through him. The air was static, electrified with emotion. I walked forward and placed my hand on Robert's shoulder. I indicated with my eyes to move to one side, this was something I needed to do. As much as Robert needed to face his demon, Father Peters, I needed to face mine. Any abuser of children, anyone who deliberately harmed a child, allowed me to do that.

It was Padriac's face I saw as I grabbed Cara's father by the hair. It was my father's body I saw as I tipped him forwards. It was my mother, my sister, and Carrig I heard when he screamed as his hands were shredded by the spinning blades. Blood splattered over my face and chest - hot blood, pieces of flesh and bone - and it felt cleansing. It felt fucking good.

Was it the act that I enjoyed the most, the act of hurting, killing someone? Or was it the sense of empowerment I felt? Whatever it was, a wrong had been righted. Justice had been served and I loved it. In that case, I loved being judge and jury.

We walked outside the shed and the sound of screaming followed us. The woman stood, minus the child, waiting.

"Thank you, Robert," she said before turning and walking back to her house, ignoring the pleas of help from her husband.

As we strode back to the car I pulled a washcloth from a clothes line. I used it to clean that man's blood from my hands and my face. Throwing it to the ground, we climbed into the car and drove back to DC.

Robert lowered his seat, closed his eyes and slept all the way back. I got lost in my thoughts. Thoughts of the abuse he had suffered, memories of my own and when I glanced over at him, I knew, there would be nothing that could ever separate us, not now.

We had murdered, we had harmed, we had served our own brand of justice and we would continue to do so. We were bound together by a force that would never be broken. Blood had been spilled by our hands and I owed him. I owed Robert my life; I would do anything he asked of me. I would be by his side no matter what.

Chapter Eight

It was an evening a few nights later that Robert and I decided Joey needed to know we were still around. We followed him to the club, then parked opposite with the lights off and waited. Shortly before closing, we saw him leave, pulling his coat tight around him to ward off the chill and flipping his collar up. He lit a cigarette, the lighter illuminating his face. We were a little surprised that he headed back to Joe's on foot, and we had to make a quick change in plans. We let him get a little way ahead before leaving the car and crossing the road. As silently as we could, we followed, gaining on him with every step. As he neared the corner he paused, perhaps he sensed someone was behind him. The road was empty and dark, the streetlights long since shut down. There was a slight drizzle and the air was damp and cold.

Robert reached forward, grabbing him by the collar and spun him around. His shock was evident when he realised who we were - and that we were alive.

"What the fuck do you think you are doing? Get your fucking hands off me," Joey said.

Robert dragged him back to the car. I popped the trunk and as we got him close, I kicked at the back of his knees. He fell face first into the trunk, and with a chuckle I slammed it shut. We could hear him shout and bang his fists, trying to escape. His voice was muffled as we started the car and drove to the same warehouse Joey had selected for our demise. It seemed fitting to choose that same spot.

"Grab that tyre iron," Robert said as we climbed out. The warehouse door was locked to with what looked like a new padlock.

Once we had the door open Robert walked to the rear of the car and released the trunk. Joey had quietened but tears ran down his cheeks. We dragged him out and marched him into the warehouse. It was dark - there was no moon to illuminate the centre of the room that time - and it took a moment for our eyes to adjust. As Robert threw him to the floor my foot connected with his ribs. A sickening crack echoed around the cavernous space. I took a deep breath and I could smell the metallic tang of blood from the previous occupants. By the look on Joey's face, so did he.

"You prick, you think you can set us up?" I said with a laugh.

"What are you idiots talking about?" Joey stammered, his eyes darted between us.

"You hurt me, Rob, and dad will kill you," he added.

I saw Robert's eyebrows rise in surprise and a smirk form on his lips.

"What do you think will happen when Joe finds out what you did? What will happen when he finds out you paid people to kill us? One of them still lives, Joey, only one, but what do you think will happen if he talks? You got three men killed that night," Robert said, his voice low and deep.

It appeared Joey hadn't bothered to find out what had actually happened, as the look on his face suggested it was news to him.

"No, you hadn't thought that far ahead, had you, you fucking idiot? Are you that fucking dumb? Do you think you could threaten us, set us up, try to get us killed and then just walk away? And what's more insulting is that you thought all we were worth was a kilo of coke."

I smiled as Robert's fist connected with Joey's face; blood spurted from his broken nose. He covered his face as his bladder gave way and piss soaked the front of his pants. As he lay on his side I kicked him repeatedly, aiming for his kidney. He curled up in a ball trying to protect himself, but his eyes widened in fear as Robert knelt, grabbed his hair and with a knife, sliced through his eyebrow.

"Every time you touch that scar, every time you see it, you'll be reminded of this night," Robert told him.

We left him there sobbing on the dusty floor, crying for his mother and knowing he'd be pissing blood for the next few weeks. He would never forget what went on and, I hoped, would be constantly looking over his shoulder. We climbed back in the car and with the lights left off, drove away from the warehouse.

"Where did you get that idea?" I said as we hit the freeway.

"What idea?" Robert replied.

"The slice through the eyebrow. That's the second time you've done that," I said with a chuckle.

"Don't know, maybe I saw it in a movie or something," he replied.

"You've never watched a movie."

He laughed. "Thought it might make a bit of an impact. You know, when you look in a mirror you look at your eyes first, that scar will be the first thing he sees every morning."

"You, my friend, are a fucking genius," I replied laughing. "Where to now?"

"The club, I need to fuck someone."

With that, Robert settled back and we gunned it to the club just in time for closing. We walked in and I watched as Robert headed straight for Christy. He grabbed her by the wrist and dragged her back to the car. I motioned with my finger for Carly to join us. With a giggle she staggered after her friend - too much booze and high heels didn't make walking easy for her, but it was entertaining for me.

We stopped at a liquor store to pick up a six pack before heading to the girls' apartment. Carly giggled as we practically fell through her bedroom door, stripping off clothes as we did. I pulled her top over her head as she fumbled with her jeans, shaking her hips so they would fall. Grabbing the hem of my T-shirt she dragged it over my head before her hands ran down my chest to the top of my jeans. She popped the buttons and slid her hand in, freeing my cock from the confines of my tight shorts.

"Your mouth around my cock, now," I said.

She did as she was told and fell to her knees, dragging my jeans and shorts to my ankles. I stepped out of them and wrapped my hands in her hair, guiding her. She had such soft lips and a hot mouth. Boy, she could suck. He mouth would tighten around my cock from the base to the tip as she rolled my balls in her hand.

I pulled her up by her hair, turned her around and pushed at her shoulders until she leant down onto the bed. I dragged her panties to her ankles and she stepped out of them. Holding her hips, I fucked her hard. Reaching around with my hand my fingers drew across her clitoris, so swollen and wet. I pinched and squeezed until she was screaming out my name. Her legs were shaking from her orgasm and her hair stuck to the sweat that had formed on her brow. I wasn't done though. Letting her fall on the bed, I told her to roll on her back. I buried my face in her pussy, tasting her and lapping up her come.

Her hands gripped my head, she wrapped her legs around my shoulders and I felt her thighs quiver. She was close to coming again. I raised her hips, forcing my tongue deeper as she dug her fingernails into my scalp. Just before she came, I pulled my head away and moved up her body. Her legs slid from my shoulders to my waist and I slammed into her, fucking her as if it was the last time I ever would. Just as I was about to get my release I pulled out, my come pulsing onto her stomach.

A knock on the bedroom door startled us. "Bro, we need to go," I heard Robert say.

Carly sighed. "Are you always at his beck and call?" she said.

"He's my brother, if he has to go, I have to go," I said as I rolled off the bed. I dressed and gave her a brief kiss before leaving.

Robert was waiting, alone, by the front door to the apartment. He didn't look happy.

"You okay?" I asked.

"Sure, just need to get the fuck out of here."

"What's up? Christy didn't want to suck your cock?" I said, laughing.

"Oh believe me, that girl had my cock every which way, I just can't stand the pleading to stay that comes after," he replied.

I was a little surprised. Until then the girls had understood it was just a casual fling, or so I thought. We never took them out, there was no need. We fucked them and maybe bought them a beer or two, but they wouldn't get anything more from us. Neither of us was capable of an adult relationship and we didn't want one. We were having fun, well, at least I was. It was impossible to tell about Robert.

We had only driven a short distance when the blue flashing lights of a cop car lit up the inside of ours.

"What do you want to do, bro?" I asked. If we'd been aware of their presence in time I probably could have outrun them.

"Pull over, let's see what they want?"

I pulled the car to the kerb and waited. A cop tapped on my side window.

"Permit," he said.

I handed it through the open window and he took a while studying it.

"Exist the car, slowly, both of you," we were instructed.

Two police officers, who had obviously been waiting, gestured for us to get out of the car. As I did one of them grabbed me by the arm and slammed me face first on the hood. He pulled my arms behind my back and cuffed me. Robert and I looked over at each other; he gave a very slight nod of his head. Being picked up by the cops had always been his worst nightmare, but that nod told me he was okay. I wasn't too worried, the police could do nothing to me, I was too old to be sent back to New York.

In silence they placed me into the back of a car, with Robert in another, and we were driven back to the station. The only thing I told them was my name and address as they booked me. Still cuffed, they marched me along a grey corridor. The walls, the floor, the metal doors to cells were all the same depressing colour. Apparently cheerfulness was not the look they were going for.

They released my wrists as they closed the cell door behind me. I rubbed at them, a little pissed at the unnecessary tightness of the cuffs. I could walk from one end of the cell to the other in four paces. Robert was going to freak - not that he was claustrophobic, but he hated confinement. I flipped the stained mattress against the wall, sat on the metal frame of the cot and waited. Eventually I was taken by a cop, again in silence, to an interview room. I sat and smiled at the sour-faced female guarding the door. He cheeks coloured a little.

A few minutes later she was replaced by one of the cops that had pulled us over, and his sidekick.

"Travis, my name is Detective Mallory..."

I cut him off. "Can you tell me why I'm being held here?"

"Joey Morietti has implicated you in a rather nasty assault," he replied.

I raised my eyebrows. "Really? And when did this assault take place?"

"Earlier this evening, the police were called to Sibley Memorial after he was admitted. It appears he has suffered some serious injuries. Know anything about that?"

"Not a thing, been at the club all night, want the address?"

After I had given him the address and he'd written it down, he handed it to the sidekick who left the room; the door was guarded once more by sourpuss. She kept her gaze firmly fixed to the wall above my head.

"Your friend, Robert, gives a different location for your whereabouts this evening," he tried.

"Then he may have had one too many," I replied.

"What can you tell me about Joey?"

"Not much, don't really know him."

"We know you work for his father," came the response.

"Doesn't mean I know who assaulted his son, if he has been assaulted, of course."

"So what do you do for Guiseppi Morietti?" he asked.

"Collect rent, as I'm sure you already know. Now, shall we get back to the shocking news of his son? What happened to him?"

Detective Mallory stared at me, I gave him a smile. He reminded me of Goon, in fact, such was the resemblance they could have been related.

"Do you have a brother?" I asked.

"What? No, I don't and I ask the questions here." He was getting riled.

"Oh, it's just that you remind me of someone." I relaxed back in my chair.

A knock on the door interrupted our pleasant exchange. Sidekick bent his head low to Mallory, but wasn't quiet enough for me not to overhear. They'd confirmed that we had been at the club all evening - I made a point to remember to give Dave, the manager, a 'thank you'.

Mallory rose from his chair and left. I sat there and whistled to myself for what felt like an hour before I was informed I could leave. They thanked me for my co-operation and told me that, should they need to, the detectives would catch up with me if they had any further questions.

After gathering my watch and wallet I left the station to find Robert outside.

"Hey bro, you okay?" I said.

"Sure, let's get a cab back to the car," Robert replied.

We didn't speak until we were back at the car and only after checking that the tail lights were still intact. I would have been pissed to find my car accidentally damaged, a reason we could be pulled over again.

"What did they ask you?" Robert said.

"About Joey, they wanted to know who had done him over. I told them we were at the club, and I guess they checked, but other than not too much else. Wanted to know what I did for Joe, though."

"Mmm, same," he replied.

I cranked up the radio and we drove back to the apartment.

****

A little over a month later, we came face to face with Joey again. Until that day we had been carrying on with business as usual, staying at the apartment in Columbia Heights. We enjoyed having a place to ourselves, but if we were to keep living together without fighting over it, I had to become a little more 'house proud,' as Robert called it.

We were sitting it the office and Robert was detailing his grand plan to Joe. Over the past couple of years Robert had decided that Joe's businesses could be more profitable if they were legitimised. He had spent months writing down his plan, encouraging the guys to understand how it could work before calling a meeting with Joe to discuss it. Joe was getting on in age, and his health had started to deteriorate. Evelyn had encouraged him to see a doctor, but being the man he was, Joe had refused at first.

Our meeting was going well, Joe seemed keen and the guys looked impressed with Robert's proposal. However, there was one issue that needed to be resolved.

"Joe, you know that night?" Robert said, there was no need for details, Joe understood.

"Yeah, Mack is still looking into that," Joe replied.

Robert glanced over to me and gave a slight nod to his head. It was time to tell Joe the truth. Mack knew, we had confided in him some time ago, but because of Joe's declining health, we didn't want to add more stress to his life. But now it was important to cut Joey loose if we were to go ahead with the plan.

"Well, there's no need. I know who set us up and I've dealt with him. He'll walk around with a permanent reminder not to fuck with me," Robert said.

The comment that our attacker would walk around with a 'reminder' for the rest of his life caused Joe to look up and stare at us. His face hardened but then sadness crept into his eyes. He knew.

"Joey, get the fuck in here," Joe shouted, his face red with anger.

A very timid Joey entered the office, his eyes darting between his father and the rest of us. Joe jumped from his chair and strode towards his son. As he did he seemed to struggle for breath. Robert rose and stood by his side. There was a change in the atmosphere in the office. Robert towered over Joe, and when he placed his hand on his shoulder, Joe took a slight step back. It was noticeable and I saw the guys look at each other.

"Joey, what you did was wrong, and for what, jealousy? You can't be trusted. You skim money off every collection you make, you're stealing from your own father. And did you know, that the crack you sold to Macy's son..., he died, Joey?" Robert said.

Joe looked sharply at Robert. Macy was a woman who lived nearby. When her pay check ran out she would borrow a little money, always paying it back on time and without any fuss. Joe was fond of her. She was a single mom trapped in a dead end job, just trying to make ends meet. We had kept the details of how her son died from Joe until we could prove it was the drugs Joey was peddling that had killed him.

"This is what's going to happen, Joey. You're going to leave, you're no good to us. You want the drug business, you take it, but you will not peddle your shit on our streets. You get on with your life doing whatever the fuck you want, but if you so much as breathe a word about what you know, what has gone on here, I will fucking bury you," Robert said.

Robert telling Joey that he was out of the family secured our future and informed everyone in the room that things had changed. There had been a shift in leadership. Robert had made a decision and his decision was final; he was now in charge. Joey didn't take it well.

"Do you agree with this?" he shouted at his father. "Are you going to stand by and let him do this, take what's mine? Listen to him, since when has he been in charge?"

Turning to Jonathan, Joey said, "You're the Consigliere, do your fucking job and advise. This is bullshit."

"I work for your father, Joey, not you. Joe, Rob is right, you need to cut him loose," Jonathan replied.

It was clear Joey had started to panic; his head swung from person to person, his eyes pleading for support.

"We can earn money, dad, lots of it. People want the drugs. You get them hooked and they have to come back for more. You're letting him take this away from us and if you do that, you're a spineless prick," Joey said.

The tension in the air crackled as Robert took a step towards Joey. The guys looked nervously from him to Joe. Jonathan half stood as if to intervene then thought better of it.

"Dad, you don't want this, you guys don't want him running the family do you?" Joey said.

No one answered him.

"Joey, my son. You are my flesh and blood and I love you but, as Robert has said, you are a liability. I know what you do and it pains me in here," Joe placed his hand over his heart.

"It pains me, Joey, that you think I am fucking stupid, blind and without ears. That shit you sell kills."

Joey was panicking as he shouted back; he called his father a murderer, his sister a Saint, but when he accused Joe's lifestyle killing his mother, that kicked it all off.

"Don't you dare mention your mother. The cancer killed her," Joe said. His breathing was rapid, the veins in his neck bulged and once again, he clutched at his heart.

"You are dangerously close to seeing how angry I can get. Your father loved your mother, she died from an illness," Robert said in such a low voice it reverberated around the room.

"What the fuck would you know, huh? You think you're his son, you're nothing but a fucking street kid. You should be kissing his feet - he took you and that prick in," Joey looked over to me as he finished his sentence.

I pushed myself off the desk and moved towards him, but as I did so Mack stood, blocking my way.

"Not here, not now," he said to me.

Joey backed up a few steps closer to the door and pointing his finger he said, "You won't get away with this."

"I just did. Remember what I said that night, Joey. Now fuck off out of my sight before I change my mind and bury you now," Robert replied.

Joey turned and walked away, slamming the door so hard the windows rattled in their frames. The only sound was a deep sigh from Joe, who seemed to have aged another ten years. Robert placed his hand on Joe's arm and gestured for him to return to his desk. Halfway back across the room he paused. Joe looked at the desk, at the chair he had sat in for the past forty years. He looked between the guys that sat, still stunned after the exchange they had witnessed, and he shook his head. At that moment, that day, our future was sealed.

"Rob, you sit. You have the respect of everyone here, me included. I trust you to deal with this, I think it's time for me to take a back seat. I'm tired," he said. Joe left the office and Goon escorted him to his car.

There was silence for a few moments. Robert looked at each guy until they nodded their heads, their agreement that they were with him. He was the head of the family and they showed their respect by standing and hugging him with a kiss on both cheeks.

"So here's what we are going to do," Robert said, sitting in that chair, at the desk that was to become his. He addressed the guys who would then work for him and I looked at him with a smile. His plan had finally come together. He had made it, we had made it.

To celebrate we took ourselves off to a local tattoo parlour. Robert pulled a drawing from his pocket. It was a screwed up piece of paper that looked old, that looked like it had been unfolded and folded hundreds of times. He handed it over without saying a word and lay down on a bed. I laughed as I watched - an angel was etched on his back, not just any old angel, but a fallen one. It was perfect, it was Robert.

Chapter Nine

It took a couple of years of hard work to lose the crap and turn the businesses around. For the first time Robert and I worked separately; he spent more time in the office and I still kept my feet on the streets. I wasn't as clever as he was with the paperwork side of things, I liked to 'do' rather than 'tell'. Mack and I set up a security division. We had enemies, and as we introduced ourselves to computers, I found something I was really good at.

Hacking into someone's computer was easy, hacking into the local police and authorities' systems even easier. I spent hours *playing*.

"Trav, I got a parking fine, can you sort it?" Jonathan asked. It took no more than ten minutes to have that wiped off the system.

I was often amazed at how easy I found it all. Mack and I had hours of fun changing the stop light sequence and watching the traffic pile up outside the office, much to Robert's annoyance. He had his head buried in paperwork and would look up and sigh at our laughter, or tut at the beeping of horns as people tried to navigate the gridlock.

"I need to get out of here, want to go get something to eat?" Robert said, causing my fun to come to an end.

"Sure, the club?" I replied.

He nodded, shut down his computer and we made our way out. At that point we had bought a couple of cars. Robert had chosen a Range Rover and I stuck to the car I loved the most, the Mercedes. Long gone were the beaten-up old wrecks we were forced to drive. I still needed to be the one in the driving seat, I suppose that, deep down, it was my way of having a little control.

135

Robert would sit in the back and work. I wasn't his driver, I wasn't his security, I was more than that. I was his right-hand man.

The club had been revamped. It no longer resembled the place we would go to on a Friday night to pick up girls. It was an exclusive restaurant with a bar upstairs. We kept the name just for old time's sake.

"You looked fucked, Rob, you're working too hard," I said.

"Thanks, bro," he replied in his usual sarcastic way.

"You need to get laid. When was the last time?"

"Fuck knows, too long ago," he replied.

As much as girls threw themselves at us all those years ago, women did the same. No matter where we went, eyes would follow us, lips would be licked and legs parted as easy as the proverbial Red Sea. I fucked regularly and took great pleasure in reminding Rob of my tally - he was far more cautious.

"What about her?" I said as my eyes glanced over at the table next to us occupied by two women.

"Which one? The brunette looks more your type the other has to be her fucking mother," he said with a laugh.

"Mmm, you might be right," I said, giving the brunette my killer smile.

I called the waiter over and ordered a bottle of wine to be delivered to their table. Robert shook his head.

"Bro, watch and learn," I said.

The waiter appeared at the table with their wine and as predicted, the brunette raised her glass to me as she took a sip. I watched as she fumbled in her purse for a pen and wrote on the napkin she then gave to the waiter to hand over to me. Written across it was the word Alison and a cell number. I smiled at her as I folded it and placed it in my shirt pocket. I would certainly be calling Alison, and soon.

"Seriously, bro. I'm worried about you, all you do is work. You need to let loose once in a while," I said as the waiter placed our meals on the table.

"Trav, there's still a lot to do and I want out of the office. I want somewhere we can live, too. There's a place nearby that might make a decent replacement; we can turn the top floor into an apartment."

"And live where we work? Rob, you'll never be away from it."

"I need to work, Trav. I need to make this work for us."

"It is working. Fuck me, I have a wallet full of money, we have bank accounts. Who'd ever have thought we would get this far?"

"It's not enough. I need to know we will always be secure and if that takes another few years of hard work, I'm fine with that," he said. "Anyway, I still have part of the plan left to accomplish."

"Am I allowed to know this plan?" I asked, teasing.

"When I know we can achieve it, bro," he replied.

We finished our meal and stood to leave. I think it was the first time I'd noticed the change in people around us. For years people had been wary of us, avoided us to some degree, but dressed in our suits and the best handmade Italian shoes, the looks we got were of respect. Some stood to chat and shake our hand as we made our way to the restaurant door, some just gave a nod. Many were businessmen with their fake smiles and some were people from the neighbourhood.

The following day I called Alison. "Hi, Alison. It's Travis. We met..."

"I know who you are," she replied cutting off my answer.

"Can I take you to dinner?" I asked.

"Sure, I'd like that."

"How about I pick you up at seven," I replied.

"How about you just let me know where and I'll meet you?" she answered.

After making arrangements, I smiled as I replaced the phone. Robert had been working on the plans for the completion of the office block that we were soon to move into, and he wanted to drive over to check on the work. Paul was left in charge although he was yet to gain Robert's full trust.

"So you have a date with the brunette?" he said as we made our way to the car.

"Sure do, want to come?" I joked.

"Bro, I wouldn't want to cramp your style," he replied with a laugh.

It was obvious that most of the women we met flocked to Robert. At first that was something that irked me. We were both the same height; near enough the same build, but so different in looks. I doubt I would ever figure out women. Robert never smiled, he wasn't approachable, but maybe that was the attraction.

We pulled up at the office block; it was an imposing building, all glass and stainless steel. It had been built a couple of years before, and the building company had gone broke, leaving it empty and unfinished until Robert bought it. It was to be the new headquarters. We stood outside for a few moments, admiring the view.

"Fucking amazing how far we have come," I said, looking up at the expanse of glass.

"We used to walk past this years ago. It was an apartment block, I think," Robert replied.

"Let's take a look around," I said.

We entered a large foyer, in the centre was a circular desk made of granite. To one side, a security desk and behind, a bank of elevators. There was a door that led to a private parking lot and another leading to a maintenance area. The polished stone floor gleamed under the glare of the light as it streamed through the glass wall. We took the stairs, exiting on each floor to take a look around.

Each floor contained one corner glass-walled office, the rest was open plan, with a kitchen and meeting room until the tenth storey. The whole floor was set up as a boardroom with yet another kitchen and upscale restrooms. The floor above that was ours. As we exited the door we were met by Paul and a team of workmen.

"Rob, Trav, come on in," he called.

We made our way to one of the four doors behind the reception area, passing an enormous granite desk that was identical to the one in the lobby. The largest corner room was to be Robert's office. Two walls were made of glass, and striding over, I took in the expansive view of DC below us. In the distance, but easily seen, was the White House and Capitol Hill. Next door was the office Mack and I would share with some of the security team we were hiring. It was to be a state of the art command centre, so to speak. Banks of CCTV were already installed. The rest of the floor contained restrooms and a kitchen.

"How are you doing?" Robert asked.

"On schedule, we can occupy in just over a month," Paul replied.

"And upstairs?" Robert asked.

"Completed, just need you and Trav to think about decor."

"I'll leave that to Rob. I know fuck all about wall coverings and paint colour," I said.

Robert and I left Paul to take a look upstairs - the eleventh floor and our new apartment. It was to be our first real home. There were three bedrooms and an open plan living space with those same glass walls. As we walked in, I stood in the middle of the living room and just looked around. I was going to live there, and the thought that Robert and I would have our own place finally hit me. We looked at each other and smiled.

"Want to pick paint?" he said.

"No, you choose, although I want a black leather sofa and a fucking big TV," I said.

We laughed and made a list of what we required. Paul had instructed an interior designer to furnish the apartment, but between us we wanted it kept simple. We weren't materialistic as such, never having owned anything of our own. Robert never watched the TV at Joe's but had started to listen to music a lot. He wanted a high tech sound system, one connected to speakers placed around the entire apartment. We selected our bedrooms before heading back down to meet Paul.

I left Robert with Paul going over the finer details while I played in the security room. I felt strange though; I couldn't put my finger on what I felt other than, I suppose, we had finally grown up. It was all real, and it was Robert that had made it possible.

****

Robert was to meet with Joe that night; they met nightly for their chat. Sometimes I would join in, and sometimes I had no idea what the fuck they were talking about. As Joe got older so he reverted more and more to Italian and I couldn't keep up with the conversation. Rob was a natural at the language and we often joked that he must have had Italian ancestors.

After my shower, I dressed and headed to the garden room. Joe was laughing, he had pulled Robert into an embrace.

"Vassago," he said with a laugh. I knew Robert must have just told him the name of our new company.

"And where are you off to, looking all smart?" Joe asked.

"I have a date, Joe," I replied.

"A real one this time? I hear about you, you'll catch a disease if you're not careful," he said, his laughter turning into a wracking cough.

Once he had gotten himself under control, and after Robert and I had looked at each other with worried expressions, he sat down and patted the chair beside him.

"My sons, look at you both. So grown up now. Such powerful men, I'm proud of what you both have become," he said.

"We wouldn't be where we are now without you, Joe," I said, wondering what had brought out his sentimental side.

He waved his hand and shook his head. Evelyn came into the room with a pot of coffee and a handful of medication for him.

"Hi, Trav," she said with a smile. "You're heading out?"

"He has a date, a real one," Joe answered with a smirk.

"A real one huh? Make sure you tell me all about it when you get home," she replied.

I left the three of them sitting on the couch, Robert and Evelyn on either side of Joe, and smiled. That was my family sitting there; they were all I had and all I needed.

****

I arrived at the club a few minutes early and was shown to the table reserved solely for Robert and me. It was towards the back, shielded slightly by plants to give us privacy. I sat facing out into the restaurant and watched as Alison made her way to the front desk. She handed over her coat and was escorted to our table. She wore a smart black dress that fell just below her knees, black stockings - I hoped - and fucking high heel shoes. She walked with an air of confidence. When she saw me stand to greet her, she smiled. I placed my hands on her upper arms and kissed her cheek as she came to stand in front of me.

"You look good," I said. She raised her eyebrows at me.

"I mean it, you look beautiful," I said.

"Well then, thank you," she replied as she took her seat.

"So, Travis, I take it you own this restaurant."

"Not entirely, it's complicated," I said. To anyone else I would have just said yes but there was something about Alison that had me wanting to be honest with her.

"Complicated huh? My life story," she said as she opened the menu the waiter had handed to her.

I ordered a bottle of Merlot and made a mental note to ask Robert about wines, he was the expert. Alison had an air of sophistication about her and I wasn't in a rush to make a fool of myself. As she placed her order I studied her. Her long brown hair shone, she had a healthy glow to her skin as if she spent time outdoors, but it was her eyes I studied the most. I couldn't determine if they were blue or green.

"Tell me about yourself?" I asked.

"Why don't you tell me about you first," she replied. Feisty, I liked her already, a lot.

"Since you already know who I am, I guess there's not much left to tell, back to you," I answered. I had to be a little careful, I wasn't sure exactly what she knew, or thought she knew.

"Touché," she replied, raising her glass of wine to me. "Well, I came to DC about three years ago, followed my heart, which then got broken. I'm an interior designer and the reason I know who you are, Travis, is because I'm about to start work on your building and apartment."

"That's fantastic. So we'll be seeing quite a lot of each other over the next few weeks."

"I imagine so, although my contact is Paul."

A waiter appeared and placed our starters on the table and I think I may have fallen in love at that moment. There was no pushing food around the plate or picking and nibbling from Alison, she ate normally without embarrassment. The conversation flowed, we laughed and she held her own, verbally sparring with me. I enjoyed her company and as much as I would have loved to have fucked her senseless, talking and listening to her was much more satisfying.

With our meal finished, Alison pulled her purse from her bag and before I could take the check from the waiter, she laid some bills on the table.

"Alison, put that away," I said.

"I'm not someone you pay for, Travis. Not on the first date anyway," she said with a smirk.

"Are there going to be more?" I asked.

"Perhaps."

We walked towards the front door. I took her coat from the concierge and helped her into it; then we made our way outside.

"Can I give you ride somewhere?" I asked.

"No, thank you. I'll take a cab."

Being the gentleman I was, I stepped towards the curb and hailed a cab. I opened the door and just as she climbed in, she turned and smiled at me.

"Thank you, Travis. I've enjoyed this evening and no doubt I'll see you at your office soon."

I watched the cab pull away and with a smile, walked to the Range Rover.

****

The following day Robert and I made our way to the new office block. As we entered what was to become our apartment I caught sight of Paul and Alison. They had plans laid out over the breakfast bar and seemed deep in discussion. Both looked over as they heard us.

"Rob, Travis, let me introduce Alison, she's our interior designer. We're just going over what you requested," Paul said.

"We've already met," I replied. Robert raised his eyebrows at me, no doubt recognising Alison from the club.

She was professional and mainly ignored me other than to talk through her design for the apartment. It was as we had asked, whitewashed walls with wooden floors, and I smiled at the image of the TV that I wanted. Rob and I spent a half hour finalising the decor before moving on to the rest of the building. As we walked around, Alison explained how the floor would be laid out. It was to be an open plan with just one corner office for the head of that department. She talked about acoustics and light - things I had no understanding of. She had even detailed where every power socket would be concealed. I enjoyed watching her work, she wasn't at all fazed by my scrutiny, and at the end of our meeting she shook hands with us all, collected her briefcase and made her way out of the building.

"That's the woman you took to dinner, isn't it?" Robert asked.

"Yep. She told me last night she was our interior designer," I replied.

"Whatever you do, don't fuck her about. She's highly regarded in her field, took a lot of persuasion and fucking money to get her on this project," Paul added.

"Paul, contrary to popular belief, I don't *fuck women about*. Well, not often anyway," I said.

Robert chuckled as we left. I fished about my pocket for my cell and sent a quick text to Alison, asking if she wanted to meet that evening. Her reply had me smiling. It was a no; she needed to work, but suggested another night. Why was I smiling? There was nothing I enjoyed more than the chase before the kill.

****

A development prospect had come up in New York and Robert was interested, but I was unsure. I had no desire to return there. Just the mere mention of the city brought back unwanted feelings.

"You don't have to come, Trav," Robert had said as we discussed the build.

"What's your meeting about?" I asked.

"I have to meet Massimo Gioletti. His family runs the city, but I've told Joe I'm not going there to ask his permission. I'm meeting him out of respect for the relationship he and Massimo have."

Joe and Massimo had been connected back in the day, in Chicago. I also knew nothing would get built in New York City without Massimo either knowing or being involved. But it was time to lay some old ghosts to rest. I would go with Robert and I would avoid Hell's Kitchen. I had no desire to meet any member of my family, unless it was to spit on their graves. I had no idea if my mother was still in the apartment or if Padriac and Carrig were still around. I had no desire to meet my sister again. She was the one I felt the most disappointed in, because she was the one who was supposed to come and find me — but she never did.

The trip was only one day; we would fly out, have our meeting and fly back. Paul had organised a private charter so we could fly at our convenience. Once settled in our seats, while preparing for take-off, I sent Alison a text. I wanted to arrange our next date for when I returned.

Paul had also arranged for a car to meet us at the airport. There was no waiting to collect luggage, no traipsing through arrivals; the car was waiting for us on the runway allowing us to be ushered off the jet and into the waiting Mercedes. The driver took us straight to the site in Manhattan. We spent an hour or so walking around the site, with Paul detailing where the building would be. Robert understood the plans far more than I did. I just saw a piece of wasteland full of rubble; he could picture the finished project.

We watched as three cars, all identical, arrived. They stopped, and someone who could have been related to Goon exited from the first car. He took his time to look around, and stared at us with his hand just inside his jacket, chest high. That stance made Robert and I chuckle. After a minute he opened the rear door of the second car and a very distinguished elderly man climbed out, waving away the offered hand of Goon version two. Massimo stood and buttoned up his suit jacket before making his way over to us. He was flanked on either side by variations of Goon version two.

"Roberto, it's good to finally meet you," Massimo said, pulling Robert into a hug.

I barely concealed the chuckle. It was a source of great amusement back home that Robert had been rechristened with an Italian version of his name by the older members of the other families. It was not generally acceptable to have a non-Italian as head of a family, but respecting Joe, a new name for Rob was the compromise. In any event, Robert certainly looked Italian.

Robert and Massimo chatted back and forth. Goons version two, three and four stood with arms crossed over their chests, scanning the environment. For what, I had no idea. We stood in the middle of a wasteland; any threat would be seen from a mile away.

We walked around the site, Paul detailing the outline of the plans, and as we made our way back towards the waiting cars Massimo asked Robert if he still fought.

"Only for fun and generally with Travis," Robert replied.

"I watched one of your fights, yours too, Travis. You were very angry, Roberto, if I remember," Massimo said.

"Probably, I was angry a lot back then," Robert replied.

"And not now?" he enquired.

"Only when the need arises, Massimo," was Robert's answer.

The conversation wasn't about our days of boxing; it was a subtle exploration of whether Robert was still on top of his game, whether he was willing and able to issue an order, to solve a problem. With a nod of his head, Massimo said his goodbye and climbed back in his car. Sadly, a year later we learnt that Massimo had been imprisoned under the FBI's Rico Laws. He would never be a free man again.

We arrived back in DC in comfort and record time thanks to the luxury of the jet. Robert left to catch up with Joe and I made my way to the club to meet Alison. I would have to ask Robert about a different venue for our next date, but I was comfortable at the club.

Alison was already seated when I arrived; I leant to kiss her cheek as a way of greeting her and breathed in the heady scent of her perfume.

"How was your trip?" she asked.

"Good, we have a development starting. Today was just to view the site and go over the plan." Of course I made no mention of meeting Massimo.

We chatted back and forth, ordered from the hovering waiter and enjoyed our meal. Over coffee Alison informed me that the furniture had arrived at the apartment, and that Robert and I would be moving in within the week.

"Want to come and take a look with me?" I asked.

She eyed me suspiciously. "Mr. Curran, are you inviting me back to your place?" she teased.

"I believe I am."

"You can't offer me a coffee, you have no cups yet," she said.

I signalled for the manager. "Tom, find me two takeout containers and fill them with coffee."

I smiled and stood, holding out my hand to help Alison from her seat. By the time she had retrieved her coat from the concierge Tom had returned with the two takeout containers full of coffee.

It was a short drive to the office and although not occupied, we had already installed security. I had rung through on the way announcing my arrival and found a guard waiting by the door ready to open it for us. We were silent in the elevator as it glided up eleven floors and opened into a fully decorated reception area. The front door to the apartment was yet to be fitted with a lock. I pushed it open and we walked through into the open living space. A large black leather sofa with stainless steel legs stood, still wrapped in cellophane, in the living room. The kitchen was fitted with appliances and the oak wooden floor throughout was highly polished.

There was a smell of fresh paint and, like a child, I couldn't help but place my fingertips to the wall closest to me to feel if it was still wet. I felt a strange sensation in my chest, in my stomach. This was to be my first real home, a home I knew I would be safe and comfortable in. I walked towards the bedroom I had selected. Although the three bedrooms were the same size I had opted for the one furthest away from the door, Robert the one closest, leaving the middle empty. It wasn't necessarily a conscious decision, but I wondered if we left it to buffer any noise made from either bedroom.

Alison followed, not that I had asked her to do that, and for a moment I was so lost in my own thoughts I had forgotten she was with me.

"Are you okay? Do you like what I've done?" she asked, concern lacing her voice.

"I like it. It's just... well, this is going to be my first real home, and it feels a little odd at the moment."

"What do you mean, your first real home?" she asked.

"I was a street kid for many years..., both Robert and I were. Home was an alley and a doorway to the back of a Chinese restaurant, if I recall."

"Oh, I didn't know. Where do you live now?"

"Now that's a long story," I said. How did I explain Robert and I lived at Joe's without explaining who Joe was?

A wooden bedstead dominated the room, its mattress in a cloth protector, and on either side of the bed were small nightstands. I sat on the bed and looked at Alison standing in the middle of the room. She stared straight back at me. No words were spoken as she took the few steps required before she was standing between my knees. Her hands cupped either side of my face. I ran my hands up her legs, catching her dress and raising it. She leant down for a kiss.

Her lips gently pressed against mine. I opened my mouth and my tongue tangled with hers. My hands had come to rest on her hips and I held them fast while pulling her closer to me. I could feel the lace of her panties under my fingers. Our kiss deepened; I was hungry for her.

I stood, and as I did I raised the dress over her head. She wore a matching lace panty and bra set, somehow that pleased me; I'd hoped she had *dressed* for the evening. Her tanned skin set off the white of the lace. She reached forward and unknotted my tie, sliding it from my collar, and with an agonising slow pace she undid the buttons of my shirt. Her hands brushed against my chest, lower and lower as each button was popped open. While she unbuckled my belt I shrugged the shirt from my shoulders, letting it fall in a heap on the floor. Alison ran her fingers around the waistband of my pants, her nails scraping gently against my skin. She popped the button, undid the zip and with my pants in her fists, she lowered them as she sunk to her knees.

My hand fisted in her hair as her tongue licked up the inside of my thigh. She reached to either side of my shorts and pulled them down. As my cock sprung free her lips closed around it. Her mouth was hot and her tongue slid against the underside of my shaft as she sucked. My stomach clenched as my orgasm built. I pulled at her hair, releasing myself from her mouth and she stood.

Alison unclipped her bra, letting the straps slide from her shoulders. She slowly lowered her panties until she was standing naked in front of me. Cupping her face with my hands, I kissed her fiercely. I echoed the moan that escaped her lips.

I wanted that kiss to last forever, but I wanted to be inside her even more. Breaking away, I turned her and gently pushed until she fell onto the bed. As she shuffled up I climbed on, crawling over her body. I started at her neck, my lips and tongue tasting, kissing and inhaling her scent. As I moved lower I caught a hard nipple between my lips. My hands were either side of her, holding her wrists to the bed. I placed light kisses on her stomach and worked my way down her body to the place I wanted to be. Her legs parted giving me access. Her clitoris was swollen and glistened; I swiped my tongue over it.

As I forced my tongue inside her, her body arched off the bed and she cried out. I licked, sucked and teased until I felt her thighs quiver, until she screamed out and came. She relaxed back on the mattress and a sheen of perspiration covered her chest. I raised my face to hers.

"You'll find what you need in the bedside cabinet," she said.

I gave her a puzzled look before reaching over and opening the drawer. I laughed as I noticed a packet of condoms.

"You have catered to all my needs haven't you, Miss Parkins," I said.

"All part of the service, Mr. Curran."

Opening a packet, I rolled a condom down my cock. I hovered over her for a moment; we locked eyes before I pushed into her hot, wet pussy. She wrapped her legs around my waist and raised her hips, matching my thrusts. Her hands held my biceps and her nails dug into my flesh as she came again. I gave into my release shortly after. Alison released her legs from around my waist and I rolled to her side. She turned to face me.

"That was so good," she whispered.

"That it was. I don't suppose you thought of a bin, did you?" I asked, removing the condom.

"Darn, and there I was, thinking no other designer went to such lengths. I shall add that to the list of items yet to buy."

I slid my arm under her neck and pulled her to me. She placed her hand on my chest, her fingers brushed against my skin. For a while we were silent. It was just as I started to doze that I felt her hand move down my stomach; my cock twitched in response. I kept my eyes closed but smiled. Her hand stroked and massaged me hard again.

"Ready for round two?" she said.

This time Alison reached for the condom and ripped the packet open with her teeth - fuck, that was hot. She expertly rolled it down my cock and then straddled me, lowering herself slowly. She rode me hard and fast and her nails raked down my chest as her orgasm built. I struggled to hold myself together long enough for her to come first and when she did, I felt like I had exploded. She collapsed onto my chest.

We lay for a while and as the evening drew in, the lights on the apartment automatically came on, so subtly at first that I hadn't noticed.

"I need to get going," Alison said sleepily.

"I'll run you home."

"I'm fine, I can take a cab."

"Alison, let me run you home," I replied.

"Please, Travis, we've had a great evening. I'll use the bathroom and then catch a cab."

I was concerned. Why would she not want a lift home? I couldn't force her, though. We dressed and took the elevator down to the foyer. There was a light drizzle so I wrapped my suit jacket around her shoulders and waited with her while she hailed a cab. As one pulled alongside the curb she turned to me and handed back my jacket.

"Thank you, it's been fun," she said. She reached up on her tiptoes to plant a kiss on my cheek before getting into the cab and driving away.

I stood for a while watching the cab take her home and wondering why she'd left that way. A little investigation was in order. Climbing into the Range Rover, I started the engine and made my way to Joe's.

****

Joe and Robert were sitting in the garden room, each nursing a small cup of espresso. They were chatting back and forth in Italian but switched to English as I joined them. Evelyn came and sat with us, topping up coffees. It was hard not to notice how frail Joe had become. At first we had thought it was his heart giving him problems, and after much nagging from Ev, Joe had finally consulted a doctor. He had cancer and had refused all treatment. We were all devastated by that news, and no amount of arguing with him would change his mind. He was a stubborn man and I knew, when the time came, he would be deeply missed by us all. He had been the father I would have loved - actually, he was the father that I loved.

I didn't hear from Alison for a couple of days. I knew she was busy with the final arrangements at the office, but she was there the day we moved in. She took delight in showing all the guys around, and I was proud of her; she had done a wonderful job. When we got to the apartment she gave me a sly smile and a wink. Not only had she furnished the place, she had also arranged for the kitchen cupboards to be stocked and the bathrooms to have a selection of toiletries. Nothing had been overlooked.

"You'll find everything you need, Travis, in your bedside cabinet," she whispered as we left.

"Not much good if I don't get to see you to use them, though," I replied.

"Oh you will, soon."

She left with Paul to complete some paperwork, leaving Robert and I alone in the apartment.

"Well, this is it then, bro. Grown-ups at last. Fancy a beer?" I asked as I opened the fridge.

"Sure, might as well celebrate. Feels strange though," he replied.

We sat on the sofa and clinked our bottles together.

"You didn't fuck her on this did you?" he asked, looking down at the black leather.

"Bro, what do you take me for? Of course not. I christened my new bed."

He laughed and we drank our beers, watching the lights of Washington illuminate as the night fell.

"So, what do we do now?" I asked.

"What do you mean?"

"It just seems a bit odd not being at Joe's. Do you think Ev will be okay?"

"Sure, she knows she can call us if she needs us. Probably glad to get rid of you and the mess you leave. And speaking of mess..."

"Yeah, yeah, I'll make sure to leave as much as possible, just to piss you off," I said.

****

Over the weeks that followed we moved into the apartment and I saw Alison a couple of times a week. Our schedules seemed to always get in the way. She had moved on to a new project, one that took her out of the city a lot. I would have liked to have seen her more and although at first I didn't realise it, I was really beginning to fall for her. I liked that she challenged me; she didn't fall at my feet. Yet something still bugged me. Not once had I driven her home, nor had I been invited to her house. If she stayed the night, it was always at the apartment. Robert, although he hadn't said anything, was clearly uncomfortable with that. If he knew she would be visiting, he stayed out late and was usually up and at his desk before we rose in the morning.

I decided I needed to start investigating why Alison kept me from her house. Mack and Robert were in Robert's office when I entered.

"Got a minute?" I asked.

"Of course, what's up?" Robert answered.

"Alison…" Before I could finish Mack cut in.

"On the rocks already?" he said.

"No, I don't think so. I've been seeing her for a couple of months now and not once has she invited me to her house. I want to know why," I said.

"Want her address?" Mack asked.

"You have it?"

"Of course he has it," Robert answered.

"Don't go rushing over there. There might be a good reason she hasn't taken you back home," Mack added as he rose from his chair and left for his office.

A couple of minutes later he was back with a file. Everyone we worked with, either as an employee or a contractor, had a file. I could have kicked myself for not thinking to check if one had been made on Alison. It was purely for security; Robert needed to know exactly who he was dealing with. I took a note of her address and pocketed it.

"Just drive by, Trav. Don't go knocking on her door until you know why she's kept you away. You might be over-thinking it," Robert said.

"Sure, catch you later," I replied.

I took the elevator down to the parking lot and climbed into the Range Rover. Setting the Sat Nav, I made my way out into the traffic. It was less than a half hour before I was instructed to turn into a leafy lane. Smart, tidy houses lined both sides of the street. I slowed as the annoying voice on the Sat Nav informed me I was close to my destination. The houses were detached, with a garage to one side, and I pulled up opposite one. The front yard was neat and it looked like someone tended the grass and flower beds. The one thing that struck me though was a bike leant against the wall next to the front door - a pink child's bike.

I sat for a moment contemplating its meaning. Did Alison have a child, a daughter? And if so, why not say so in the beginning? More important, how did I feel about that? Children had never really figured in my life plan. There was no sign of life at the house, and after a couple of minutes I drove on.

"That was quick," Robert said as I entered his office.

"Mmm, I think she has a child. There was a bike in the front yard," I said, as I sat in one of the chairs opposite him.

"Has she ever mentioned a child?" he asked.

I shook my head. "No, and it might answer the questions about why I only see her once or twice a week and why I never get invited to her house."

"Maybe she wants to see how your relationship goes before she introduces you to her child. How do you feel about her?"

"I really like her, Rob. I think this could be serious, but a child? I don't know if I can handle that."

I was being honest with him, but also deep down inside there was this issue with my own childhood.

"I don't think I could be a dad, Rob," I added.

He didn't speak, just nodded his head.

I was scared I would end up like my father. I was as violent, if not more so than he had been, so I already had some of his traits. I sure as hell didn't drink as much, but having a child - no, having anyone rely on me - was something that made me question myself.

Was I good enough for that?

I could be a selfish bastard, I knew that. I'd spent way too long fighting to survive. I lived a life that was fraught with danger, I'd murdered people. The thought of bringing a child into my world was terrifying. Robert and I had enemies, dangerous ones, enemies that wouldn't think twice about abducting someone precious to us. I realised I was more like Robert than I'd thought. Neither of us got too close to anyone. At first I thought that was because we liked the freedom we had, but then I wondered. Whoever I got close to had the potential to finish me - and if something bad happened to someone I loved, I'd live the rest of my life suffocated by the guilt.

****

A few days later I received a text from Alison about meeting up, it was midday and she wanted to speak to me. We'd only met for dinner until then. I agreed to meet in a coffee shop not far from the office. Leaving the car parked in a no-stop zone outside, I made my way to the table she where was waiting for me. She didn't greet me with the smile she usually did. She had dark circles under her eyes, and she looked to me as if she had been crying.

"I'll get straight to it, Trav. I think I'm pregnant. I missed a period and did a test but it was inconclusive. I've booked an appointment this afternoon at the doctors' office. I was going to wait until I'd had the test before I told you but... oh, I don't know. I kind of want someone to come with me," she said.

Holy fuck, that wasn't what I was expecting at all. I signalled for the waitress to come and take our coffee order and we sat for a moment or two in silence. I wracked my brain for a time I hadn't used a condom. There had only been one time; could we be that unlucky?

"Of course I'll come with you," I eventually said.

My heart was pounding in my chest and I wasn't sure what to say. Fuck seemed to be the only word rushing through my brain. Fuck, fuck, fuck.

"I'm not going to apologise, it was an accident but I will say this, whatever the outcome, I'll deal with it. I don't want you to feel obliged to do anything," she said.

I simply nodded my head; the words I should have said just wouldn't come out of my mouth, and what words would they have been? I don't want to be the father I had? I was scared that I would be? To be a father meant to have a relationship, and that meant telling her who I really was. She wouldn't understand, and I wasn't about to explain either. I had buried my childhood, and all of a sudden it was rushing back through my brain. We drank our coffee in silence. It was awkward and I struggled even to start a conversation. It didn't seem appropriate to bring up that I had driven past her house and seen the bike, it didn't seem appropriate to mention that the weather was great, nothing seemed appropriate.

I noticed Alison glance at her watch; it was obviously time to go. We stood, I helped her on with her coat and we made our way outside. I opened the passenger door and guided her in. As we drove she gave directions to her doctor's office. I parked and as we walked towards the reception my steps faltered.

"Go and check in, I just need to make a call," I said.

She nodded and I watched through the glass door as she announced herself and then took a seat. I pulled my phone from my jacket pocket and dialled Robert.

"Shit," he said after I had explained where I was.

"Shit indeed," I replied.

"What are you going to do?" he asked.

"I have no idea yet. I guess we need to wait and see what the doctor says, it might be a false alarm."

"Why didn't she get the test and then tell you after?" he asked.

"She wanted the company."

"Okay, fair enough I guess. Call me as soon as you know anything."

I replaced my phone and joined Alison in reception. It wasn't a long wait before her name was called. I followed as she made her way to the doctor's office, I sat in total silence as she said she wanted a test, and explained that the one she had done was inconclusive. The doctor asked questions, took notes and I stared stonily out of the window as Alison was given a bottle to pee in. When she left for the restroom, the doctor spoke.

"Doesn't look like you're too happy to be here?" she asked.

"Can you tell?" I said, a little too snappy I guessed.

"Obviously, so how about we offer just a little support to Alison at what is clearly a stressful time for you both."

I stared at the doctor, she stared straight back at me. Not a flicker of apprehension showed in her eyes. Our 'who would back down first' competition was broken as Alison returned. She handed the bottle to the doctor, who stood and moved to a cabinet. I couldn't see exactly what she was doing; she kept her back to us. I did see her remove her gloves, pour the contents of the bottle down a drain and then discard it.

As she sat at her desk she spoke. "That test was negative. I think it's highly unlikely you are pregnant. Now, do we need to talk about birth control?"

To say the relief I felt was overwhelming was an understatement. I turned and smiled at Alison, the first smile I had given her. Her smile in return wasn't a full one though.

"Thank you doctor, I don't think right now that I need to discuss birth control. Perhaps I'll make another appointment next month."

"Okay. See the receptionist on your way out."

We rose and left. Alison didn't see the receptionist on our way out, we just made our way straight to the car and drove back the way we came.

"Do you want to get something to eat? I asked.

"No, thank you though. And thanks for coming. I really should have just gone on my own."

She bit down on her lip before sighing. "Can you just drop me back off at that coffee shop?"

"Why don't I just take you home?"

"Because I have a meeting later. I want to do a little shopping first."

"So you go shopping, then to a meeting? Doesn't it look a bit odd, hauling your bags in there with you?" I asked.

"I want to shop for some sample items, Travis, to take to my meeting."

"Okay. How about I come and meet you later, at your house perhaps." I knew I was pushing it.

By then we had arrived back at the coffee shop, we sat in the idling car.

"Not tonight, I'm really tired," she said.

"Tomorrow then."

"I'll ring you," she answered.

As she reached for the door handle, I placed my hand on her arm. "Why do I get the feeling that's not going happen?"

She relaxed back in the seat and sighed.

"I have an opportunity in New York, Paul has asked me to be involved in some of the new developments Vassago has going on. It's a big deal for me and one I can't turn down. I wanted to talk to you about it, and I guess this scare kind of got in the way. It made me think about my life and what I want. I know we've never really talked about our past, but I was never allowed to do anything for myself, Travis, and now I can."

"I understand, I'm sorry this is going to end. What about your daughter?" I asked, it was time to bring it up.

Alison looked sharply at me and then smiled. "I guess I should have expected you to *check me out*. Rebecca will come with me of course."

"Is that why I was never invited to your house?"

"Partly, you're the first person I've dated since her father left. I'm sure you can imagine how traumatic that was for her, so I didn't want to introduce you until I was sure about us. She's only five and it wasn't a year ago that he left."

"Can I ask one thing? I need you to be honest with me. Did you agree to meet me because of my connection with Vassago?" I asked. A thought had started to whirl around my brain.

"I'm not sure I understand what you mean. If you're asking me if I knew who you were, then yes. I don't take on a client without checking them out," she replied.

"Do you usually date your clients?"

"Travis, I have no idea what you're getting at. No, I don't usually date my clients. If you think I've dated you to get an in with Vassago, remember I already had the contract before I met you at the club." Her eyes didn't quite meet mine when she spoke, though.

"Fair enough. Good luck, Alison," I said.

With a final smile she left the car. I sat for a moment before making a u-turn and driving back to the office. I was gutted, and I was also upset at Paul. Surely I should have known. As the elevator took me to the eleventh floor I started to get pissed, very pissed. I stormed into Robert's office; he was on the phone but looked up at me as I strode across the floor. I paced, waiting for him to finish his call. Finally, he replaced the handset.

"Did you know Paul had offered Alison a job in New York, on the builds?" I asked.

"I knew he was lining up a team, I'm meeting with him to go over those plans tomorrow. What happened today?"

I told him of the doctor's appointment and the result, of the conversation in the car, and as I did, he reached for his phone and called Paul to his office. I took a seat and waited the couple of minutes it took for Paul to arrive.

"You wanted to speak to me?" he said, as he made his way into the office.

I jumped from my chair. "Travis, sit down bro," Robert said.

"Paul, did you offer Alison a position as our interior designer in New York?" Robert asked.

"Yes, I think she replied this morning by email but I haven't checked yet. She's on the list to discuss with you tomorrow," he replied.

"Okay, did you know Travis was dating her? That was, until this afternoon," Robert said.

Paul turned to me. "Shit, Trav, I didn't know. I swear I would have run it past you first if I had known."

"She fucking called it off because she's heading to New York now," I said.

"Trav, how could I have known? I mean, I know you said you knew her, but I thought it was just a casual thing, you know, one of your one-night stands," he replied. He chuckled until he noticed neither Robert nor I were *chuckling* along with him.

"Listen, I'll tell her we had a change of mind, the position is no longer available," he said.

I slumped back in my chair. "No, she's excited about it. It's a great opportunity for her."

"What can I say? I'm sorry. She did an amazing job here, I thought she would do a better job being on board from the ground up. You can still see her though; I mean, it's not that hard to get back and forth," Paul said.

"No, I don't think so. New York isn't somewhere I want to go to regularly," I replied.

Paul offered his apology again before leaving the office.

"I'm sorry, bro. You know I like them to sort their own staff but if I'd have known I would have told you," Robert said.

"I know you would, I'm just a bit gutted really. I wondered if she dated me to make sure her contract was secure."

"Did she seem that kind of person?" he asked.

"I don't know. I'm just pissed, that's all."

"The gym is finished, want to go test it out?" Robert asked.

We had decided to install a gym in the basement of the office. The staff had been given a pass to use the facilities whenever they wanted. Robert and I made our way down and into the private changing room. Our lockers were already kitted out with clothes and gloves. The gym housed state of the art equipment and, at one end, a boxing ring. Neither Robert nor I had boxed for a couple of years; we never had the time, and the old gym had long since been closed down. It was fun to climb back under those ropes and even better to let out a bit of aggression. Neither of us had lost our skills; we may have been a little slower but it was a great workout.

Chapter Ten

Joe's health had taken a turn for the worse. Robert and I spent most of our free time with him and watched his decline; we knew the end was not far away. It was in the very early hours of one morning that Robert woke me to say he had received a call from Evelyn, asking for us to visit.

"Bro, we need to get to the house, Evelyn called," he said.

"Fuck, is he…," I didn't finish the sentence.

"No, but I don't think he has long."

In silence I dressed and drove as quickly as I could to the house. We found Joe in his bed with Evelyn by his side. Her eyes were red from the tears that gently rolled down her cheeks. I sat beside her and took her hand in mine, giving it a gentle squeeze. Robert sat on the other side of Joe, whose eyes were closed; his breathing was raspy and laboured. Robert instructed Evelyn to call whoever she needed, especially the doctor that had been monitoring his care.

The only sound in the room was the breaths Joe was struggling to take. My chest felt constricted and no matter how hard I tried, I couldn't stop the tears from falling. I had loved that man like a father, he had loved me like a son, and my heart was breaking. Evelyn returned and the doctor arrived shortly after. He took Joe's blood pressure, listened to his chest and shook his head. He gave words of comfort to Evelyn and took a seat in a chair on the other side of the room so as not to intrude. The next person that arrived at the house was Jonathan, closely followed by Mack, Paul and Richard. One by one they came into the bedroom to say their goodbyes before returning to the kitchen to wait. The last to arrive was Padre Carmelo. He was an old man and had been the priest at the local church for as long as I could remember. Evelyn helped him to Joe's side where he prayed for his soul. Everyone, except Robert, prayed with him.

It wasn't long before the rasping quietened, before the rise and fall of Joe's chest stopped, and we knew he had died. I pulled a sobbing Evelyn into my arms. I watched Robert close his eyes and his chin fell to his chest. The doctor came forward and did what he had to do for confirmation. Robert stood and escorted the doctor from the room; there were calls to be made.

The guys came and each kissed Joe on the forehead; Richard and Paul, both of Italian descent, mumbled in their own language, a prayer perhaps. Jonathan looked broken. Excluding Evelyn, he had known Joe the longest. He had been his advisor until Robert took over, and he freely cried for a man he also loved.

It was an hour or so later that the undertakers arrived to take Joe's body. Evelyn fussed, ensuring they handled him with care. Being surrounded by Robert, the guys and I ensured that he would be treated with the utmost respect. Once they had taken him, she set about to make coffee for everyone. Jonathan took the kettle from her shaking hands, led her to the kitchen table and made her sit. He filled it and made the coffee himself.

"I need to tell Maria," Evelyn said. Her sister had been placed in a home many years ago. The dementia was too bad for her to be cared for safely at home.

"Why don't I make the calls?" Jonathan said. He was also referring to Joey.

Although no one had seen Joey for years, he would need to know his father had died. What he would do with that information was anyone's guess.

"Where's Robert?" Paul asked.

"Garden room, let him be please," Evelyn replied.

Robert needed a little time alone, I knew that, although Evelyn took his coffee and sat with him for a while.

"Is there anything we should be doing?" Paul asked.

"I have his will, I'll speak with Robert later and we can instruct our lawyers to deal with that," Jonathan replied.

As the morning broke the guys left, each hugging Evelyn as they did. Robert and I sat for a while and Evelyn dozed on the sofa beside us.

"What do we do now?" I whispered.

"We need to organise his funeral, I guess. We'll talk with Evelyn about that later. You want a coffee?"

I nodded and Robert and I left Evelyn asleep. We sat in the kitchen just reminiscing about our lives, and talking about Joe. We laughed and I cried some more. Although not an overly affectionate person, Robert placed his arm around my shoulder to offer some comfort.

A week later the funeral was organised. It was a lavish affair, and one that attracted the local police, something that stressed us all. Massimo had a day pass from prison to attend - how he had managed that in spite of his charges was beyond me, I realised he really did have friends in high places. Joey attended but stood on the fringes. It was clear to everyone he kept himself away from the main party, and to see the constant smirk on his face, we were unsure whether he was there to mourn the passing of his father or to spit on his grave.

Joe was laid to rest with his beloved wife, Maria, and when it came time to leave, mourners filed past us, offering their condolences to Evelyn and shaking Robert's hand. It was yet another example of how he was regarded as the head of the family.

The wake was held at the hotel Vassago owned; a private function room had been set to one side. It was good to meet old friends of Joe; many would tell their stories of their time with him and it was a pleasure to meet Massimo's family from New York. As the evening wore on, Evelyn started to flag somewhat. It was time to take her home.

Robert and I stayed at the house for a few days after the funeral, until Evelyn ushered us out, telling us it was time to get back to work and back to our apartment. Joe wouldn't have wanted a long period of mourning, and deep down I also thought she wanted some time alone.

****

The businesses were growing, and with that came requests, primarily for Robert. Requests to attend functions, most of which he declined, and many requests for donations; but one day he showed me a letter he had received. It was another donation request, and one that had probably been sent to hundreds of businesses in the DC area. A children's home was looking for funding. Something about the request resonated in both of us and we took a drive to Arlington to check it out.

Perhaps it was fate, because as we drove through a gap in a low stone wall we couldn't help but notice a sign, Stone House.

"Bro, see that sign?" I said.

"We'd need to change that if we get involved," Robert replied.

"Why?"

"This needs to be kept under the radar. We don't need my surname attached to this, we have too much history, and that doesn't need to be brought here."

I understood what he meant. We were greeted at the door by a friendly but harassed-looking older woman. She introduced herself as Nancy Pearson and seemed thrilled that we had taken the time to visit. I thought to myself that she probably hadn't had much support from her fund raising campaign. We took a tour of the house and the grounds - it certainly needed some repair and modernising - and then sat in the kitchen for coffee and homemade cookies. Once Nancy explained that the home took in homeless children, something changed. Without even knowing Robert's thoughts, I wanted in. I wanted to be able to do something to help, and because of Robert and his grand plan, I had a bank account with enough money to last me my lifetime. It was time to give something back.

"Nancy, this house needs a lot of money spent on it, repairs, redecoration and some modernisation," Robert said before looking briefly at me, we smiled and I nodded.

"We want to buy this house from you. It will stay as a home and I would like you to stay here, but with help," he added.

"We'll have it valued and give you a fair price for it," I said.

Without hesitation she agreed, confirming that her fund raising hadn't been successful We arranged for our lawyers to make contact and start the process. We left Nancy shortly after and as we walked back towards the car I paused, looking over at the grassed front yard.

"Rob, let's do this, just us. Keep it outside of Vassago, this is personal," I said.

Robert agreed, it wasn't something we wanted associated with Vassago and some of its shadier dealings.

The purchase went through fairly quickly and modernisation started. Paul was pulled off a development to help organise the work team and with as little disruption as possible to the children, we created a place fit for habitation.

"I've had a thought," Robert said one day. "I want Ted in there. Look what he did for us all those years ago, he'd be perfect for handling those boys."

"Brilliant idea, maybe the kids can come to the gym one night a week, get them boxing," I added.

Boxing was not just a way to learn to fight; it was a lesson in discipline, in control of emotions such as anger. It would help the stay fit and healthy, and more importantly it would give them children what it gave us, a sense of self worth, a purpose.

Once the modifications were complete we had an 'opening ceremony', something small. Jonathan had wanted to use the home for a little publicity, probably show the world that Vassago had a heart somewhere, but Robert and I disagreed. Ted was amazing with the kids, he was a man able to give a hug when needed, separate a fight if necessary and he was tough enough to stand up to their tantrums. He was the perfect choice and he worked well with Nancy.

****

"Boys, I want to be involved in the home. I'm bored rattling around the house all day and that's another thing, I want to downsize," Evelyn said as she prepared a meal for us.

She came to the apartment on a regular basis. Despite our insistence that she take things easy for a while, she couldn't stop looking after us. She cooked, not every night, but it was nice to have a home cooked meal and she tidied up after us. Okay, me more than Robert. She made sure our suits were cleaned and she fussed, just as she had since we were twelve years old.

"Okay, what do you want to do?" Robert asked.

"I'm going to help Nancy clean the place and cook. Not every day but it will give me something to do," she replied.

"Don't you think you already do enough?" I said.

"Travis, I have the energy of someone half my age and I'm bored. I want to do something other than pick up after you. Although having seen some of those boys, they could do with a little re-educating on how to look after their things," she raised her eyebrows at me and I was taken back fifteen years.

One thing we had learnt about Evelyn over the years, if she made her mind up about something, there was no changing it. There was no point in arguing with her and she was right, since Joe had died she had been a little lost. Looking after people was what she did best, it's what she needed to do.

"What do you want to do with the house, Ev?" Robert asked.

"I'm going to sell it. I'll put a third of the money in trust, just in case he ever shows up and the rest I'll use for Maria's care," she replied.

There was no need to use Joey's name and as the son of Joe he was entitled to a third of the property. It had been stated in Joe's will that the house was to be divided among his three children and the money he had in various bank accounts around the world became Evelyn's. She was a wealthy woman. The properties Joe had not already sold to Robert were gifted to us. Joey had not attended the will reading, despite being invited, so he was unaware that his father had opted to leave a large portion of his wealth to his 'adopted' sons.

"Okay. Speak to Richard, he'll handle that for you," Robert said.

"Ev, you can move in here until you find something else," I offered.

"I know, but I'll probably just get a rental for a little while, until I decide what to do," she said.

"Before you do that, I might have a plan," Robert added.

Evelyn and I looked at each other, raised our eyebrows and laughed. It was a source of great amusement to us that Robert always had his plans - plans he never shared, but plans we knew included us. Plans that always came to fruition and we benefited from. Never once had he done wrong by us.

****

It was a month or so later that Robert's latest plan was revealed. He wanted to build a house, he wanted more space and was getting stressed at the amount of women I brought back to the apartment. I had teased him many times, he just wasn't getting enough of the ladies - jealous, that's all. But deep down I knew the reason. The more successful we became the more private and reclusive Robert was. At first I worried about it; he dated, he fucked women, but he never opened himself up to any one of them.

Many a woman would cry on my shoulder wanting to know why he wouldn't love them back. It was something Evelyn and I had a private discussion about.

"You need to leave him be, Travis. Stop interfering. He'll meet the one, one day," she said as we sat at the small table in the kitchen with our coffee.

"I know but he worries me. It's like mindless sex for him. He takes them to dinner then to the hotel, he never brings them home" I replied.

"You know he doesn't want them here, and I think you should be mindful of that as well. He's trying to protect us all, himself more than anyone, and we need to respect that privacy." I felt like I was a teenager again and she was scolding me.

"But this is my home, too. I can't just run my life around how Robert wants to behave," I protested.

"And he has never said a word to you about the amount of women you bring back here, has he? This is me speaking, Travis. I'm just asking you to be a little more considerate. I've picked up three pairs of panties, a bra, one shoe and God knows how many..., well, I don't even want to go there," she said while giving me one of her piercing stares.

I had the good grace to be embarrassed. Sometimes I missed the bin, that was all.

"You know Robert, he wants the best for everyone and he will always put himself out for that. He stays out of his home so you can have your women here. He runs his life around you, me, everyone. Let's give him a break from that for a while," she added.

I hadn't thought about it that way. "Maybe I'll take them to the hotel as well."

"I think that's a good idea. Now, this house he wants to build, have you seen the plans?" she asked.

"Only a plan of the site, looks like there are already a few old stone buildings there. We're going to take a look around soon. In the meantime I know he has found a house we can move into. As much as I love the apartment it's too small for us now."

Although the apartment was three bedrooms and the living space fairly large, for some reason it often felt claustrophobic. As much as Robert and I enjoyed living together neither of us wanted to be in each other's company all the time. It would be nice to perhaps have a separate TV room. We had very different ideas on what entertainment was, and although he never complained, if I was watching a movie or a chat show, Robert would take himself off to his bedroom.

"Is Robert still dating Miranda?" Evelyn asked.

"Well, if you can call what they do dating, I guess so," I replied.

Miranda worked at a museum and Vassago had been involved in donating to their outreach programmes. They wanted children from inner city environments to have a better education. It was the only charity Vassago donated to. She also happened to be a friend of his PA, Gina. I think it was when Robert took Gina to a meeting that he met Miranda.

"Toxic, that one. I hope it doesn't last. She's a little too up her own ass for my liking," Ev said.

I nearly choked on my coffee. Evelyn very rarely cursed but when she didn't like someone it showed. I'd often joked with her that she would never make a great poker player, she wore her emotions like her clothes. But Evelyn and I had met Miranda at a lunch, and I agreed. She was snooty, looked down her nose at everyone and clung to Robert like a leech. No matter how rude he was to her, she took it. He had not one ounce of respect for her, all I could guess was that she had some special skills in the bedroom to keep his attention for as long as she had.

We heard the key turn in the front door and Robert entered the apartment. Under his arm he had a set of documents.

"Rob, can I get you a coffee?" Evelyn asked.

"Sure, that would be great," he replied.

"What have got there?" I said.

"This, bro, is where we are moving to." He laid a brochure on the table.

It was a house that Vassago had acquired and was in the process of being remodelled. We would move in until our build was finished, then it would go into the property department as a rental. We had slowly been building up a portfolio of exclusive properties that were often let to companies for their executives when they were in town on long-term business.

The three of us sat and looked through the brochure. It was a large property on the outskirts of the City. It contained four bedrooms with en-suite facilities and dressing rooms, two living rooms, a huge kitchen area and a home office. Beside the house were two garages, and the front and back yard were to be landscaped.

"Ev, you're welcome to move in as well, your house sale is likely to go through quickly," Robert said.

"You boys don't want me hanging around," she replied.

"Of course we do, at least we know we'll be fed," I said, earning a slap to the back of the head from Evelyn.

"I'll think about it," she replied.

Robert and I were unhappy with the choice of apartment she moved into as a temporary measure while she decided what to do. It was in a great block in Columbia Heights, one of ours of course, but we worried about her. The area was still up and coming and although there were massive improvements in the quality of tenants, we were still *weeding* out the rough ones.

****

Robert and I took a drive with Paul to see the land in Great Falls that was to become our home. Plans had been drawn up; I was yet to see them but I knew as we pulled into an unpaved road and through a gap in a wall that it was a perfect location. I parked the Range Rover and we took a walk. The land was mainly woodland and there were three stone buildings in varying degrees of disrepair. The one that caught us unaware was a chapel.

"That looks old," I said, as we stood outside.

Scattered to one side were headstones, some had fallen down and the remainder looked like they were about to. They were too old to make out the engraving, and were covered in moss. Robert pushed open the large wooden door at the entrance. Birds flew from their nests, having been disturbed most likely for the first time ever. Their panic created a haze of dust, its particles picked out by the sunlight streaming through the broken windows. Oak pews lined both sides, and as we walked a few paces down the aisle Robert came to an abrupt halt.

I followed his gaze to an arched stained glass window in the back wall. The sight took my breath away. For a moment no one spoke. Looking down at us was an angel, God in the background casting her away. She had tears on her cheeks, her head was bowed and her hands were clasped in front of her naked form. What took my breath away wasn't the window itself, but that the angel was a replica of the one Robert had tattooed on his back; a tattoo he had designed himself many years ago.

"Leave this building standing, Paul," he said quietly before he turned and walked out.

Paul looked at me. "What was that all about?" he asked.

"That window. Look at the angel. Have you seen it before?" I said.

He took a moment to stare. "Fuck me, that's the same as his tattoo, isn't it?"

"Yeah. That would spook anyone."

We found Robert walking around the chapel; he'd stopped to study a gravestone. His fingers ran over the mottled face as if trying to understand the words, like a blind person would read braille. He was pensive, quiet. Robert had learnt to bottle up his emotions as a child, and it made him hard to read as an adult. There was no point in asking if he was okay. After a moment or two, he turned towards us and we carried on exploring the grounds.

We came across another old stone building, its windows too grimy to see through. The wooden door had a padlock that was so rusted it disintegrated in my hand when I shook it. Inside was a workbench and some old tools. The walls were sturdy though, this building was in a far better condition that the rest.

"Leave this one too, knock down the rest," Robert said.

We made our way to the car. "Paul, I want most of the woodland left, just clear enough space for the house, the buildings I want, and a parking area out front. Have the plans done as soon as possible," Robert said as we drove back to the office.

It was only a few days later that Robert presented the plan. What had been drawn up was stunning, a main house with all the living accommodation on the top floor and the front wall made of glass. Beside it were four garages with two apartments above. To the side, there was a pool house and gym with a small guest apartment. Without hearing the words I knew what Robert was about to propose.

"Trav, it's about time you had your own place, you can keep it as messy as you like and it won't stress me out," he said with a grin.

Robert and I had lived together in one place or another since we were twelve and the thought of living separately was a little daunting but he was right, it was time to live apart. We were nearing thirty and an apartment suited me better than a house. I found myself rattling around the one we were staying in. I didn't like the expanse of space and I wandered from room to room not really comfortable in any of them. I liked the plan, I liked the thought of having an apartment over the garage and still within a short distance from each other, and I loved the thought that Evelyn might move in too.

"Ev, what do you think? Will you move into the apartment?" I asked.

"I have to say, it looks amazing. Yes, I'd love to," she replied.

It was obvious Robert was worried about this announcement, to soften the blow, he'd said, he had a surprise for me. We took a walk to the garage and when the doors opened, standing there were two identical Ducati motorbikes.

"Oh fuck, Rob, where did you get them?" I asked as I strode over and ran my hand over the gleaming black metal.

"Rome, believe it or not. Remember Luca, Massimo's son? He has a contact. Come on let's go see what these beauties can do."

"Boys, helmets please," Evelyn said as we mounted the bikes.

The noise of the engines was immense, a low growl that echoed around the garages. With a wheel spin that kicked up dust and stones, we roared down the drive. We raced each other through the lanes of Great Falls and had fun. Even over the noise of the engines I could hear Robert laugh, something I hadn't heard in a while.

Eventually we pulled up alongside a bistro, well, more of a café, and the one we used to frequent when we were younger and needed to sober up. Fredrico, the owner, greeted us with his usual exuberance, embracing us and fussing around. He cleaned a table for us and rattled off the menu in part Italian and part English. We sat as two espressos were placed on the table

"Fuck me, that was amazing," I said.

"They're something else aren't they?" Robert replied. "You okay about this move?" he added.

"Sure, I guess it's time to grow up a little," I laughed. "Seriously bro, I'm looking forward to it. People will talk if we continue to live together."

****

The house took just under a year to build, the plans changed frequently, and it was fun to watch Robert get stressed every time Evelyn or I changed our minds about something. I wanted a shooting range and a gun room. We kept guns in the house, not that Evelyn was aware, or she would have freaked. We hadn't totally shed our old way of life, and every now and again it reared its ugly head. We had enemies from the past and far more dangerous ones otherwise known as businessmen and politicians.

The new house was fixed up with a state of the art security and intercom system so we could communicate from one property to another. The cars were fitted with sensors to allow them to pass through the electronic gates, and the whole system was linked to the one at the office so it could be monitored twenty-four hours a day.

The day we moved in was strange. I didn't ask who designed the interior, I knew it wouldn't have been Alison; she had long since made the move to New York. It was laid out exactly as I wanted. The apartment had two bedrooms, both en-suite, open plan living space with the kitchen at one end. A bar separated the kitchen from the seating area. There were windows overlooking the woodland to the back and the gravelled parking area to the front. It was a light and airy space and I immediately felt comfortable. However, that first night was odd. I climbed into bed and although I knew my family were close, I missed being in the same house with them.

The following day I called on Robert, he was sitting on the sofa reading a paper with music playing in the background. He looked content and happy. I opened his fridge and took out two beers, popping off the caps as I joined him.

"There's a game on," I said, as I handed him a beer.

"So go watch it then," he replied with a smile.

"I'm bored, it's too quiet."

"Trav, if you really hate it then move in here."

"No, I'll get used to it. It's just strange at the moment," I replied.

"I know it is and I mean it, if you don't like the apartment move your things in. But the TV is in the other room and staying there."

I laughed; I did like the apartment, I figured it would just take a couple of days to adjust. I finished my beer and left the empty bottle on the coffee table, knowing it would piss Robert off. He tutted.

"You got old too quick," I said as I stood. I flipped him the finger when he laughed.

"No bro, I grew up, big difference," he called out to my retreating back.

I went to visit Evelyn; she was always a lot more fun and I was hungry. I was hoping she might feed me.

Chapter Eleven

It was autumn when my past caught up with me. I hadn't thought about my family for a long time. Robert and I had travelled to New York many times over the years to check on developments, and although I made an effort to avoid Hell's Kitchen, as time went on that fear of meeting up had changed into something else. I was a different person to the one back then, and deep inside there was often a little disappointment when we boarded the jet to return home. I would love to meet my brothers, especially in a dark alley late at night.

We were in Manhattan checking out a site that was to become our largest development to date. A complex of apartments and stores, restaurants and coffee shops framed a courtyard that was to house an elaborate water feature. The architects had done well with this project. It was high-end and expensive. We were a long way off from the start of the build; planning applications had to be submitted first.

It was as Robert and I exited the car to make our way into a restaurant for dinner that I saw her. She was leaving the restaurant on the arm of a suited man; he held the door open for her and she was laughing. She wore what looked like expensive clothes, her face expertly made up; even I knew her shoes and bag were designer. I stopped short and took a sharp breath in; I felt the colour drain from my face. Robert stopped beside me.

"You okay, bro?" he asked, concern laced his voice.

Robert's voice caused her to look up and she gasped too. Her companion stopped and looked at us. Her red hair was still beautiful, and under the lights of the entrance canopy, it shone. Her blue eyes immediately filled with tears, tears that ran down her cheeks, and she raised a hand to her mouth as a sob escaped.

For a moment there was silence. She reached out for me and I took a step back, away from her.

"Travis?" she croaked.

"Aileen, are you okay? Do you know this man?" her companion asked.

She nodded. "He's my brother," she said.

"Was," I said. "I was your brother, not anymore," I added quietly.

"I tried to find you, as God is my witness, Travis. I went to DC, I tried to find you," Aileen said between her sobs.

She reached out and took a step towards me. That time I let her touch my chest and her hand fisted in my shirt.

"Honey, why don't we all go back inside, we don't want to make a scene here," her companion said.

At that, Robert stepped forward. "You and I will step to one side, they can make whatever scene they wish. Shall we?" he said as he gestured with his arm.

And then I was alone with her. I didn't know what to say, and I was totally confused. My brain was awash with emotions, endorphins, adrenalin, every high and low flooding through me simultaneously. I could smell her perfume; it reminded me of home and a pang of hurt hit me in the chest.

"I went to DC, to the address Dan gave, and you weren't there. I asked the neighbours, I walked the streets for two days, Travis, and I couldn't find you. I couldn't find Dan, either. There were people in that house, no one knew what I was talking about when I mentioned your name," she said, rambling.

"I was there, Aileen. I lived on the streets for years. I begged, I was hungry, dirty and sick sometimes. I wasn't that far away, all you had to do was look down the nearest alley and you would have seen me. I was the kid lying on the ground in the piss and dirt. I was the kid that cried because my mother and my sister had abandoned me." My voice had started to rise in anger and pain.

"Please, Travis, I spent two days…"

"Two fucking days," I hissed. "I spent years, Aileen, fucking years on those streets. You spent *only* two days looking for me. DC isn't that big, maybe if you had stayed one more day you would have found me."

"I came back, time and time again. I just couldn't find you," her voice had grown to a whisper.

I didn't care about the tears that ran down her cheeks; I didn't care about the tears that ran down mine. After all this time, my sister was standing in front of me. I had hated her for so long, but I loved her so much. I pulled her to me; I cradled her head in my chest as she sobbed. I looked over at Robert and her friend; both were standing and watching us in silence. I nodded to Robert; he understood what I wanted and he made his way back to the car. I placed my hands on Aileen's arms and took a step away from her. She looked up at me and smiled, it was a sad smile. She reached up with one hand and placed in on my cheek.

"Look at you, all grown up, a man now." We stood in silence for a minute or two.

"Goodbye, Aileen," I said, the words stuck in my throat. I very nearly choked on them but I walked away.

"Wait, Travis, please. Give me your address, please. I can't lose you again," she begged.

I climbed in the car and she grabbed at the door handle, trying to open it. I closed my eyes and let more tears fall as we drove to the airport. Robert made a call to move up our flight time. I couldn't look behind me, and I sat in silence until the car pulled alongside the jet. It was only after takeoff that I finally spoke.

"Well, that was pretty fucked up, wasn't it?" I said as I took a sip of my beer.

"Yep," Robert replied with a sigh. "Do you think you should have...?"

I cut off his question; I knew what he was going to say. Robert found it hard to accept that I refused to acknowledge my family, as he had none. But I'd never really told him the extent of the pain my family had caused me, especially my brother, Padriac.

"No, bro. I've spent years getting my family out of my system, I can't go back there. If I kept in touch with her, she would tell my mother, and my mother would tell the rest because she's too fucking weak to keep it a secret."

"I think you'd find that she already knows where you are, who you are," he said.

"Why do you say that?" I asked.

"Her companion? He's on the city's planning board, he knew who we were, the company name, everything. He may tell her."

"Then I'll cross that bridge when I come to it, I guess. I don't think I can have a relationship with her, Rob. Too much time has passed."

"She did say she had come to find you, though," he said gently.

"She spent two fucking days, Rob. For the first few days I stayed local, she didn't look that hard."

There was no way I was going to be convinced my sister had come looking for me, she may have made it to DC, but she could have found me if she really had tried. She clearly wasn't that concerned about getting away from the family herself. There she'd been, in all her fine clothes, leaving a restaurant no more than a few blocks from the slum where we had lived.

It was less than a week later that a letter from Aileen arrived at the office; her companion had indeed told her where I was. I wasn't sure whether to be furious or not, I wasn't sure whether to even read the letter. It had been left on my desk unopened, as it was marked private. I unlocked my top drawer and dropped it in. That letter stayed unopened for over a month.

****

I still dated, or had fuck buddies, I suppose would be the more precise term. Sometimes I would take one out for dinner, and only on very rare occasions Robert and I double dated. It was unusual for him to spend more than a couple of months with the same woman; he got bored of them very easily. Miranda seemed to be the longest for a while.

I was sat in my office with the door propped open when I saw him exit the lift. Behind, and standing as far away from him as possible, was Miranda.

"What are you laughing at?" I said as he strode towards me.

"Just had a session with Miranda," he replied.

"What did she call you this time?"

Miranda had a habit of using nasty words; my guess was she wanted to rile some sort of emotion from Robert. Trying to be seductive and nice hadn't worked, so now she was trying the 'I don't want you' route. If she thought she would have him running to her, she really wasn't as intelligent as she made out to be. Robert could take or leave women; he had no feelings towards them and only wanted them for one reason.

"A mean bastard. Pretty tame for her," he said, answering my question.

"I really don't know why you go there," I said shaking my head.

"Neither do I. It was a cock ruling the brain moment."

Robert left and made his way to his own office. I decided to move her file from the current drawer to the past one. As sad as it sounded, everyone we came into contact with had a file. They were all checked out; even the woman I was currently dating, Shelly, was about to get a file. I had wanted them colour coded - red for hot, blue for not. Should I ever want to revisit one, it would certainly make it easier to pick one out.

Shelly was a manager at a local restaurant, so she told me. I never took anyone at face value, but she was fun and the more time I spent with her, the more I liked her. She could be a bit trashy sometimes, especially after a glass or two of the cheap wine she insisted on drinking by the bottle, but I laughed with her. And maybe having some fun was what I needed right then.

I struggled as the business got more successful. I wasn't as educated as the other guys although my talent lay elsewhere. If there was a *problem* to solve, it was usually passed to me and not Mack anymore. The guys were getting older, and weren't able to deal with a threat as well as they needed to be. In fact, Jonathan was priming his son to eventually take over from him. He was the oldest of the guys, well into his sixties, and I wondered how long he would stay on board before he finally decided to retire. Patricia, his wife, had nagged him to slow down a little over the past year.

"Lunch?" I said as I walked into Robert's office. My stomach had been grumbling for hours.

"Thanks. I just had an interesting conversation with Luca Gioletti. He wants to meet to discuss our new development," Robert replied.

"Discuss what?" I asked.

"He wants in, can't afford to pay though, I've seen his accounts. He wants to trade, his team for apartments."

"Do you trust him?" I asked.

"About as far as I can throw him," Robert replied with a laugh.

My phone beeped in my pocket and looking at the text I saw it was from Shelly.

"You need me for anything? That was Shelly, she wants to meet for lunch," I said.

"No, you go. I'll have Gina get me a sandwich or something. Mark can run me home."

I headed to the apartment to freshen up a little and grab a change of shirt before making my way to the parking lot. It was as I'd pushed through the lot door that I saw Shelly enter the foyer. She stopped at the reception desk and spoke to one of the girls before making her way to the elevators. She wore heels much too high, stilettos that made her look like she was tottering on her tip toes. Her makeup was garish and her shirt tight across her chest. It was the skirt that I noticed more, far shorter than she normally wore. I frowned. She had sent me a text with a place to meet, so why was she at the office? I waited until the elevator doors closed and watched the illuminated numbers climb, coming to a stop at the eleventh floor.

I took the next elevator, but exited at floor ten; something was amiss, something didn't feel right. I then took the stairs up to the last floor. The door to the stairwell was in the corner of reception. Had I chosen the elevator I would have been seen as soon as I exited. As quietly as I could, I made my way to where I could hear her voice, ducking under the window in the door of my office. I shook my head at the sight that greeted me.

Shelly was perched on the edge of Robert's desk and he was not pleased. Just the look on his face was evidence of that. His scowl was deep, and even from where I was I could see his eyes darken. She was coming on to my brother. It wasn't the first time that had happened, and I trusted Robert with my life. I knew he had no interest in her, but it stung a little.

"Isn't Travis on his way to meet you?" I heard Robert say.

"Yes, I just wanted five minutes to meet the elusive Robert Stone," she replied, trying to sound as seductive as she could.

"Well now you have, perhaps you should get going," he replied.

I heard a noise from my office. I guessed Mack and one of the security guys, Mark, were recording this event. A chair scraped and I held my breath, half expecting one of them to leave the room.

"You coming on to me?" I heard Robert say. His voice was low, a sure sign he was angry.

"If you want me to," she replied.

"Get the fuck off my desk. You are dating my best friend and you walk in here looking like a cheap whore to come on to me?" he said.

At that point I walked back to the stairwell. I'd heard all I needed to. I took my time walking down the stairs and went straight to the gym. I changed and opted to run a mile, trying to clear my head. Robert would never take her up on her offer, and I would never do the same to him. I was pissed though; I had liked her far more than I should have, really. She wasn't my type and she certainly wasn't long-term material, but after all that had happened with Alison, I guess my emotions were still in turmoil.

After my run I hit the heavy bag, a satisfying dent appeared as I punched as hard as I could. I wouldn't tell Robert what I had seen; I would wait and see what happened. It would be hard for him to tell me straight, he knew that I'd liked her. Something would be arranged, a way for me to see the kind of woman she really was, and I was grateful for that. I didn't want to hear that my girlfriend had come on to my best friend.

Showered and changed, I decided to take a drive. As I crossed the lot to the Range Rover I noticed something on the windshield, a piece of paper. I read it and when I did I wasn't sure whether to laugh or scream out loud. Yet another piece of my past was back, and this time it was serious.

Chapter Twelve

I read the note over and over before folding it and placing it in my top pocket. All thoughts of Shelly immediately fell by the wayside. I sat in the Range Rover for a little while, deciding what to do. I needed to find out if it the note was genuine or not before bringing anyone else into this.

I planted a fake smile on my face as I made my way back to the office, passing Robert's on the way. His door was open and he looked up.

"Hey bro, how was lunch?" he said.

"Shelly had to cancel, there was a problem with one of the chef's at the restaurant," I said, it was the first thing that came into my head.

"Where did you go then?" he asked.

"Gym, thought I'd have a quick workout."

He nodded and picked up the ringing telephone from his desk. I made my way to my office.

"Mark, take a break will you."

I took a key from my pocket and unlocked the drawer to my desk; nestled near the top was an envelope, the letter I had received from my sister. I held it in my hand awhile, debating whether to open it or not. I needed to know if the note I'd found on my car was genuine, and the only way to know for sure was to call her. I slid my finger under the flap and pulled out the page.

Dear Travis,

I understand why you ran off, and I hope you will read this letter and let me explain. I didn't come for you immediately, I couldn't. As soon as dad knew you had gone he went mental. He beat mum to a pulp and put her in the hospital. I had to stay; I thought you would be okay with Dan for a few more days, a week at most. It took two weeks before the hospital would release her, before the police would stop harassing us to find out what had happened.

Padriac was arrested, he never went to jail, but we didn't see him again. No one knows what happened to him. Carrig left shortly after, although he got in touch a few years later. I had to stay, I had to protect her, and I honestly thought you were fine. I tried to call, to speak to you or Dan, I was desperate for news.

As soon as I could, I got a lift to DC, I went to the address I was given and you weren't there. A family lived in the house and when I asked, they had no idea who I was talking about. They gave me the landlord's details and I called him. He was Dan's father. He had no idea about you but I managed to get a number for Dan.

I called Dan and he explained. He had been arrested, it was a mistake. His brother was dealing drugs and when the police raided, Dan was caught up in it all. He was held by the police for a few days and then released. He tried to find you too. I met with him; we walked the street, Travis, solidly for two days. We thought we had covered every alley, every block, everywhere we could think of. We checked the hospitals and with the police. I couldn't find you and it broke my heart to have to return to NY. And why did I have to return? I can't hate her, Trav, like you can. I would love to, I would love to not feel anything towards our mother, I would love to walk away and never think of her but the guilt was crushing and I was torn. I was so bitterly torn I couldn't think straight. You were tough, I made myself believe you would survive and you would be okay. I even made up stories in my head - a family had taken you in, a loving family that cared for you.

I came back a month later. There was a day I thought I saw you. A gang of kids were running up the sidewalk and laughing. I called out but they never heard. I ran after them but as I turned the corner they were gone. I began to believe I had imagined it. I began to see you on every street corner and knew it was my mind playing tricks, or so I thought. Now, I'm not so sure. Maybe I did see you, maybe it was you running along the sidewalk and my heart breaks more knowing I might have been so close to finding you.

I don't know how to say how sorry I am, I don't know that you'll ever forgive me. When you saw me that day, I wasn't out enjoying myself, as such. I don't live in the US anymore, Travis. I moved back home. Dad died, we don't know how, he was found dead in a ditch. That was the first day I had smiled in a long time. It sounds so callous, but I needed to leave right then. I wanted to build a new life and get away from mum — she didn't need me anymore. I return though, once or twice a year I come to NY, and always to DC, in the hope I might bump into you. In my heart I knew you had survived, I always felt you. I never believed I would see you in NY again.

If you can find it in your heart to forgive me, please call.

Your ever loving sister, Aileen.

Attached to the letter was a card with her overseas address and a cell number. I was torn. Was she the woman I thought I had seen on occasions? I had a vague memory of seeing a redhead, and I remembered one time it wasn't her, but there were other times I thought I had seen her from afar. How different would my life have been had I not given up hope and approached her?

I made the call. I could hear the long distance ring, and a sleepy voice answered. I hadn't thought to check the time difference. Once I announced who I was, there was a pause and then a sob.

"Aileen, I can't talk for long right now. I will call back another time, but something has happened and I need your help. Padriac may be in DC, and I need to know if that's true. Who would know, Aileen?" I said.

"Travis, I'm just so glad you called. Did you read my letter?" she said.

"I did, but like I say, right now I need to track Padriac down. You owe it to me to help."

I was trying not to sound harsh, but I was rushed for time . My oldest brother had left that note on my windscreen and I wanted to get to him before he made his next move. In fact, I was looking forward to it.

182

"Dan or Carrig might know, let me get their numbers for you."

I heard a rustle, perhaps she had climbed out of bed, and then she came back on the line and gave a contact number for both.

"Please let me know what's happening, Trav," she said.

"I will, when I know myself. I'll call you again Aileen, I don't know when, but I will."

With that, we said our goodbyes. I looked at the piece of paper in my hand, wondering who I should call. Who would be the most surprised to hear from me? I was unsure if I wanted to speak to Carrig, so I opted for Dan.

"Dan, you might remember me. It's Travis, Aileen gave me your number," I said once he answered.

For a moment, he was silent.

"Travis?"

"Yes, Travis. This isn't a social call, Dan. I just want some information, and for some reason Aileen thought you might be able to give it to me."

He cleared his throat. "Okay, what do you need?"

"I need to know if my brother, Padriac, is in DC."

"I can probably find out. You're still in DC then?"

"Never left, lived on the streets for years after you fucked off, but I don't have time to reminisce with you." I was aware of how harsh my voice sounded.

"We came for you, Trav, I swear. I got locked up for a few days but Aileen did try to find you."

"Not hard enough. Now, Padriac is in town and I need to find him quickly. You get back to me as soon as you can."

"Carrig might know, he's looking for him too."

"How would you know that?"

"He..., you might want to speak to him, Trav."

"He what, Dan?"

183

"I don't know for sure, but I think he killed your father. He's not the person you knew, he went to jail for a long while and now he's out."

"What did he go to jail for?"

"Fraud, embezzlement, you name it. He called it fund raising…, he works for the Irish, Trav."

"The Irish?" As much as I only wanted the briefest of conversation with Dan, I settled back in my chair to listen.

"The Real IRA," he replied.

"Fuck."

"Why do you think your sister is in Ireland? She supports them too, it's how she got to leave. She was given money in return for her assistance."

"Well, I'd like to say it's been fun chatting but…, just get me that information as quick as you can."

I finished the call, and as I did a memory surfaced. I picked up the letter from Aileen.

'Dad died, we don't know how, he was found dead in a ditch….'

I wracked my brain for the right words. Carrig had told me he would kill my father, his body would be found in a ditch one day. Had he done that? I looked at the piece of paper on my desk. Carrig's cell number stared straight back at me.

It was a couple of hours later that I received a text. I wasn't surprised to receive the text, I doubted Dan was in a hurry for a second conversation, and neither was I. Padriac had indeed made the trip to DC; he had been picked up by the cops for being drunk. How Dan would know that interested me, so I made a note to do a little investigating. If Dan could get that kind of information he could prove to be useful in the future. I deliberated; we had contacts in the local police but I wanted no association with Padriac, nothing to connect me with him - what I had in mind for my *dear brother* meant I had to stay as far away from anyone connecting us as possible.

****

Robert and I drove home, and it was clear that he thought something was up. I was quiet, but he didn't press for information.

Being pushed to reveal what was on his mind was something he hated, so he never did the same to others. He knew I would tell him when I was ready. Instead of heading into the house with him, I made my way to my apartment. I needed just a little time alone to decide what I was going to do. I would tell Robert, I had to. It was possible he would get caught up in my past. I took Padriac's note from my pocket and read it again.

Guess who, brother? I see you've done well for yourself and it's only fair you take care of your family. You fucked off and left us to deal with the shit that was our dad. I bet you don't care but he beat the shit out of mum and then Aileen. Broke mum's heart, you did. He wouldn't let her come find you and we all paid the price. So, it's only fair you pay now. I know where you are, who you are. Think you're some big shot, huh? Well, brother, time to face the past. I'll be in touch.

Padriac

I chuckled a little at the thought that Padriac had been *left to deal with the shit*. Aileen had said in her letter that he had disappeared shortly after so I knew Pad hadn't dealt with anything. His threat didn't bother me as such, I certainly wasn't afraid of him. What bothered me was the statement that he knew *who* I was. If that was true then he knew of Robert as well. I made my way over to the house; it was time to talk to Robert.

I found him sitting on the sofa with a glass of wine in his hand. I grabbed a beer before I joined him.

"You okay?" he asked. He knew me well enough he could practically read my mind.

"Rob, I have a problem, a big problem," I said.

"What's wrong?"

I reached inside my jacket pocket, pulled out the note and handed it to him. As he read I slumped forwards a little, resting my chin on my hands, my elbows on my knees.

"Trav, when and how did you get this?" he asked once he had finished reading.

"It was on the car windscreen, at the office."

"Why didn't you tell me earlier?"

"I wanted to check it was legit first."

"We need to know what he knows. It might be that we do nothing until he gets in touch again, but you need to tell me about your family so we can prepare. We need the guys in on this as well."

I then told him about the conversation with both Aileen and Dan, including the information that my brother was involved with the Real IRA.

That was the part I had dreaded the most. In all our years together I knew far more about his past than he knew about mine. He knew there was more to the story of why I ran away from home, I was sure. But now it was time to tell him the truth. While I grabbed another beer, he called Mack.

I'd already told him about my dad being a drunk, of Padriac and Carrig and the beatings they dished out on a regular basis and how I had stabbed Pad. So I told him about my mom, the many times she had just watched and not intervened, and how I felt nothing for her. There was a pause; Robert must have thought I had finished my story.

"Okay, let me scan this so we have a copy," he said as he made his way to the home office.

When he returned, I continued. "Rob, there's something else. Padriac didn't just beat Aileen and me."

He looked at me and waited for me to continue. I swallowed hard.

"Do you remember when we paid your Father Peters a visit? I wanted to deal with Cara's dad for a reason. I never got to pay Padriac back for what he did to Aileen and me."

I hadn't looked at Robert while I spoke, I didn't want to see shock or disgust on his face. My brother had abused both Aileen and I, her far more I imagined. I felt no shame for myself; neither did I feel embarrassed as such. I had a lot of anger inside, but what I didn't want was pity. I never wanted to see pity in his eyes. If I saw that he felt sorry for me, I think that would have finished me.

"Do you want to talk about it?" he asked quietly.

"I don't want it to go any further than us. Maybe, one day, I'll talk about it, but not now."

Robert rose to grab some more beers, and as he did a pair of headlights swept across the room. Mack had arrived. The front door opened and closed and he joined us on the sofa. Robert went through what had happened and showed him the note.

"Trav, do you want to tell us about him?" Mack asked.

"Padriac is the oldest, ten years older than me, I think. After him came Aileen, then Carrig. They were all born in Belfast, I was born in New York. My dad was a drunk, beat us kids and mom. The older boys take after their father. Padriac was the worst. Me, mom and Aileen took the brunt of his beatings," I said.

"We need to find out who else knows you are here," Mack said.

"Aileen's old boyfriend, Dan, brought me here when I was a kid. I contacted him. He found out Pad was in town."

The conversation went back and forth for a while as we decided on a strategy. Mack left to check the CCTV cameras for the parking lot and I could have kicked myself for not doing that when I had the office to myself.

"Trav, you know this will get sorted and how, don't you?" Robert asked after he had shown Mack to the door.

"I don't have any feelings towards him, Rob. If I catch up with him myself, he'll wish he never started this for sure. I'm just worried about dragging you into all of this."

I finished off my beer and left to walk back to my apartment. I felt exhausted.

Chapter Thirteen

"Hey, bro. You okay?" Robert said as he crossed the drive the following morning.

I'd left the Range Rover idling, waiting to make our way into the office.

"Ready to take on the world," I replied.

I'd slept fitfully the previous night. Thoughts of Aileen, Padriac, her letter and his note had whirled around my brain. I had needed to speak to her but I began to wonder if I would actually call her back. She knew where I worked, she could contact me if she wanted to, and I thought I might leave it to see if she did - to see if she was serious enough with her apology to make the effort.

Because of the early hour, the foyer was empty save for Stan, who rose from his security desk to greet us. I often wondered if he ever left the building. We travelled up the eleven floors and were met by Mack, Richard, Paul and Jonathan. They were already waiting with coffees in Robert's office.

"Thank you for coming in early, we have a problem that I want to discuss with you," Robert said as we sat.

He explained about the blackmail note and Mack passed around a copy. Robert asked Mack if anything was found on the CCTV and Mack handed out a grainy photograph of a man, overweight and in a dark jacket. He wore a baseball cap pulled low to shield his face. Mack explained that the CCTV clip showed the man walk to the car, place the note under the wiper and walk away again.

"There are some things I should tell you, a bit of family history. But first you should know, I have no idea if this is true or not. My parents fled Northern Ireland in the mid seventies with three kids. My mom was heavily pregnant with me at the time. They were taken in by a family and for a couple of years they moved around. I was told my dad was a butcher and the reason they fled was because the security forces were after him. He'd had something to do with the Shankill Butchers, part of the Ulster Volunteer Force, and responsible for some horrific deaths. Death by a butcher's knife," I said.

"Fuck," Paul said. His wife, Rosa, was Irish and he understood what that meant.

"Exactly," I replied.

Paul had met Rosa on a trip to Southern Ireland; her family were connected with the IRA in some way. Joe wanted no part in dealing with the Irish and no matter what the deal was, he wouldn't touch it.

"I found all this out over a period of time, when I was a kid, but I wouldn't have been old enough to really understand what it meant," I said. "Anyway, whether it's fact or fiction, Padriac loves to tell a story when he's drunk and he might be running out of an audience for 'my dad's a Shankill Butcher'. I might be his next source of bar talk."

I left out any reference to Carrig; what to do about *him* was something I wanted to ponder on some more.

"Mack, get hold of Tony, let's get to Padriac before he sobers up and decides on his next move," Robert said.

Tony was an *investigator with special skills*, shall we say. He was someone we used when we needed to track an individual that perhaps had information we wanted. He was a strange man. To look at him you would think he was a kindly old grandfather, always smiling and happy, but his skills were not something even a hardened criminal wanted to see.

The guys stood and left. They made their way back to their respective floors to start their day. Mack left to contact Tony and I sat with Robert, finishing off our coffee.

"Didn't get very far, did we?" I said.

"What do you mean?" he asked.

"We think we've shed our old lifestyle but it's always there, in the background."

****

It was about midday when Mack called. Tony had already located Padriac. Seemed he did have a big mouth after all. He had been in a bar the previous night just around the block and had been thrown out after he started singing Irish rebel songs.

It was also midday that my 'issue' with Shelly was resolved. She had gone out of my mind for a few hours, although I had received a text from her the previous evening, a text that I had ignored. After I returned from making coffee I found a brown envelope on my desk. There was no writing on the front and I took a cautious look inside. I pulled out two large photographs of her sitting in a bar, her hand resting on a guy's thigh. She wore the same clothes she had on when she visited Robert. I guessed what had happened; Robert or Mack had given me a way out. I played the game.

Storming into Robert's office I threw the photographs down on his desk. "Fucking bitch," I said.

He looked at the photographs before speaking. "Shit, bro. I'm sorry. What are you going to do?"

"Finish it, obviously." I collected the photos and as I walked towards the door and back to my own office, I deposited them in the bin.

About ten minutes later, I received a text from Robert, wanting to know if I wanted to box a few rounds. I was up for that. We met in the gym, and no matter what time of day it was the 'Oh my God, he's in the gym' message had spread around the office. Fully made up women without a bead of sweat on their brows were *working out,* and by working out, I meant checking *us* out. Eyes followed as we made our way to the treadmills and ran side by side.

"You're getting a bit loose there, bro," I said as I tried to outrun him.

"Loose?" Robert replied.

190

"Yeah, not as ripped as me anymore. Too much dining out, my friend," I said with a chuckle.

No matter how hard I worked out, no matter how much weight I lifted, I would never have the muscles Robert did. He was the proverbial brick shithouse, but it was fun to tease him every now and again. After our run we climbed under the ropes of the ring. We sparred for a half hour or so and I tried desperately not to show my chest heaving from the exertion. Every now and again Robert would smirk, he knew I was getting out of breath and he pushed me a little harder, upped the pace a bit.

Workout over, we showered and changed back into our suits. We took the elevator back to the eleventh floor. I was glad, my legs were still sore from all the boxing. Mack came out of his office once he saw us in reception.

"Meet your brother," he said as he crossed the room.

In his hand he held a photograph of an older man, unshaven and looking like the drunken bum I was expecting.

"You sure it's him?" Robert asked.

I stared at it for a while. "You know what? That could be my fucking father standing there. I'm looking forward to meeting him again."

****

I was sitting in my apartment after a dinner Evelyn had prepared, nursing a beer and watching some trash on the TV - a celebrity and I use the word loosely - reality show. There were times when I totally got Robert's aversion to TV, but sometimes I just wanted noise in the room. I was comfortable living on my own, it had taken time but I didn't like silence. I loved to annoy Robert at times with either whistling or some inane chatter in the car.

My phone vibrated on the coffee table I was resting my feet on, and picking it up I saw a call from Robert.

"Think we are on for tonight, bro. You up for this?" he said.

"For sure, I'll be outside in five," I replied.

Of course I was up for it. That night I would meet my brother for the first time in over twenty years, and I was looking forward to it. I knew Mack had told Tony to ply Padriac with drink, get him to talk, and that way we'd know for sure what he knew, or thought he knew. I dressed in black jeans with a dark T-shirt, and pulled a black hoodie over my head. As I entered the garage I took a licence plate from a drawer and exchanged it for the real one on the Range Rover. If checked, the plate belonged to a Mr. Hardy in San Francisco. Mr. Hardy did indeed own a Range Rover, of the same year and the same colour.

I heard the crunch of gravel as Robert, dressed similarly, crossed the drive. "Ready?" he said.

"Always," I replied.

Before heading off, Robert checked the glove compartment to make sure we had what we needed and on his nod, we left.

"Where to?" I asked.

"14th Street Bridge," he said with a smirk.

"Very appropriate."

Robert and I had met under the 14th Street Bridge, it was a place the drunks slept, a place most ending up falling in the Potomac and drowning - yes, a very appropriate place. I whistled softly to myself as I drove. During the journey Robert brought me up to speed. Tony had been plying Padriac with beer and once he got the point of being kicked out of the bar, Tony offered to walk him home. That walk would detour beneath one of the busiest bridges in the city.

We pulled across a grassed area and stopped the car. With the lights off, the Range Rover was difficult to see from either the road or the traffic making its way over the bridge. We walked down the bank and towards the pier. I could make out two figures, one standing and one lying on the concrete.

"Robert, Travis, charming brother you have here," Tony said as we approached.

"What did you get from him?" Robert asked.

"Well, he knows who both of you are and that you have money, Trav. He boasted that his brother owned a big company and that he got his money from crime. He didn't go into details and when I pushed, he just tapped the side of his nose. He certainly knows something, or rather, he thinks he knows something. I didn't have enough time to get it out of him before he got kicked out. I'm more than happy to take him to my *'operating room'* for further investigation if you like," Tony said.

He had a gleam in his eye that reminded me that the guy was a total psychopath.

"Did anyone hear him talk?" I asked.

"No, the bar was empty and to be honest, the staff kept away from him. Until he grabbed the barmaid's ass of course. Then they hauled him out."

"Okay, thanks, Tony. I'll be in touch," Robert said.

That was Tony's cue to leave, and as he left I walked over to the slob of a body lying under the bridge. Every now and again I'd hear him groan. I looked down at his face; there was no family resemblance at all. The guy lying there was grossly overweight and stunk of piss; the front of his pants was stained.

Robert handed me the gloves he had found in the glove compartment and we put them on before rifling through his pockets. There wasn't much, just a scrap of paper and some coins, which I put in a plastic zip-lock bag. We rolled him over to check his back pockets; we didn't want anything left on the body that could easily identify him. Finding nothing, we rolled him towards the river. I would have liked to have sobered him up, beat the fuck out of him and see the fear in his eyes, but this would look more like an accident, another drunken bum that had fallen into the river.

The sound of the traffic drowned out the noise of him hitting the water and we stood and watched as he floated away, the current quickly taking him from the bank. The cold water must have revived him, though. His head came up and he sputtered. His arms flailed as he tried to fight the current and get back to the shore. But there was one moment when his eyes locked on mine, he recognised me, and he knew exactly what had happened to him. My only hope was that he saw my smile as he was pulled under the dark cold water of the river.

We walked back to the car and I reversed onto the side of the road, waiting for the traffic to clear. We drove back to town.

"Okay?" Robert said.

"Yeah, shame the fat fucker was so drunk. I think he recognised me, I hope so anyway," I replied.

"Let's go see what he has in his apartment," Robert said. He read an address from a text he had received from Mack.

As we pulled into the alley that ran down the side of a run-down block, I reached under my seat. I pulled out a small revolver; one that had a silencer fitted to it. As we exited the car, I fired at the one streetlight, plunging us and the car into darkness.

"You could have just thrown a fucking stone," Robert said.

"Not as much fun, bro, and I doubt you would have gotten that high," I replied with a chuckle.

With a shake of his head we made our way into the apartment's front entrance and up two flights of piss-soaked stairs. The stench was overwhelming and I pulled my hoodie up to cover my mouth and nose. I picked the lock of the apartment door and quietly pushed it open. Although Tony had found Padriac's address, we had no idea if he was living there alone. Knowing Tony, if he'd had a little more time, we would have received a twenty page report with every detail.

Silently we walked through the rooms. The kitchen sink was full to the brim with dirty dishes and takeout containers. Something certainly shared the apartment with Padriac, I heard the scuttle of rodents running across the kitchen counter. As I pushed through a door I saw a mattress on the floor and a towel nailed to the window to block out the light from now 'broken' streetlight. I rummaged through a pile of clothes on the floor while Robert opened the drawers of the one cabinet. Finding nothing, we moved back into the living room. On a small table we found a pad, the jagged edge showing where a page had been torn out.

"Sure knows how to live, doesn't he?" Robert whispered.

I chuckled. "Reminds me of my childhood home, although at least my mom kept it clean."

After adding the pad to the zip-lock bag we left, there was nothing else of use in that disgusting apartment.

****

Arriving back, I changed the plate back to the correct one and followed Robert into the house. I emptied the bag onto the breakfast bar. There was just over a couple of bucks in coins, a few receipts from a liquor store and a piece of folded paper. That piece of paper contained the address for Vassago. Robert flipped through the notepad. He showed me page after page of scrawl. Padriac had made a list; he documented the office address, our home address and even the details of the cars we owned. Underlined were two words, Guiseppi Morietti. He had made the connection between me and Joe. It wasn't a secret that we had known Joe; many of the locals still remembered us as kids and would stop and chat for a minute or two. But they were older people, not someone from New York.

"So he knew something," I said.

"Seems that way," Robert replied.

"Fucking shame we didn't sober him up."

"Not worth it, bro. He's out of the way now, that's all that matters."

In one way I was glad, a sober Padriac had a vile mouth. Did I really want to hear what he had to say. More important, would I want Robert to hear what he had to say? *No.* We took all the papers and the notebook and set them on fire in the hearth, watching until they were nothing more than a pile of ash.

"I'll see you in the morning, bright and early," I said, as I made my way out.

Robert nodded and locked the front door behind me. I made my way straight to the fridge for a beer. I sat for a while, just thinking. I felt no remorse for what I had done. That brutal man had hurt my mom, my sister and me for many years. I raised my bottle of beer and smiled, making a toast. *Revenge, dear brother, revenge.*

I pulled the piece of paper from my pocket and stared at the two cell numbers. Should I tell Carrig? I sent a text.

'You can stop your searching for Padriac. Travis'

An hour later I received a reply. I had showered and was about to climb into bed.

'We should meet, compare notes. C.'

'One day.'

****

The following morning we were back to business as usual. I had the car ready, and as Robert walked across the drive I greeted him with a smile.

"Morning, bro," I said.

"You sleep okay?" he asked.

"Best night's sleep I've had in ages," I chuckled.

We stood and looked at one another for just a moment, and gave each other a nod. No words were necessary. We had done what we had to do; another threat had been eliminated. Maybe I would call Aileen and tell her Padriac was not around anymore, maybe not.

I knew Robert had a stressful day ahead, a board meeting scheduled to last most of the day to finalise what had turned out to be a hostile takeover by Vassago. It hadn't started that way, they never did. This particular company had borrowed money from Vassago. It couldn't afford to pay back that loan so Robert had decided the company had to convert its debt into shares that Vassago would own. The CEO of the company disagreed. They had been locking heads for months, and Robert was at the end of his tether. It was make or break day. The CEO complied, or the company would be forced to close, its assets sold to pay back its debt.

Robert had explained the process to me many times and I got it, but there was no way I could do what he did. I couldn't sit in that boardroom day after day and listen to the abuse the CEO threw at him without rising and punching the prick square in the face. Mack and I watched some of the proceedings with a smirk on our faces. Robert had a wonderful knack of making people feel uncomfortable, of having them baying for his blood to start with, then subduing them enough for him to go in for the kill.

"How does he do it?" Mack asked as we watched a little in awe.

"He has no emotion, Mack. They can't rile or intimidate him, and the cooler he is, the more panicked they are," I replied.

"Makes him a very dangerous man."

"That it does," I replied.

We watched a little longer before boredom took over. I had no idea what the fuck they were talking about, shares, figures, assets, stock values - it meant nothing to me, and I was quite happy with that. Mack needed to run an errand and I was left with Mark. There was something about Mark that was beginning to niggle at me, he was a little too shifty for my liking. He rarely spoke to anyone, just sat and played with the CCTV or drove one of the guys around occasionally. I wondered if we should have had a camera installed in the command centre and made a mental note to talk to Robert when things settled down again.

I needed a coffee, and entering the kitchen, I saw Gina waiting for the machine to filter. We had an uneasy relationship, we just never clicked. I imagine it hadn't helped as she overheard me constantly running down her friend, Miranda. Gina never mentioned her private life, but of course I knew most of it. She lived alone in one of the apartments Vassago owned Robert liked the staff to rent his apartments, he felt it kept them tied to the business in exchange for a discounted rental.

"Can I pour you a coffee?" she asked. If nothing, she was always polite.

"Thanks, Gina, that would be great," I replied.

We stood in an awkward silence until the coffee was ready; she poured me a cup, added milk and handed it to me with a tight smile. I gave her a broad smile back as she left the room.

I pulled my mobile from my pocket briefly wondering if I should call Aileen I scrolled through my contacts until I found her number, then paused my finger over her name.

What good what it do now? I thought. It seemed we had both chosen a life of crime; in theory, we had something in common. But then I realised that too much time had passed, with too much pain. *Did I want to be involved in the life she had chosen any more than she would want to be in mine?* With a heavy heart, I deleted Aileen from my phone and walked back to my office. I had her address, I would send a card sometime, but right then, at that point in my life I didn't think I had anything to say to her.

We had some new staff members join Vassago over the past few months; the company was expanding at a rate I couldn't keep up with. I set about to catch up on my background checks and create their security files. We asked for consent from each person for most of the checks; but not for all. Everyone had a skeleton or two in their closet and I liked to dig away until I found them. I could only hope no one had slipped through the net.

****

It was late in the day, long after most people had left for the night that Robert and I headed for home. We were about to walk through the parking lot door when I noticed Robert immediately stiffen and turn his head slightly to one side. I followed his gaze.

Striding across the foyer was a woman. She faltered slightly, looking around her before smiling and heading towards Stan. She was beautiful in an unusual way; it was very hard to describe her. It was the contrast of her fair skin, and the deep blue of her eyes against her raven-coloured hair that gave her an unusual, exotic look. Her hair was so black it was almost blue. I was about to button up my jacket and ask the young lady if she needed any help when I saw the look on Robert's face. He didn't blink, he focused totally on her, even staring at the elevator long after the doors had closed. His stare was more intense than I had ever seen, his features were rigid and his nose slightly flared as if he was inhaling her - like a lion having just focused on its prey.

"Bro?" I asked, trying to revive him from his obvious trance.

He shook his head slightly; he had a strange look on his face. His brow was furrowed as if in deep concentration.

"Sorry. Do me a favour, wait for me in the car," he said.

I watched as he strode over to Stan and asked who the woman was. I laughed as the elevator door closed behind him.

"Mr. Stone likes that one, I think," Stan called across the foyer.

Stan was the only person, other than the guys, that could joke with Robert. It was because Robert had a fondness for the old man; he was a trusted member of the staff that had been around since we opened the building.

"Seems that way, Stan. A dollar she tells him to get lost? She looks a little too refined, that one," I said.

"No, Travis, I saw the way he looked at her, she'll be on his arm in no time," Stan replied.

What Robert wanted he usually got, but I wondered. Maybe I was being a little snarky because I had quite liked the look of her myself. I chuckled. I couldn't recall a time both Robert and I had ever liked the same woman, but there was something compelling about her that had captivated him, and it went beyond her looks. Even I'd felt a pang of want when I saw her.

I sat in the car, the radio was blasting with a song by Evanescence *Bring Me To Life*. I was so into the song that I didn't hear the car door open; I was alerted to it by the blast of cold air. I turned down the song.

"Well?" I said, after a moment of silence.

"Well, what?" he replied.

"Who was she, and did you get her number?"

He didn't answer immediately, but kept his face towards the window as I drove home.

"She's someone I feel like I know," he said quietly.

"Huh?"

"I can't explain it right now, Trav. Let's just get home, shall we?"

We drove the rest of the way in silence. Occasionally I glanced in the rear view mirror; Robert was still staring out the side window. I recalled the woman's face. She didn't stir any memories for me, and I think I would have remembered that one. I was sure I'd never met her before.

We pulled into the drive and I killed the engine. "Rob, you sure you're okay? You seem quiet," I said.

"Sure, Trav. Sorry, I've just got something on my mind, that's all. I'll see you in the morning," he replied.

I knew exactly what was on his mind. Why he felt he couldn't talk wasn't necessarily unusual. Robert was a man who kept his thoughts to himself until he was sure about them, but I began to wonder what had happened when he caught up with her.

Shortly after we had arrived home, Evelyn came through the apartment door; she had plated a meal for me.

"Evening, Trav," she said.

"Did you see Robert?" I asked.

"I did, what happened today? He's in a very strange mood."

"I'm not entirely sure. We were about to leave when a woman came into the foyer and that was it. He saw her, followed her to wherever she was going, and wasn't the same after."

"And he never said who this woman was?"

"No, but, hold on...," I picked up my phone and called the office. The night security guard took my call and I asked to be put through to Stan.

"Stan, sorry to bother you. That woman, the black-haired one? Can you tell me who she was visiting?" I said.

"You're not bothering me, Travis. She was a friend of Sam Crawley, he had called down earlier to say she would visit. Let me just check my log..."

I heard a rustle of paper before he was back on the line. "Her name is Brooke Stiles."

"Okay, thanks. You have a good night," I replied.

I grabbed my laptop and fired it up. Evelyn sat beside me at the kitchen table.

"Her name is Brooke Stiles and she's a friend of Sam Crawley. I think he works in marketing."

I brought up the employee records. I read aloud what I'd found. Sam Crawley had been employed for about three years and was recruited from the UK.

"Is she British then?" Evelyn asked. "It's just Rob said something very strange. He said, 'he'd found her'. I have no idea what he meant but he had a broad smile when he said that," Evelyn said.

"He's found her? Do you think he knew her before he came to the US?"

"I don't know. He added that he had no idea what that meant himself, though. If it was someone he'd known, wouldn't he have recognised her? He was so young when he left the UK, though."

I did a general search using the name *Brooke Stiles*. Nothing in particular came up; no social media accounts, just a vague reference to a woman of the same name involved in marketing with a motorbike manufacturer.

"I'll do a little digging in the morning," I said.

There was a computer in my office specifically set up so it couldn't be traced back to Vassago. It was the computer I used if I needed to delve a little deeper into someone's background or access government departments I had no clearance for. I wrote the information I needed down on a pad. I took note of Sam's previous address, it would give me a location to start with. If she was a friend she possibly had lived near him.

Brooke Stiles stayed on my mind most of the night, even in my dream. I saw her face when I closed my eyes and I woke anxious and frustrated. What was it that had compelled Robert to follow her? What was it that had her image seared into my brain? Did I have feelings for someone I saw for less than a minute? My only thought, as I climbed into the car the following morning to travel to work, was that it was going to get awkward.

****

Robert was stressed; he had been working much too hard over the past couple of months so when he called through to me at lunchtime asking if I fancied a match, I agreed. We made our way down to the gym; there had been no mention of the previous evening, but he was still quiet and pensive. The only chat between us had been work-related. I decided to give Robert another day before I pushed him about what was wrong. I was concerned.

As we made our way into the gym I noticed her. Brooke Stiles was running on a treadmill, the one in the furthest corner. I couldn't fail to notice her pert ass wrapped in Lycra. She obviously kept herself fit; although not muscular, her shoulders were well-defined. She wore a cropped top that showed flawless skin, her long hair was tied up, although tendrils had escaped and were stuck to the side of her neck, a neck that glistened with perspiration. She stood out amongst the other women 'exercising'; she really was having a work-out. She ran at a pace I didn't think I'd match. Yet again Robert stilled as he noticed her.

"Ready to have your ass kicked?" I said, giving him a nudge with my shoulder.

"Whatever you say, bro," he replied, his attention finally drawn from her.

"Afraid I'm going to hurt you?" I said, chuckling.

"No, just worried about marking your pretty face," he replied.

We climbed under the ropes and, as usual, the fully made up, not a bead of sweat women changed the machines they were on to ones closer to the ring. The one thing with Robert was that he could switch his focus and attention in a millisecond. His eyes bored into me and a slow, wicked smile formed on his lips. I raised my eyebrows as a challenge and we boxed. I managed to get a few good hits in; nothing that would serious hurt but might leave a bruise or two. We were always careful around the head. Years ago Ted would force us to wear head guards when we trained, but we had dropped that a long time ago. We boxed for fun and fitness, nothing more.

I held my arms up as a sign of needing a time out, and pulling out my gum shield I rested my hands on my knees to relieve the stitch in my side.

"Worn you out, have I?" Robert said. I could only nod my head.

We laughed as we climbed back under the ropes. Instead of making our way to the gym door, Robert diverted to the treadmill Brooke was still running on. She must have been running for an hour. I stood and watched as he approached her and although she was facing the mirror she startled when he spoke. They had a brief conversation before a funny thing happened. She walked away from him. He smiled and shook his head; that was a first for him. Most women fell at his feet and he was the one to walk away, leaving them panting for more.

"Crash and burn, my friend," I said as he joined me.

"Not yet," he replied. He had a smile on his face, one that stayed put the entire time we showered and changed back into our work clothes.

****

Later that day we were in the car, heading out to a lunch appointment. Robert was in the back going over some paperwork when something caught his eye.

"Pull over, quick," he said.

"Huh?"

"Pull over, now."

"Okay, calm down," I said as I pulled straight across the lane cutting off the car on my inside.

Before I'd even come to a stop he was out of the back door. I turned in my seat to see what had him so agitated. Brooke was standing on the sidewalk, about to take a photograph; Robert must have seen her ahead of us, as I had pulled over exactly where she stood. The rear door was still open and I could hear him as he asked - no, demanded - that she get in the car so he could take her to lunch. She clearly wasn't impressed, and for the second time that day she blew him off. I couldn't stop the laughter.

"Trav, do me a favour, fuck off," he said as he got in the car. That made me laugh more.

"Well, bro, you could have handled that a little better," I replied.

"Drive to Mansion House," he said.

"Why Mansion House?" I asked.

"She's a friend of Sam Crawley, she's visiting from England and that's where he lives."

"Bro, you can't start stalking her."

"I'm not *stalking* her but she is coming to dinner with me, whether she likes it or not."

"And if she doesn't want to? What are you going to do, drag her out by her hair?"

"If need be."

I fixed my gaze on the road; the laughter was gone and replaced by a feeling of worry. Robert had never behaved this way before. He'd never, in fact, been turned down by a woman, but I wasn't so sure about his approach with Brooke. I caught sight of him in the rear view mirror, writing on a business card.

I pulled up outside the apartment block and he pressed the intercom for the supervisor. He was let in and just a few minutes later he returned. I left the car idling and turned in my seat to look at him.

"Well?" I said.

"Well, what?"

"You, chasing after her, it's a first, Rob. I'm just a bit surprised."

"Guess there's a first time for everything," he answered.

It was clear he didn't want to get into a discussion about her, and again I wondered why. I watched as he picked up his mobile.

"Sam, Robert Stone. I would like to know if you have plans for Brooke this evening?" he asked. There was a pause as he listened to the answer.

"Don't make plans, I would like to take her to dinner," he added before cutting off the call.

"You really are going to have to work on your manners," I said.

"Yeah, yeah, pick her up at seven, bring her to the club," he said before settling back and continuing to read through his papers.

As soon as Robert left the car for his meeting I got straight on the phone to Evelyn. It wasn't that I wanted to gossip about him, but he was acting completely out of character. I relayed the day and the dinner invitation.

"I don't know whether you should interfere, Trav," she said. "He obviously wants to meet with this woman, leave him be and just see what happens. I agree, he is acting strange, but let's just wait. It may come to nothing," she said.

****

At exactly seven p.m. I parked outside Mansion House, an apartment block Vassago owned in Columbia Heights. I liked to revisit the Heights, it brought back fond memories. The old office was still there, although rented out, as was the old gym, which had been converted to a grocery store.

I saw her silhouette through the glass door as I exited the car. She smiled briefly although she looked a little agitated.

"Miss Stiles, would you like me to take your coat?" I asked.

"Thank you, but I can carry it," she replied.

She settled into the rear seat and we drove in silence to the club. She waited for me to open the car door for her, and I doubted that was because she expected it, it was more that she had started to look a little nervous, and she didn't appear to be in a rush to meet Robert. I was glad when she entered the club, I was glad to have her out of the car and not so close to me. She affected me, and not in the way women normally did. If I was a little confused about *my* feelings I was dreading what Robert felt. I understood emotions - he didn't. Somehow I knew a bomb was about to go off and she was the fuse.

I sat in the car the whole evening. I could have gone for a meal myself, I could have stayed in the bar upstairs in the club, but I didn't. I just sat and worried. All I hoped was that this would be Robert's usual dinner and a fuck, maybe see her again, maybe not. It was with a little relief that, when they left the club, he whispered for me to drive them to the apartment, or the 'fuck pad' as it had been renamed.

It was typical for Robert to take a woman to dinner, then her back to the apartment and call a taxi when he was done with her. No one had ever stayed the night with him. He wouldn't even fuck them in his own bed, choosing the spare bedroom instead. I'd joked many a time with him over it. I gave him a wink and a smile and did as he requested, hoping my earlier worries were unfounded.

****

To say I was surprised by Robert's text the following morning would be an understatement. He had messaged me to say he would be late to his desk, and to ask if I could take Brooke home.

"Good night?" I texted back but received no reply.

I waited in reception and watched as she came out of the elevator, she had pulled her hair into a loose bun on top of her head and she was stunning, even without makeup.

"Good morning, Miss Stiles," I said, as I pushed myself off the desk.

"Good morning, Travis."

I was surprised she knew my name, another first. "No Range Rover this morning?" she enquired with a smile.

I laughed; I liked her sense of humour already. "No, Miss Stiles, that's normally for the evenings."

"Please, call me Brooke. Miss Stiles makes me sound old. How long have you been with Robert?" she asked as we left the parking lot.

"Many years," was all I answered.

A half hour later I was back at the office. I switched the camera on my desk so I could see into Robert's. I watched as he picked up his phone and made a call. As he spoke he ran his hand through his hair, a sure sign he was stressed. Once his call was finished, he just sat for a few moments with his eyes closed. I left my office, bumping into Gina hovering outside.

"Is Mr. Stone okay?" she asked.

"Sure, Gina, just had a stressful few days, that's all. You want me to take those in to him?" I asked.

She nodded and handed me his messages.

I sat in the chair opposite his desk. He didn't speak at first but when he did I was dumbstruck by his request.

"Travis, pick Brooke up and bring her to the house later."

I couldn't speak at first. "Are you sure, Rob?"

"Yes, I'm sure. There's something about her, Trav. I might be making the biggest mistake of my life here, but pick her up for me. Do a quick check as well."

I nodded and left him to his messages. It was a half hour later that Evelyn called me. She told me that she'd had a conversation with Rob, he'd asked her to make a meal.

"I don't know what to say. I might talk to him about it," I said.

"Trav, I think it's a great thing. He has finally found someone that might be important to him. We need to encourage this. The fact he wants to bring her home is a huge deal, let's not spoil it for him. If it all goes wrong, then we'll worry," she said.

After our conversation I switched on the computer. I searched record after record for her, printing out anything I found. She appeared to be just a normal woman with a job and a rented house. There was a man's name on the lease of the house and I started to check him out too.

Robert was ready to leave an hour before he normally would have. He had rescheduled his appointments that day, yet another first. I dropped him off at the house before heading back to Columbia Heights.

"Good evening, Travis. As it's the evening I guess I get the Range Rover," Brooke said as she walked towards the car.

I had left the Mercedes at the office; it was in need of a valet.

I chuckled. "Miss Stiles, you most certainly do."

"So, am I allowed to know where we are off to tonight?" she asked. I detected a little mischief in her voice and I began to like her more.

"Ah now, it's more than my life's worth to divulge such secrets."

We fell silent as I drove out of the City and towards home. As I pulled onto the drive, Robert was at the front door waiting to greet her. I thought he might have made an effort though; he was dressed in a shirt and jeans, his usual lounging around the house attire. Robert caught my eye and gave a very slight nod of his head. I retrieved the file I had started on Brooke and caught up with them in the kitchen. He was introducing her to Evelyn and it looked like they were getting along well. I strode to the home office and Robert followed.

"Anything?" he asked.

"She has a rented house, there's a guy's name on the lease, different surname though. She's not and has never been married. Works in London for a marketing agency and from what I can tell, has some big accounts. Other than the guy, nothing that sparks any interest."

"Okay, thanks. I'll talk to you later."

"Text me when you want me to take her home."

"I'm hoping she'll stay," he replied leaving me standing open-mouthed.

A couple of hours later I remembered I had left my laptop in the car. I made my way down to the garage, the door of which was still open just in case I needed to drive Brooke home. As I was leaning into the car I heard the front door open and I looked over. I saw her run and fall to her knees.

"What the fuck?" I said out loud. I walked over to her.

"Please take me home," she said. She was crying.

I helped her to her feet, then noticed Robert at the front door. He looked distraught as he called out her name. Leaving her standing, I walked over to him. I placed my hand on his chest.

"Leave her, let me sort this out," I said.

"I just want to apologise, I fucked up big time, Trav."

"Okay, let me deal with this, go back in."

I'd never, in the years I had known him, seen Robert look that devastated. I helped Brooke into the back of the car and drove down the drive. I handed her a tissue from the pocket of the side door, not knowing how long it had been there and whether it was clean or not.

"Thank you and I'm sorry for dragging you out like this," she said as she wiped her eyes.

"Brooke, he's not a bad person, things have happened to him and he's just fucked up," I said.

"You're right about the fucked up part," she answered. "What has happened that's so bad?"

"Ah, Brooke," I sighed. "I can't tell you that, that's for him, but I will tell you one thing, he might have only known you for two days, but you're the first woman to have gotten to him."

We chatted a little more before I left her at the apartment. She had left her purse at the house, and I watched as she pressed the intercom, then seconds later as she pushed through the door. My phone was vibrating in its cradle and a ringing filled the car, both Evelyn and Robert were calling, one on my cell, one on the in-car phone. I took Evelyn's call first.

"Ev, I've just dropped Brooke off at home, I take it you've spoken to him?"

"I have, he won't speak about it, only that he fucked up, what on earth has happened?"

"I don't know. I was in the garage and she ran from the house, she fell and was crying. I'll go see him as soon as I get back."

"Okay, please, Trav, let me know," she said.

I then called Robert.

"I'm on my way home, okay? See you in five."

208

"Sure," was all he said before cutting off the call.

****

Robert was sitting at the breakfast bar when I climbed the stairs of the house. His head was in his hands. He didn't look up as I sat beside him.

"What happened?" I quietly asked.

"She asked me about my aunt and I flipped, I guess," he replied.

"Did you hurt her?"

"No, yes, sort of... I don't fucking know what I did. One minute she was standing in front of me, the next I fucked her like she was nothing. I can't explain it, Trav. I have to have her. I need her and I don't know why. It's fucking my head up big time."

"We have to go to New York in the morning, get some sleep and we can deal with it when we get back," I said.

"I'm not going to New York, I have to deal with this now. I'll drive over there," he said as he stood.

"Sit the fuck back down. One, you're in no fit state to drive. You scared the shit out of her, how will you make it right if you barge over there now? Give her a day or so to get over whatever the fuck you've done."

I was angry at him, and not entirely sure why. I liked her, that much I knew. Was I angry because he had made her cry? Or was I angry because, deep down I saw, no I felt, the connection - as strange as it was - between them, and I didn't want him to fuck it up? I needed to come up with a plan. I left him an hour later; he was exhausted, so I made my way to Evelyn's.

I told Evelyn what little I knew and we agreed that she would go and see Brooke the following day. She could use the return of Brooke's purse as an excuse, and between us we agreed on one thing. Brooke had to know a little of Robert's past. It would be a massive gamble to take and could backfire on us but, if this was to work, Brooke had to know what set Robert off.

Chapter Fourteen

Robert and I drove to the airport the following morning; he was quiet all the way. I tried to engage him in some conversation, but he wasn't having any of it. He sat through planning meeting after planning meeting and thankfully we had Paul with us; he was able to answer the many questions fired at Robert. Periodically Paul would look at me, his eyebrows furrowed in question, and I would gently shake my head - don't ask.

The meetings went on long into the day. It was late at night before we were able to return to DC, and the early hours of the morning before we finally made it home. I had taken a call from Evelyn to tell me she had met with Brooke, explained about his aunt, and that, unfortunately, she wasn't sure Brooke would want to see Robert again.

The following morning I left my apartment with the intention of seeing Robert, checking whether he had managed to get any sleep. As I crossed the garage I saw one of the bikes missing. He must have pushed it from the garage and some way down the drive. The noise of that thing starting would have woken me.

"Ev," I called out as I knocked on her door. Our doors were never locked and I pushed it open.

"Morning, any news?" she said.

"He's gone."

"What do you mean, he's gone?"

"The bike's gone, so I guess that means he has too."

"Shit. I wonder if he's gone to visit her." Evelyn's curse, despite the situation, brought a smirk to my lips.

"He's a grown man, Travis. We'll just have to wait until he comes home," she added.

We both hung about her apartment, pacing, sitting, checking our phones until eventually we heard the bike. We scrambled to the window to see Robert help Brooke off the back, and she was laughing. A simultaneous sigh of relief left both our lips.

"I'll pop over there later, pretend to make some dinner or something and find out what's going on," Evelyn said.

I laughed. We didn't want to know because we were nosy, we needed to know because Brooke was obviously someone important to Robert. Whether he understood what that was or not was debatable. We needed to know both were okay.

****

Later that night Evelyn called on me. She had been over to the house and found Robert and Brooke wrapped in each other's arms, dozing. Brooke had gotten up, and they had spoken. It seemed all was resolved, for that moment anyway. I watched as they made their way to the garage, heard the Mercedes leave the drive, and I assumed he was taking her home. A half hour later he returned. Instead of heading to the house he climbed the stairs to the apartments, opened my door and grabbed two beers from the fridge. He sat beside me on the sofa.

"You okay?" I asked.

"I am now."

"So?" Getting information from Robert was an arduous task.

He laughed. "I'm taking her to a function in a couple of days, the one at the museum."

"And then what? She's only here on holiday, Rob," I said.

"And then we just have to see," he said with a sigh.

"What it is with her? What's got you this fucked up?"

"I honestly don't know. When I'm with her I feel something in here," he poked his chest. "I can't explain it, Trav. I feel like I know her yet I've never met her before. There's so much shit rushing around my brain I can't think straight other than to know I can't let her go home."

211

"You can't keep her here," I said.

"I know that, but I'm going to work damn hard to see if I can change her mind," he said with a grin.

"Be careful, Rob. Don't break her heart, she's not your usual airhead, there's something special about her."

He looked sharply at me. "I don't intend to." He studied me for a moment as if expecting me to say more and I picked up my beer.

"I should go, talk to you later, bro," he said as he placed his empty beer bottle on the table.

I sat for a while just thinking. I was happy for him. I wanted him to find someone he had that depth of feeling for - even if it was only after a few days. The thing with Robert, I realised, was that he didn't do half measures. He was an all or nothing man; life was black and white for him. Was I a little jealous? Perhaps.

****

A couple of days later Robert and I drove to collect Brooke. As she left the apartment block I had to control the gasp that tried to escape my mouth. She looked stunning. Her hair was pinned up with loose tendrils framing her face, her makeup subtle except for ruby red lips, and her dress... It clung to every curve of her body.

"Scrub up well, don't I boys?" she teased as she passed, obviously aware of our gaping mouths.

I was going to have to be very careful; she was not mine, and never would be. Regardless of what happened between her and Robert she would always be off-limits. She was dangerous in one way, though. Whatever it was about her, it ensnared men. The strange thing was she had no idea she had that power. If she could reduce the likes of Robert to a wreck she would destroy a lesser man. She had grace, she was quiet but strong; she had to be to forgive Robert. She was funny and entertaining, she was... She was fucking with my head, that's what she was doing. I shook it to rid myself of her and drove to the museum. I had opted not to attend the function. Sitting with the guys was fun, but being surrounded by the pompous and wealthy fake patrons wasn't my cup of tea. A few bottles of beer and there was no telling how I would behave.

I found a bar and settled on a stool. A few years ago Robert and I would never have travelled alone, we always had some sort of security, but times had changed, we had changed. The businesses were legitimate and it was very rare that we encountered anyone from the past. We kept an eye on everyone, naturally, but from a distance.

I nursed a beer, lost in my own thoughts. It was the overpowering smell of cheap perfume that seemed to bring me around. Perched on a stool next to me was a woman with over-bleached blonde hair and too much makeup. Maybe a year ago I would have fucked her just for my release, but as I looked at her, my stomach turned.

I didn't want a cheap thrill, a quick fuck, anymore. I wanted a relationship, I wanted what Robert seemed to have found. Even knowing this 'thing' with Brooke might not last, even knowing it was less than a week old, it was a relationship for sure.

I gulped down the last of my beer, and with a scowl, walked out the door. I needed fresh air and a chance to get a grip. I'd met Brooke for no more than an hour in total. How the fuck could I feel something for someone I'd met for such a short period of time? I was glad for my brother, I wanted him to have a relationship, and I wanted him to be happy. Whatever was going on with me would stay with me; I just needed to get over it.

****

My pledge to keep my feelings to myself didn't last long. The following morning while deciding whether to go for a shoot or not, I heard the garage doors open; looking out I saw Robert. The first thing I noticed was his bare feet... Why was he walking across the gravel in bare feet? I watched as he backed the Mercedes out of the garage, at speed, and roared off down the drive. Something had gone terribly wrong. I looked across to the house; the front door was left wide open. I ran down the stairs and across the drive.

Brooke was sobbing and Evelyn was cradling her to her chest. The sight and sound of her cries tore something apart in me. Evelyn left her and walked towards me; with her head bent low she told me what had happened.

"He's lost it, again. They were chatting, Brooke brought up the aunt and..." She shook her head.

"What did she say to him?"

"She said she knew about the fire. Oh, Trav, what have we done?" Evelyn sounded so sad, I placed my arm around her shoulder. I could feel her tremble.

Robert had totally flipped. It seemed he and Brooke had had a fantastic evening and at some point during the night, I guessed, his emotions had started to run wild. He had no idea what to do or how to understand what was happening to him. He'd never been in love and there was no doubt he was in love with the woman he had left crying on the sofa. Our plan had backfired. We thought that by telling Brooke about Robert and his aunt it would help her understand him more. What had happened was, when Brooke said she knew that he had killed his aunt, that was it - total meltdown.

It was my fault; I was the one to persuade Evelyn to tell Brooke. I was the one to encourage her to visit while Robert and I were in New York, and I had to put it right. I made my way down the stairs. I called his mobile; I heard it ring in his bedroom. I called the car phone, it was switched off. I called the security desk and asked them to track the car, it was fitted with a tracker and they soon had a location for him. But I was torn a little. I wanted to get to my brother, but I had also seen how shaken Evelyn was, although she'd hidden that from Brooke. I walked back upstairs.

"This isn't the first time he's behaved this way, is it?" Brooke asked.

I sat on the coffee table in front of her.

"All I can tell you, Brooke, is that he's never had a normal relationship, he's never brought anyone back here. He's done things over the past few days we've never seen him do. You could have knocked me over when he said he was taking the day off. You've done that to him. I know you guys have only known each other a week but you've changed him so much already. Ev and I were talking about it, we're scared for him and for you. We want him to have a normal life, but what will happen to him when you leave? I don't mean this to hurt you, but you're going to break his heart," I said.

A silence followed. "What about what he's going to do to me? He could break my heart, too. I love him," she whispered.

I closed my eyes and sighed. She loved him and he loved her, I was sure of that.

"All I can say, Brooke, is that if you take on Robert, you do it for life, and you're leaving in a couple of weeks."

"Do you think I can take him on for life?" she asked.

"I don't know if I can answer that. He'll fuck up often - Can you deal with that? Can you deal with his mood swings? More importantly, Brooke, can you forgive him anything?"

I made a point of emphasising the word *anything*. If this relationship was what I thought it was, she was going to have to know who Robert Stone really was. Who all of us really were.

My phone beeped; a text had come through telling me that the Mercedes had stopped and was in a parking lot. I stood and nodded to Evelyn before taking the Range Rover out to find my brother. I found the car but Robert was nowhere to be seen. The car had taken a beating, the side window was punched through, and I saw drops of red on the door. I touched one of them and brought it to my nose, the metallic smell told me it was blood. I scanned the parking lot. An old guy sat in a payment booth; he looked at me, and before I could make my way over he signalled the direction Robert had taken. I waved my thanks and left the Range Rover to follow on foot.

I don't know what compelled me to walk the way I had, to take the alley to my right or cross the road when I did, but I instinctively knew where to go. I felt his pain, and as I closed in on a beat up old bar I knew he was inside. I took a breath and opened the door. Sure enough, with his back to me, Robert was standing at the oak bar, a line of empty bottles in front of him. I signalled to the guy behind to bring two more.

We stood side by side for a while, not speaking. He knew I was there, I'd heard him take a deep breath in and release it. I'd seen the slight glance to his side. Eventually he spoke.

"Has she gone?" he asked.

"No," I replied.

"What do you mean, no? Get her out of my fucking house, Trav."

I placed the bottle to my lips. "No."

He looked at me.

"If you want to deny how you feel, deny yourself this one fucking chance at a normal life, you go and tell her to leave. I've left her heartbroken but for some fucking, stupid reason, she loves you, she won't leave. You're one giant prick, Rob," I said.

"Prick, you call me a prick?" he said, spinning around.

He needed to lash out, he needed to release the pent-up frustration, anger, sadness, whatever the fuck was going through his mind and body. He was pushing for a fight. I didn't give him a chance; I punched him clean on the jaw. Believe me, Robert was a lot stronger, and much more aggressive than I was; he could knock me out with one punch if he really let loose. But I banked on the fact that he would rein himself in, get himself under control, and only then could he talk through what he felt.

"Come on, fucking hit me again," he growled at me.

People scuttled from the bar; just the sight of him was enough to terrify anyone close. His eyes were black, the veins on this forehead and his neck bulged as the blood pumped around his body. I lowered my fists.

"That's what you want isn't it?" I said quietly.

"What the fuck do you know what I want? Huh?" He was like a caged animal, pacing in front of me.

"You want me to hit you, you want to be punished don't you? You fucked up and you need to feel something? You want to feel pain, you're desperate just to fucking feel something, and pain is all you know. But you do feel, Rob, you just don't understand it yet."

He lowered his own fists, his breathing was ragged as he stood and stared at me. I started to see something in his eyes though; I was getting through.

"What's going on in here?" I said, tapping the side of his head.

He took a moment to answer. "I don't know."

"Shall I tell you? You have finally fallen in love, bro. You just don't know it. You've been conditioned to think you are not worthy of love, you've suppressed your emotions to such a degree that you haven't *felt* for years and somehow that wonderful woman has broken through your brick wall. She's gotten in here...," I tapped his heart.

"What do I do?" he asked.

"You get your fucking ass back there and you tell her how you feel."

"I can't do that. I'll fuck up again, Trav and next time I might hurt her."

"Then you'll live the rest of your life a coward with regrets. She is an amazing woman, you will be a fool if you pass this one up. If you do, you don't deserve another chance at a woman like Brooke."

"You like her, don't you?" he asked.

"It doesn't matter whether I like her or not, and yes, for your information, I wish I had been the one to walk across that foyer. I wish I had been the one to take her to dinner, but I wasn't. I wish someone looked at me the way she looks at you. I wish I felt the connection you two clearly feel with someone. But you know what? She loves you, so don't fucking waste this."

We stood in silence. "I'm sorry you feel that way," he said.

"So am I. So now what?" I replied.

"I don't know, let's just go home."

We walked the short distance back to the car. I sent a text to Mack, someone would need to collect the Mercedes and have it fixed. We drove home in silence. I loved Robert and I hoped he would make the right decision. It wasn't going to be easy for him; it wasn't going to be easy for any of us. Hopefully we had a new member in our family; hopefully Brooke could find the strength to forgive him his past, to accept us and our way of life - to love us all.

I sat by the window all night. I watched Evelyn walk over to the house the following morning, and I breathed a huge sigh of relief when I saw her leave. She looked up at me, she had a huge smile on her face and she raised both thumbs - it was going to be okay, they were going to be okay. And I would do *anything* to make sure they stayed that way.

Dear Reader

Was I in love with Brooke? Possibly, in the beginning. But as time went on I realised it wasn't her, the person, that I was in love with, it was the idea of her. It was the change in my brother. It was the shift in the family dynamics. It was how she balanced Robert - that was what I was in love with.

To say their relationship is odd is an understatement, but then they are both unique people. I never believed in love at first sight until them. I never believed two people could be so in tune with each other, so connected, until them. They give me hope for a future for myself. They've shown me what love actually can be. Don't get me wrong, I'm still chalking up my conquests, but maybe deep down I'm looking for someone to love, someone who will love me back unconditionally - someone like Brooke.

But there is always one thing holding me back. No matter how many years have passed, I can't forget. I thought I had buried my childhood, but thanks to Aileen, thanks to Padriac and to Carrig it has all come rushing back. The fear, the pain, the abuse, it was all there whirling around in my mind. Perhaps I need to deal with that before I can really love or be loved. Am I just too broken? Who knows?

Life has changed dramatically. For a long time it had been the three of us, Robert, Evelyn and me. Now, as Brooke called us, we were the Four Musketeers, and she was the toughest of us all. She withstood a lot from Robert in the beginning with a quiet strength that won us all over.

Life has settled a bit. Well, I say settled - it is as settled as the kind of life my family is ever going to get. We still have our enemies - there was one that proved to be more dangerous that we imagined - and another one that caused the family a lot of stress and 'inconvenience' for a while; but we did what we always do. We pulled together and dealt with it the only way we could.

I occasionally hear from Aileen, she's married and has children. She's never come back to America, but she kept sending letters until I finally wrote a reply. We have never spoken since, but who knows, maybe she'll visit one day. I work hard at forgiving, understanding and believing her and I'm getting there. Did she try hard enough to find me? I don't know. That question and answer has to be buried now. I need to move on.

And move on I shall, there's a rather attractive blonde - Caroline, I think her name is - waiting for me to take her to 'lunch'.

Travis x

40538210R00128

Made in the USA
Charleston, SC
06 April 2015